SHIFT

Book One of the Faceless

RIKKAINE THOMPSON

For Dan

ACKNOWLEDGMENTS

There are so many people I want to thank; my family, my friends both new and old.

First and foremost, my husband, Robert, with his quick smile, clever remarks, shoulder to cry on and a cup of tea when I need it.

My Mum, who taught me the beauty of words and my Dad, who turned them into pictures. My sister, Felicia, for being both an inspiration and a brat with the wittiest of banter, a rare combination. My brother, Daniel, who never got to read this but is still with me on every word. My wonderful children for understanding that sometimes I need to spend time with my word babies too.

Katie Luisier, my first reader, for being the best of friends and always ready to flail with me. Her advice and love over the years has been invaluable.

Elle Tharp, for her vision and humor and the wonderful book cover she designed.

Sally Aniscar of Full Proofreading Services for her professional advice and assistance in polishing this manuscript.

Amanda Boniface, Cheyenne Phakousonh, Chelsea Deaner, Haideé T. H, Karyn Sands, Laura Reed, Emily Combs, and the Ladies of the Tiger Bra chat room, for their advice, patience and confidence boosters when I needed it most.

CHAPTER 1

A twig snapped.

Hidden from view among luscious, green foliage, Noah braced his rifle, peered through the scope and stilled.

A deer. Soft, dark eyes and its ears twitching with every noise of the forest. Noah fixed the crosshairs of his sniper rifle on the deer's face. Timid, the deer sniffed the air before it took a step toward the small stream ahead of it. Then another. Entranced, Noah watched as it looked every direction it could, seeking danger. Its ears flicked in agitation and its nostrils flared, then slowly it lowered its head to drink.

It was still a distance away, if he could get closer he could see more of the delicate creature—

Gunfire. The deer bolted, only to collapse farther down the stream.

A small widening of his eyes was the only reaction Noah allowed himself as he moved his scope to determine where the shot had originated.

A man emerged from a clump of ferns. Holding his rifle high in triumph, his mouth moved, but Noah was too far away to hear what was said. Adjusting his tinted sunglasses, Noah continued to scope.

Motion to the left alerted him and Noah swung his aim to another man who stepped from behind a tree. The man leaned against the trunk with the muzzle of his gun pointed toward the ground.

A third figure came into view behind the man against the tree. Noah's instructions echoed through his mind: *Three targets. Kill one.* Without another thought, Noah pulled the trigger. The man's head jerked and he collapsed into the ferns.

Aware there were others in the forest, Noah picked up his shell, stowed both it and the gun in his bag, and ran. Noah kept low as he ran, keeping to areas of ground that wouldn't show his tracks; dry ground, rocky areas, and logs. He had a head start on the men and he needed to lose them as quickly as he could, preferably before they determined their friend was dead and started looking for the culprit.

They were soldiers fighting on the wrong side of this war, but they weren't his orders. There were other things Noah needed to worry about.

A traitorous crunch beneath her boot and Aly dropped to a crouch. She couldn't afford to be spotted now, not this deep into enemy territory. Holding her gun against her belly, she scurried on three limbs to reach the trunk of a tree. Heart in her throat, she pressed her back to the rough bark and listened to the sounds of the woodlands.

Birds chattered. Wind whooshed through branches. An idle insect chirped. No sound of enemy footsteps or movement through the woodland, nor the rustle of something moving through the undergrowth. She turned her head, using her eyes and ears to check everything she could before she peeked out from behind the trunk.

Nothing in her immediate area. Lifting her gun, she peered through the scope to increase her sight range. Finding nothing on the right, she twisted and skimmed the left side.

Free and clear. Her moment of inattention hadn't given away her location. Taking a deep breath, Aly pushed away from the tree and set out again. She scurried from tree trunk to bush, hyper-aware of her surroundings and vigilantly checking for any sign of the enemy.

A voice carried on the wind alerted her and Aly dove for cover. Bracing her gun against her shoulder, she scanned and waited.

They were closer than she expected. Three figures moving through the underbrush, oblivious to the danger lurking in the foliage. Tilting her head, she sighted. Her gloved finger poised over the trigger as she waited for the right moment to strike. Inhaling deeply, she allowed herself a controlled breath out. Tingles ran down her arms as she fired.

With a soft pop, yellow paint splattered across the chest of her target. While her victim stared at his chest in surprise, Aly fired again. Her two remaining targets dove for cover and this time, her shot dispersed against a helmet.

Flynn, who she'd hit in the chest, grinned and gave a thumbs-up. Ethan, who'd taken one to the helmet, swore. The third hid in the scrub and Flynn cheated by indicating in her direction to alert his teammate.

With a groan, Aly shouldered her gun and prepared to make a run for it. As she pushed away, her best friend Fletcher darted out from behind a tree to take out the last remaining man. Without pausing to gloat, he ran for Aly.

"Kill stealer!" he teased as he approached.

"I know a good diversion when I see one!" she retorted.

"Lies," he scoffed. "You didn't even know I was there. C'mon."

She kept pace with him. "One left?" she asked. She'd kept track of the beeps from their referee, Latisha, whose horn signaled the beginning of the game and marked each "death". So far there had been nine, but there was no way of knowing which side until Latisha indicated the end of the match. Fletcher, being roamer and therefore the communicator of the team, should know. "Or two?"

"One. It's Tyrell." Fletcher gave an exuberant laugh, then continued in a sing-song tone. "And I know where he's hiding."

Grinning, Aly picked up her pace as much as she could considering they were running through woodlands. "Should've picked us for his team then."

"Absolutely. Dean," he said, indicating their team captain, "will be on his way but I know we can beat him. You can be the diversion this time."

Laughing, Aly clenched her fist and extended her forearm. Fletcher bounded closer and bumped his forearm against hers.

Seventeen-year-old Alyson Gale, known to her friends as Aly, loved Tuesday afternoon paintball. She'd played on the local Bellhollow team ever since she'd discovered the sport at fourteen. There were twenty of them who played once or twice a week, and the best of them would attend tournaments in Redding and other cities in California.

On Tuesdays, they split into teams of ten and played capture-the-flag, which rarely resulted in a flag capture and tended to become a free-for-all hunt for the other team. Fletcher Norman was their best player. He knew all the tactics and he had a reputation for being the last man standing.

A single beep sounded and Aly and Fletcher exchanged a glance. "Think it was him?"

"Dunno," Fletcher replied. "Stick to the—"

Another three beeps, followed by a long one to indicate the end of the game. Slowing to a walk, Aly turned in the direction of the parking lot and grinned at Fletcher. "Victory."

He rested his gun against his shoulder. "Well, that was anticlimactic. I only got four today; you stole two."

"You can't always get the kills," she teased, amazed that four out of ten wasn't enough to satisfy him.

He grinned. "Wanna bet? Twenty seconds head start."

Aly's eyes widened. "We promised Dean we wouldn't—"

"Fifteen seconds. Don't delay."

Leveling her gun at him, she took the first shot. Yellow paint splattered against his chest as she turned and bolted. Fletcher's laugh rose in increments, sounding both delighted and devilish. She glanced over her shoulder and grinned as Fletcher charged after her.

Penelope Gale, Aly's mother, was not pleased when Aly and Fletcher arrived at Aly's home. She blocked the doorway and shook her head at the yellow and orange paint splotches clinging to their hair and faces. "Really?"

Aly shuffled as she opened the trunk of her little yellow hatchback to pull out their soiled gear. Her mother always made Aly feel disheveled. Pristine curls, sculpted makeup and glamorous dress suits, Penelope was a real estate agent who always liked to look her best. While Aly got her brown hair and copious freckles from her mother, she'd inherited her untamable locks from her deceased father. Her mother always said she either had too much curl or not enough and her hair couldn't decide which way to go. No matter what hair product Aly used, her hair always ended up a tangled brown mess. It was even worse when clogged with paint.

Fletcher spread his arms wide. "Give us a hug, Aunt P."

Taking a step back, Penelope raised her hand stop to him. "I have to meet clients soon. Don't you dare."

Aly's six-year-old half-brother Tim called from inside, "Mom! Your phone's ringing again."

Pulling a face, Penelope shooed the pair. "Go around the back. I don't want paint in my house."

Disgruntled, Aly muttered, "When do we ever get paint in the house?"

"All the time," Fletcher replied, cheerful as he took their paintball guns from the trunk. "Your room's a mess of paint."

Aly mock glared at him and locked her car. "So not what I meant."

He smirked. "Shoo, go shower. It's going to take you a while to clean that rat's nest."

The mock glare turned into a real one and she made sure to take extra-long in the bathroom. By the time she finished, Fletcher had rinsed their gear, cleaned most of the paint from his dark hair and sat maintaining their guns at the small table in the laundry. Tim sat opposite him, swinging his feet on the chair and talking non-stop about his favorite TV show.

"Hey squirt," she said, leaning on the door frame.

Tim beamed, "Hi Aly-phant! Fletcher says we can go to the arcade this weekend!"

She raised her eyebrows at Fletcher. "Did he now?"

Fletcher gifted her with his lopsided smile. "Did you have other plans?"

"I'm working Sunday," she said. "So, we'll have to go Saturday."

Tim whooped. "Yay!"

"If you're good and Mom says it's okay. And we go to the art shop too."

Tim deflated while Fletcher laughed. "Aww. But that's so boring."

"No art shop, no arcade. I'm not driving to Redding without going. Your choice."

Tim flopped in his seat and appealed to Fletcher.

"No dice, bud," Fletcher said, lifting away from the table to store the paint guns in a lockable cabinet in the laundry. "She's the boss."

Smiling, Aly told Fletcher, "Shower's free."

"Did you save me hot water?"

She grinned. "Nope. You can shrivel."

He bopped her on the head as he went past her and bounced up the stairs.

"Just for that, I'm hiding my notes!" she called after him. "You can go without tonight!"

"Can't hide them if I find them before you do!" he replied, veering into her bedroom instead of the bathroom.

Aly bolted after him. "Don't you dare!" she yelled as she thundered up the stairs, earning a warning yell from her mother about noise.

Fletcher met her at the doorway, grinning. "As if I would. More fun to wrestle it out of you later."

Ducking into her room, she lashed out an over-exaggerated swinging kick at him for good measure. "Ass."

Crossing his eyes, he poked his tongue out at her and went to the bathroom.

Ignoring the mess of half-finished research papers on her school desk, Aly went to her drawing desk. Her final acrylic submission for her AP Studio Art Drawing class was due soon and she still wasn't satisfied. The shading wasn't what she'd envisioned and needed more work. Landscaping wasn't her passion, nor were more traditional forms of art. She preferred character design and movement and using digital art over hand-drawn, especially since she'd chosen animation for her career goal. Her school portfolio needed a landscape so she picked a fantasy alien forest, full of purple and white trees and pink grasses.

Glancing up at the clock above the pin board on her wall, Aly decided she had time before study group.

"Aly, a word?" Penelope asked a short time later.

Without raising her head, Aly removed the fine paintbrush from between her teeth and dropped the one she'd been using in cleaner. "Hmm?"

"I wanted to talk to you about Fletcher."

She stored her paintbrushes and swiveled her chair until she faced her mother. "Sure. What's up?"

Penelope was a picture of motherly concern. "He seems down lately."

Aly swung her feet. "Finals. College apps. General stuff."

"Are you sure?"

"Pretty sure," Aly replied and shrugged. "We're all feeling it. The teachers are really packing on the homework."

"Homework that he does at our kitchen table first thing in the morning."

"He's always done that," Aly pointed out.

"The anniversary is in a few weeks."

Aly's eyes widened. "No, Mom, don't."

Penelope's gaze was mournful. "He doesn't talk about Lee. It's not healthy."

Fletcher and his uncle Lee had breezed into Bellhollow when Aly was eight and had stuck around. The always-absent Lee had drifted from town to town until Fletcher came and forced Lee to settle.

Lee took a job stacking shelves at the local supermarket and he often worked as a seasonal lumberjack. Aly thought Lee was a curt, scary kind of man with intense eyes, and she never interacted much with him. He never came to school events, never did anything parental, and left Fletcher to his own devices. In all her memories, she only remembered meeting the man a total of five times and each time she did, she always felt weird around him.

Lee died when Fletcher was fifteen. His car crashed on the way to Redding and left Fletcher without a guardian. Penelope had been adamant that Fletcher should come to live with them, but Fletcher had refused. When Penelope approached social services, she discovered Fletcher had hired Cassidy Cook, the mother of their friend Del, as a lawyer to help him become legally emancipated so he could live on his own. After that, Roger, Aly's adopted father, helped Fletcher get a part-time job as a janitor at the regional hospital where Roger worked as a doctor.

Since Lee's death, Fletcher had an open invitation to every Gale event and every mealtime.

Smiling, Aly shook her head, "Fletcher's okay, Mom."

"Course I am," Fletcher said, flouncing in carrying two glasses of orange juice. "Why are we talking about me?" He placed a cup beside Aly and pressed his chest to her back to be annoying as he leaned over her. "Looks good."

"Thanks."

"At least it did before you started fiddling," he said as he flopped on Aly's bed with his glass, then put his feet up. "You can't just leave things alone, can you?"

Aly scowled at him. "If you spill that—"

He wriggled his shoes at her and grabbed her favorite yellow bee plushie to cushion his back as he leaned against the headboard. "I've got mad skills."

"Bumble-butt," she smiled, shaking her head at him, which only made Fletcher poke his tongue at her as he pushed up the sleeves of his oversized blue flannel shirt. Aly often teased Fletcher's love of flannel and clothes that were too big for him, just as he teased her love of yellow and bees.

"Since you're both here," Penelope said, "there is something I want to talk to you both about."

Aly and Fletcher turned their attention to Penelope obediently. "What's the buzz, Aunt P?"

"Roger and I have been talking," she said, then addressed Fletcher. "We know you must be worried regarding the money side of going to college. We have more than enough for Aly saved up, we'd be happy to supplement—"

Fletcher choked on his juice. He swung so he sat on the side of the bed away from Penelope and coughed.

Rushing over, Aly pounded between his shoulder blades.

"I'm good," he ground out through a raw throat. Wiping his eyes, he waved Aly away. "I'm fine."

She wouldn't be dissuaded and sat beside him with her

hand on his back.

Undaunted by Fletcher's overdramatized choking, Penelope continued, "We've plans to purchase a small, two-bedroom apartment as an investment near whichever college Aly decides to go to. The help we'd offer you would be to live there rent and utility free. You would, as Aly is, be expected to provide your own food and amenities, so it's not a free ride. We are also willing to help offset some of the debt you'll incur—"

Fletcher's body was stiff, like he braced for a blow. "I can't—"

"Mom, you can't spring this on him," Aly complained. Fletcher had always been proud, never accepting handouts or charity. To spring something like this on him, Aly could only imagine how he felt.

"You both have been so busy; you've been hard to pin down and college starts in August."

"It's April," Aly snapped. "We have time."

"And you know how long it takes to close a deal on an apartment. You knew about that offer."

The offer was one of the reasons why Aly hadn't told her parents she was accepted into Otis College of Art and Design yet. She wanted to do a year or two there, then transfer to California Institute of the Arts, assuming she could get in. She hadn't known about her parent's intentions regarding Fletcher. "Yeah, but that doesn't mean Fletcher's going to go to college anywhere near me."

Penelope sighed as her phone beeped. "We'll discuss this, I only wanted to let you know."

Her mother disappeared out the door and Aly turned to Fletcher. "I'm sorry. I didn't... I mean, I heard them discussing money lately, but I didn't know—"

He shook his head, hunching his shoulders. "I can't accept money from them."

Aly nodded. "I know." She bumped him with her shoulder and attempted to tease. "It's not like you applied for anything anyway."

Fletcher glanced up. "Huh?"

The nudge turned into a lean. "You never talk to me about the future. You know all my hopes and dreams, but every time I try to talk college and future, you evade. All I can get is 'I dunno. Something with computers'."

"It's never been on the cards, Als," he muttered, pretending he was engrossed in looking at the floor. Leaning away from her, he put his glass on her bedside table.

She sighed at his admission. "All that hard work."

"Yeah, yeah. Submissions are closed by now."

She gave him a bland expression. "You know there are colleges still accepting submissions. If you could be anything, what would you be?"

The phrasing caught Fletcher off-guard and he lifted his head. "Does Superman count?"

"You don't have his looks," Aly quipped, grinning.

He scoffed. "I'm hurt."

"You need a spit curl."

Fletcher ran his hands through his dark hair and yanked it onto his forehead in a messy semblance of what could be a curl if she squinted.

"Perfect. If I threw you out my window, would you fly?"

He grinned and puffed out his chest. "Course I would; I'm Superman."

Aly kept her smile. "So, Clark, what are you going to do at college to support your superhero days?"

Fletcher sighed. "You don't let up."

"Nope."

"I don't know; I really hadn't thought about it. I suppose…" He shrugged. "An astronaut."

She gave him a flat expression. "That'd be awesome if we were still sending people into space."

"You mean we don't?" he said, faking surprise. "Shucks. I'd better catch a lift with Russia."

"Or work for SpaceX."

He brightened. "That'd be fun! Playing with rockets all day."

"Can we be real for a moment?"

Fletcher scowled. "Don't put me on the spot. I just finished saying I haven't thought about it. What do you think I'd be good at?"

She leaned back, pursed her lips and considered him. "Pest control."

He snorted and laughed. "Awesome. Thanks."

She giggled. "Sorry, couldn't help myself. You can do anything you put your mind to."

His smile was more sincere. "Thanks."

Aly studied Fletcher and decided to go for it. "You know… I've been thinking about taking a year off before college."

"Oh?" He raised his eyebrows at her, inviting her to elaborate. "Stalling about telling your mom you got into Otis?"

Aly rolled her eyes. "You heard Mom. She wants to buy an apartment. Which'll suck if I can get into CalArts. They're too far apart."

"Lucky," Fletcher muttered.

She ignored that. "Think about it, go see the sights and such. Backpack across Europe." She sighed wistfully. "Imagine the places and people I could sketch!"

Fletcher made a rude noise. "Roger would never agree. He'd be worried about some European boy stealing your virtue and you never returning."

She snorted. "Probably. I have money saved, and there's the money my dad left me that I've been saving—"

"Which you're supposed to use for college—"

She wished he'd stop interrupting her. "Roger and Mom have already said I could use it on whatever I wanted. There's more than enough for Otis. So, I was thinking…"

Fletcher narrowed his eyes. "What?"

"What if we went together?"

Recoiling away from her, he stood up and retreated across the room. "What?"

"Roger wouldn't get in a huff then," Aly said, earnest. "Or at least not as much of one. I could defer for a year. We can do odd jobs, stay for a few weeks in each place and really see the world. Just imagine you and me in Paris. Wouldn't that be amazing? All the additions to my portfolio if I've actually been there! The culture and the people. It'd be a great adventure!"

He stared at her in disbelief, then shook his head. "Aly—"

"Think about it," she insisted and babbled because she knew what came next. "I'm sure there'd be others at school who'd be interested in backpacking. Del and Grace! Imagine Del in France, he'd have such a bad accent! Lloyd and Tamara for sure, Lloyd'd love the chance for traveling journalism. And Kate! She's doing fashion design; she'd die for a chance to—"

Fletcher couldn't look at her. "I don't have that kind of money."

Aly chewed her bottom lip. This would be the hard part. "I'd help you—"

Fletcher stalked toward the door. "We'll be late for study group."

"Fletch—"

Fletcher didn't answer. He made it all the way to the front door before she caught up to him. He scowled at her and yanked the door open. "I'm not a charity."

"When, exactly, have I ever treated you like one?" she snapped in return and snatched his arm to stop him from leaving.

He dragged her out onto the porch before he halted at the top of the stairs. "Your whole family is conspiring— I'm not going to— I've gotten this far without handouts—"

"It's not a handout," Aly insisted. "This is something I want to do and I want to take my best friend along for the ride. Why is that so hard for you to understand?"

He ran his free hand through his hair. "I can't take this from you too."

Her brow furrowed in confusion. "Take... what have you taken? When have you ever taken anything I've offered?"

He shuffled and gave her the impression of a caged animal. "Look... there are things... I can't go to college. They'll find out."

She frowned. "Who will? Your family?"

He hesitated, his gaze sliding from her to the floor.

"The same family who doesn't care about you?" she continued, her voice rising. "Who has never visited, never sent money, never even called?" His family didn't care. None of them even showed up for Lee's funeral. Fletcher didn't speak about his past and the time before he came to Bellhollow, and Aly believed it was because of his family. She hated them on his behalf. When she was younger, she often daydreamed about confronting them. "Who gives a frick if they find out?"

"I've already taken a huge risk staying here this long."

She stared at him. "I don't understand. What risk?"

Fletcher closed his mouth so fast his teeth clicked.

"What's with you?" Aly asked, bewildered.

He sighed and scuffed the wooden porch with his shoe as he fixed his eyes on the ground.

She squeezed his arm and ducked her head down to coax his gaze back to her. "Fletch, it's okay."

"No, it's not. I shouldn't be taking it out on you. Penelope's just trying to help... I guess... with college looming... I've been taking a long, hard look at my life... and not really liking what I see."

"'Bout time," she said, smiling. Being sympathetic, she shucked off the humor to console him. "Don't stress too much; we'll figure something out. There's all sorts of grants you can find if you need it, plus deferred payment. I have heaps of lists and contact names. We can sit down and sort through things if you want. It's not too late."

He studied her for a long moment. "Yeah. I'd appreciate it."

Smiling, she continued, "Europe was just an idea; you don't have to come. I'd like it if you did, but it's no big if you're afraid of a little plane flight."

He snorted. "Not afraid of planes." Another sigh. "You always have to have an answer for everything, don't you?"

"Yup," she said, her smile taking up most of her face. "I'll start an advice column in the school paper called 'Ask Aly'."

Fletcher shook his head in dismay. "Dear Aly, I have this annoying best friend who always gives me the wrong advice, what do I do?"

Pretending to ponder, she mock-scribbled on her hand. "Dear perpetual loser, your best friend knows best and one day you'll realize this. Love, Aly."

Fletcher laughed and gave her a spontaneous hug. "Get your ass on the bike or you'll be walking to Grace's."

She scoffed, returning his hug with enthusiasm. These were the best sorts of hugs from Fletcher. "Like you'd leave me."

He lifted her off the porch to squeeze her, something he knew she hated and did it anyway. "I'm tempted."

"Will you consider Europe?"

He groaned. "Pushy."

"Please? Pretty please with a Snickers on top?"

"Yeah, yeah," he muttered, "I'll consider it."

"I don't want to leave you behind."

"You're going to, one day."

Caught by the sadness in his voice, she made a promise. "Nope. Won't happen. We'll be friends forever."

He squeezed her and said with more sincerity, "You're my favorite person."

Her heart betrayed her with an annoying, leftover flutter that she covered with a laugh. "Dork."

"Hurry up and get your stuff," he said.

CHAPTER 2

"You will remain quiet and confined until we arrive. Is that clear?" The words were routine and Noah remained compliant.

The smell of the hessian bag over his head was reminiscent of old socks. Voiceless movement circled him. His hands were bound together in front of him and there was a tracking device strapped to his foot. He was forced up into some form of rumbling vehicle.

His stomach dropped away as the seat he sat on ascended. Helicopter, judging by the forces acting on his body as well as the sound of the engine and the blades cutting the air. Although he'd never been in one, he could fly a simulated one. Not having anything else to do, he counted the seconds to their destination.

Two hours and thirty-six minutes later, the helicopter hovered.

"Get out. To the left," the voice beside him instructed, and something thumped as it hit the ground. Hands shoved him and forced him through the door. The drop was greater than Noah anticipated. He stumbled and sprawled onto some sort of soft foliage.

Rolling onto his back, Noah offered up his bound

hands. The helicopter lifted away without anyone untying him. Listening, he gauged the direction it headed while he fumbled for the ties of the hood. By the time it was off, he didn't care about the helicopter anymore.

Open air. Trees towering into a gray sky. He knelt in a small ferned meadow surrounded by forest. Around him, the ferns were windblown by the helicopter and the ones beneath him crushed. A bird flew overhead and Noah traced its flight, his eyes watering from the glare of the sky. He traced the path of a breeze as it flowed down from the trees and skipped across the top of the ferns. So many sounds, too many to follow.

Freedom. Sunshine. He closed his eyes to the sun and let it dance on his face.

Something beeped and reminded Noah of the mission.

Pressing his bound hands to the wet soil to give himself more balance, he heaved to his feet. Once standing, he turned toward the bag left for him.

The usual survival gear. A knife, a heavy camouflage jacket, a small pouch of food, a canteen, a compass, a cap to cover his hairless head, sunglasses, a sniper rifle and ammunition, a watch with a countdown of six hours remaining, and a manila folder. Written on the outside of the folder were the words, *Return to the drop-off before the timer on the watch depletes. Do not remove the sunglasses. We are watching. Failure to comply will result in death.*

Glancing at the device strapped to his ankle, he opened the folder. The folder contained a limited map of the surrounding forest with a red circle and a small piece of paper containing his orders. *THREE TARGETS. KILL TWO.*

The sunglasses diminished the glare from the forest as he slid them on, as well as muting the color so brilliant green dipped to various shades of dull gray. Gathering the bag and with compass and map in hand, Noah set out.

Noah was efficient. The kills were clean and conducted within moments of contact, then he vanished into the forest like a ghost. Exactly like all his other kills.

Waiting at the rendezvous point allowed him to gaze upward and peek beneath the sunglasses to watch the sky come alive with color, fade, and then tiny pinpricks of light dotted the heavens. When the tranquilizer dart came, his last glimpse of the outside world was the twinkling stars.

They didn't find the daisy hidden in his sock. His sister's smile was worth the risk.

Lijuan Locklear, or Grace to her friends, opened the door to her home and beamed. Long raven hair, dark eyes and an infectious laugh, she'd been Aly's friend for two years. Her mother, Lan, was both head chef and owner of the Happy Dragon, a local Chinese restaurant, and her father, Jonathan, was a deputy at Bellhollow's sheriff's office.

Aspiring to compose, Grace's major instrument was piano and she played trumpet in the school marching band. She produced some beautiful pieces, which she sold for a pittance or released on YouTube. Sometimes she and Aly would create a small cartoon to showcase both their talents. To show her grandmother she strived for academic excellence, Grace held weekly study groups. Lan always made sure the group was well fed and even tested new dishes on the bottomless pit of Del.

"Hi guys!" Grace chirped, accepting Aly's greeting hug and ushered them into her foyer. "You're the last; even Del beat you today."

Fletcher pretended to stagger and slump against the wall in shock while Aly rolled her eyes. "Yeah, sorry," she said. "Someone decided he wanted to free-for-all. Took me ages to get the paint out of my hair."

"I am not the one who started working on her portfolio while I was in the shower," Fletcher complained. "*She* had to store her paints." He turned his voice falsetto to mimic Aly's. "Hang on! Just one more thing!"

Aly poked her tongue out at him.

Grace's house always smelled delicious and tonight was no different. Walking through the massive kitchen, Aly greeted Lan, who was cooking, and Jonathan, who was following his wife's gentle instructions. Jonathan, believing himself to be of American Indian descent and never knew his parents or his heritage, had embraced Lan and Grace's love of their Chinese heritage and was often found helping out in the kitchen.

When Del spotted them entering the dining room, he sat back and tossed his pen on the table. "Finally! Now y'all can ask him the math questions. I literally got no clue." Dark skin, mischievous grin and rows of tightly braided corns that ended just above his shoulders, Delwin Cook was a gamer at heart. He ran a YouTube channel dedicated to gaming in his spare time. He and Fletcher had met aged fifteen after Del's parents divorced and his mother, Cassidy, decided small town living would benefit her boys. Quick both to smile and to flirt, Del fitted into their little group with record speed.

Fletcher bumped his fist against Del's and nodded to Lloyd and Tamara in greeting. Lloyd and Tamara were a longstanding couple of Bellhollow High. Polar opposites, Tamara was outgoing and bubbly while Lloyd was serious and geeky.

"No Zek and Kate?" Aly asked, indicating the two missing members.

"Kate's grounded," Tamara said, throwing her auburn hair over her shoulder. "And Zek's got something in Redding."

"Bar mitzvah prep for his brother," Lloyd added.

"We doing Math?" Aly asked, disappointed as she dumped her bag on the floor and took a seat beside Grace. She'd already finished that homework. "I thought it was Lit tonight."

"Jenkins' assignment is due tomorrow, Aly-cat," Del

reminded her. "The word from Zek is that there's a pop quiz." He jerked his thumb at Fletcher. "And he's the one with the know-how."

"Math is easy," Fletcher said, getting out his books. "It's all logic and remembering equations."

"And stealing Aly's notes," Grace commented and poured herself a glass of water.

"Her handwriting is prettier than mine," Fletcher said with a lopsided smile. "Als?"

Pretending to be huffy, she flipped through her book. "Nope."

Fletcher placed a Snickers bar before him and licked his lips. "That's a shame, cause—"

To the amusement of their friends, Aly's notes replaced the Snickers before Fletcher finished his sentence.

Aly doodled while Fletcher took the lead of the study group. She appropriated parts of his seat for her feet, bending her knees so she could use them as a slanted table. Feeling brattish, she jiggled and poked him with her toes until Fletcher gripped her ankle to keep her feet still.

Fletcher pushed her notes toward her. "You jotted down one of the equations wrong."

Aly frowned. "Which one?"

Fletcher pointed with his pen. "D slash dx, tan x equals sec squared x. You forgot to square the sec."

"She forgot to square her sex?" Del asked with a crude grin, deliberately mishearing.

"Del!" Grace complained and whacked his arm. "I think those cornrows are braided too tight—" she reached out to tug one. "Jerkface."

"Aww," Del said, warding away her hands. "C'mon Gracie, I didn't mean it like that."

"Sure you didn't."

"Damn," Aly said, looking at her notes and ignoring Del. Reaching into her bag, she pulled out her assignment.

"Only makes one question wrong," Fletcher assured her as she checked her work. "Easy fix."

Lan poked her head through the door and smiled at them. "Ten minutes."

Del whooped and tossed his pen on the table, ready to give up on his homework right then. "Can't wait! Smells delicious, Mrs. Locklear! Let me help you."

"He's only helpful when there's food," Lloyd joked.

Unable to study any longer, a flurry of activity erupted from the teens as the table was cleared of homework in favor of food. Conversation uplifted, turning to the gossip of the day and the party Madison-Lee Campbell threw on the weekend.

Carrying several plates along her arms, Lan placed the various dishes around the table. "How is it going?"

"Good, thanks," they chorused.

Rubbing his hands together, Del looked pleased. "You spoil us. Where do I begin?"

"There are two new dishes," Lan said, pointing to two meat plates. "Please let me know what you think."

"Can do," Del said as he reached for the new dishes first and heaped some into his bowl. The others around the table followed his example.

Lan pointed to two of the dishes. "Tamara, those two are vegan."

"Thank you!" she sang as Lloyd reached for them to serve her. "I appreciate that."

Del stuffed his food into his mouth. Chewing with a thoughtful air, Del gave Lan a nod and two thumbs up. "'licious." Del swallowed. "I really love the heat. Wowzers. That's some bite."

Lan smiled, proud, and bopped Del on the head. "Thank you."

Lloyd coughed and took a drink, then breathed out. "Wooo."

Lan looked at him with concern. "Too strong?"

"Only for me," Lloyd said, fanning his mouth. "But I'm a baby when it comes to spicy food."

"He really is," Tamara said. "Mamá has to make a

separate meal when he comes to eat. You, on the other hand," she said, indicating Del and his abysmal display of table manners, "need a bib."

Del slurped. "Waste."

"At least your food won't end up on your shirt," Grace told him with a meaningful glance down.

Aly shook her head. "You need a massive beard so you can store food in it."

Del laughed. "Now, there's an idea." He stroked his wispy chin. "I bet I could grow this out."

"Shit, Aly, don't give him ideas!" Lloyd complained while Fletcher groaned.

"There's not even enough there to grow yet," Grace teased.

Lan left them to their own devices and chatter remained on things other than homework. Del, Fletcher and Lloyd discussed some first-person shooter game, while Tamara and Grace discussed fashion, with Aly joining in with both conversations. As it invariably did with Grace and Tamara, the conversation turned to prom and three themes ready to be set to a vote.

"Hoops," Tamara said as Grace battled Aly with her chopsticks over the last shrimp. "Corsets. Those pretty lace gloves. I'm definitely voting Victorian. Think of all the accessories we could do. Kate's already doing designs for each."

Grinning at Aly, Grace popped the shrimp in her mouth and overdramatized how delicious it was. Aly flopped back in her seat. "Why do we even need a theme? It's not a costume party, everyone's going to dress how they like."

"But it's an English thing," Grace complained, ignoring Aly. "Southern belle's sort of the same kind of thing; why couldn't we do that?"

"Victorian sounds more… upper-class?" Lloyd suggested.

"What about a masquerade ball?" Tamara said. She

waved her fingers in front of her eyes. "Feathered masks."

"See, now that could be fun!" Grace commented. "If we're quick, do you think prom committee will accept it?"

"At least it's not 'under the sea'," Aly mumbled, talking to her bowl.

Fletcher poked her in the ribs.

She turned her head to glare at him.

He poked her again, talking in hushed tones. "Cheer up. Prom's not that bad."

"Maybe for you," she said, slouching on her chair. Folding her arms on her chest, she refused to look at Fletcher. He was a guy, he had it easy. For a girl, there were expectations and Aly didn't like it.

"What's that supposed to mean?"

"Nothing."

"Yeah, right." Fletcher squinted at her. "Are you afraid you won't get asked?"

"Nope."

"Are you afraid you *will* get asked?"

An embarrassed heat flooded her belly and she glared at him for pressing. "After Homecoming? I'd rather go alone," she muttered. Homecoming had been the worst idea she'd had. She'd been so thrilled Carter had asked her but the whole thing had turned into a disaster because the guy didn't understand the word "no". But he'd understood a knee to the groin and the pepper spray Grace's dad had supplied them both with.

"Then go alone," Fletcher said as if it were the easiest thing in the world.

"Yeah, sure. Like that'd work. I'm aware of the things that will be said about me if I do."

"Aly, you're above petty gossip."

Her lips thinned into an untalkative line.

Fletcher shrugged. "Or come with me, if it's really worrying you."

She frowned at him, waiting for elaboration. "No cute guys you want to ask out?"

"None that swing my way," he said as he poked around his bowl with his chopsticks. "Slim pickings in Bellhollow. Rather have a fun night with my friends. If you're worried about appearances, just say you're going with me."

Going with Fletcher would solve all her concerns. She could go to prom and guarantee a fun night. Curling a piece of hair that had fallen from her ponytail over her ear, she looked at him. "And what about expectations on you?"

"You mean the limo crap?" he asked, surprised. Food slithered off his chopsticks and back into his bowl. "You want a limo?"

She scoffed, even though she smiled at his joke. "Dork."

"And here I was going to show up in torn jeans and flannel," he teased.

She laughed and plucked the sleeve of his flannel shirt. "You better not. I expect some class if you're taking me to prom, you know."

"So, that's a yes?"

She shrugged. "Sure. Sounds fun."

"Do I have to wear a tux?" he whined.

"Depends," Aly teased. "If we get Disney princess, you can dress up as the Beast."

Fletcher laughed. "Okay, *Belle*."

"If we get that, I'm stuck as Prince Naveen," Del included, adding himself to the conversation. "Since we don't got any other black princes. Really, all the options literally make me wanna suck balls. I should complain."

Aly screwed up her face. "Eww."

"That's really gross," Lloyd complained. "I'm eating here."

"Oh, you know what I meant," Del grumbled.

Hiding a smile, Grace nodded. "Boycott prom for their lack of diversity and have our own. I don't want to be Mulan or Pocahontas."

"We don't *have* to dress based on the color of our skin or heritage. Elena's an awesome princess, but I liked the idea of going as Lottie," Tamara said. "She's sort of a combination of the two prom ideas."

"Please don't tell me you're going to wear a hoop dress," Lloyd whined. "How am I supposed to get close to you?"

"I'm hoping for superheroes," Del continued and puffed out his chest. "Superman."

Aly fought not to laugh and shared a knowing glance with Grace. Lloyd lost the battle to hide his laughter and Fletcher didn't even try to hide his.

"You can be Catwoman," Del suggested to Aly, waggling his eyebrows.

"I don't think so," Aly said, shaking her head.

Del pouted. "Aww, c'mon."

"I already have a Batman costume," Aly said, and thumped her hand down on Fletcher's shoulder. "And here's my Robin."

Fletcher groaned and rubbed his face with his hands.

Del burst into rambunctious laughter.

"Why do you have a Batman costume?" Tamara asked, amused.

"Halloween, three years ago," Fletcher said, resigned. "We dressed up to help Roger at the children's ward."

Del snickered. "That's literally the best thing ever." He leaned forward to leer. "Did you go the tights or the hot shorts?"

Aly giggled as Fletcher refused to answer. "Poor Fletch," she said as she shook his shoulder. "He'll never live it down."

At the end of the meal, they engaged in the epic battle of rock-paper-scissors to determine dishes duty. When everything was clean, they continued the study session, splitting to their various electives.

Since Fletcher had a night shift, he and Aly bid the others farewell at nine and clambered onto Fletcher's bike. About halfway home, he became irritated and preoccupied with something occurring behind them. Aly glanced behind only to be blinded by the headlights of a car.

Wrinkling her nose, she lifted her hands from the hold behind her and wrapped them around Fletcher's waist, curling against his back. It was easier for her to predict his movements if she held him and she knew it always made him feel better. It was common for cars not to see a bike or behave erratically around them, but this car engine sounded close.

Fletcher turned without warning and she gripped him tighter. They darted down a side street he didn't often take to reach Aly's home. The headlights didn't follow as the car roared down the road away from them. Relieved, Aly loosened her grip but didn't release it.

He remained agitated until they reached her home. Instead of waiting for her to get off, Fletcher braced his legs on either side and stood, twisting to face down the road behind them.

She shivered, a mixture of nerves and a tingle she couldn't explain, and rubbed her arms. Fletcher flicked his gaze toward her and a flash of light caught his eyes. For a brief moment they appeared to shine like a cat's in the darkness. Unsure what he had seen that could affect him like that, she turned her head but was met with an empty street.

The tingle vanished. "Either someone's drunk or they're pulling a prank," Fletcher said.

"Tailgating assholes," she muttered and got off the bike. "Drive safe."

He bumped his helmet against hers in goodbye then sat back down. "Always do."

CHAPTER 3

Forced to hold the same position for hours while staring straight ahead, Noah's muscles ached. Smith, their invisible handler, showed no sign of releasing them. As far as he knew, Noah's last mission was successful. Since he wasn't permitted to speak with his siblings, he didn't know which of them had displeased Smith and required discipline.

His peripheral allowed him to view his siblings. Eight other souls condemned to share his life of white walls and endless drills. Soldiers dedicated to the Institute. Four brothers: Solomon, Moses, Ruth and Adam, and four sisters: Seth, Jonah, Elijah and Boaz. If he was honest with himself, he didn't know much about any of them.

Adam was the bulkiest while Boaz was the tallest. Moses' ability to learn languages and Ruth's mathematical equations were often commented upon by Smith. Elijah's aim far exceeded the accuracy of the rest of them. Jonah had the most strategic mind. Solomon always endured. Little Seth smiled the brightest when given flowers and, because of a speech impediment, was considered broken in the eyes of Smith.

They stood in the small hallway lined with eleven doors, five to each side and one door at the end. They had their own bedroom, equipped with a slated bed, a set of drawers in the wall, and a shower and toilet.

There were ten bedrooms. For reasons never explained, one remained empty.

The hallway emptied into the main hanger, a large two-story room with a one-way window on the second floor. Within the chamber stood an elaborate obstacle course, a combat mat, a metallic table with bench seats for eating, and a set of desks. Under Smith's verbal instructions, they ran themselves into exhaustion on the obstacle course. They faced each other in hand-to-hand combat. Academic instruction included Anatomy, Mathematics, Chemistry, Weaponry, Explosives, Simulated Combat, and Tactics. They ate. They learned. They slept. Round and round in endless monotony and silence. Recruits in a war they knew nothing about. No history. No knowledge of the enemy. Nothing about what existed beyond.

Noah's earliest memory was waking, covered in ooze, on the slated bed in his bedroom. He had no idea how he came to be there or why he was covered in the clear goo. He suspected his siblings shared the same memory, but he couldn't ask. He measured time by how fast his hair grew before gas would fill his room while he slept and he would wake up shaven again. It wasn't only his hair that was taken; there were other noticeable differences. Pinprick marks on his arms. Sometimes there would be pen marks as well. All pieces to a puzzle Noah filed away for analysis.

"At ease," Smith's voice said, breaking the silence in the hallway.

Noah breathed out and allowed his limbs to relax and change position. Across from him, Elijah did the same and Noah allowed his eyes to meet hers instead of staring at the wall.

"Noah. Clean execution. Well done."

Noah inclined his head at the rare praise. "Thank you."

"Execution?" Jonah blurted, jerking her head up. "His mission was an execution? After all the personality dissection you requested of me, you have him—"

"Silence," Smith replied in his emotionless tone.

Jonah clenched her hands into fists and glared at Noah, who stared resolutely back. It took Jonah a few moments to control her expression and return to staring at the empty door across from her.

Missions were a regular occurrence with varying objectives. Sometimes Noah dismantled a bomb, sometimes he created one. He was tested, physically or mentally, in a room filled with mirrors. He ran on treadmills until he collapsed from exhaustion, or was given complex puzzles to solve for hours on end without sleep.

Occasionally he was commanded to take out a target related to the war. Sometimes these assassinations were quiet—sniper from a distance. Others were to set an example, done with as much evidence as possible as long as he wasn't seen. Once he even used heavy artillery to take out a vehicle full of passengers in the middle of a convoy of cars.

None of Noah's missions involved direct contact with another person. He never spoke to them, never saw their faces, and was never allowed to touch his handlers. His targets were always viewed through a scope from a distance, through sunglasses that made the world gray.

Now, thanks to Jonah's outburst, Noah wondered at the difference in their missions. If she reacted with surprise that he received executions, what was she given? It brought many questions to his mind, among them was the absence of Ruth.

Ruth's space beside him was empty and had been for eight sleep cycles. Noah had completed a mission during that, so had Elijah and Adam.

Training continued without answers to Ruth's disappearance. When Seth's spot emptied as she partook in her mission, Noah discovered there was a word for the emotion he experienced. Worry. Something new and alien, it ate away at him. His mind conjured images of moments that could have gone wrong in his missions, and placed Seth in his steed. What would she do? She was different to him and her skill set varied. How would she overcome? He ran simulations in his mind, but it didn't help him overcome the feeling.

She returned two days after she'd left and his relief was palpable. Except Ruth's place was still vacant.

After Seth's return, Noah noticed the others reacting to Ruth's empty place. Boaz's eyes went there first as she exited her room. Adam frowned daily at the closed door before him, but he quickly hid the expression. Seth's head turned to look at Noah across the empty spot between them. Elijah's eyes drifted in the direction of Ruth's door instead of staring straight ahead.

Training made Noah's tongue lead in his mouth. Days passed and the training kept him silent.

In the end, Seth broke, raising her hand the moment she exited her room. Smith didn't respond and Noah counted the minutes in his head.

Then Solomon raised his hand. Boaz followed moments later. Adam threw back his shoulders and lifted his hand. Within seconds, everyone except Jonah had their hand raised.

Finally, Smith answered with a dispassionate, "Yes, Seth?"

She struggled with each word. "W-w-whe-where is R-rrrr—" She clenched her fists in frustration as she became stuck on the "r".

Impatient, Boaz took over, "Where is Ruth?"

A long moment of hesitation. "Ruth failed his mission."

"What does that mean?" Boaz asked.

Smith answered in his same emotionless tone, "You were all warned of the penalty for failure. Ruth failed."

Noah felt an eerie, sinking feeling in his stomach.

"He's dead?" Solomon asked.

Elijah gasped, her fingers rising to her throat. "You

killed him?"

"He fell victim to our enemy," Smith replied.

Boaz cried out in shock, her hands covering her mouth. There were varied reactions and outcry from his siblings, but it was Seth's reaction that stunned Noah the most. Tears rolled down her cheeks before she released a strange choking sound and covered her face with her hands.

Noah stood frozen in place and looked at each of his siblings to judge their reactions. None of them seemed like they knew what to do either. Solomon made the first move, traveling to Seth's side. Some instinct pushed at Solomon as he gathered Seth into his arms and held her.

"Seth," Boaz murmured, morose.

Jonah made a loud noise of disgust. "She is weak. She is unsuitable for—"

"You are not being fair," Solomon said with a scowl.

Jonah thrust out a hand to gesture Seth with utmost scorn. "She cannot even speak! She is a *soldier*, not a sniveling child—"

Smith's amplified voice cut across theirs. "Silence."

Even though he had not spoken, Noah snapped his eyes forward and waited for Smith's punishment.

"You will not disrespect me," Smith continued. "Your instructions for the day are canceled. Instead, you will stand at attention until released."

Missions ceased as a result of Ruth's demise. Training increased. Noah collapsed on his bed in exhaustion daily. Sometimes one of the others would collapse during training. Seth, Solomon and Moses were more likely to, but when Adam began to succumb to the over-exertion, Noah grew concerned.

Their brief outburst had been the only time they got to speak. Smith ordered silence when any of them dared speak out of turn. Days and days of silence.

Ruth's absence didn't concern Noah in the same way Seth's grief did. She was silent, not only of her voice but her body language as well. The flashing, tongue between teeth smile didn't appear as they exited their room. The delight in her eyes no longer shone. She barely ate. He worried, and his worry surprised him.

Solomon fretted most of all. He broke protocol to be near Seth as much as he could. He piled his own food onto her plate in an attempt to make her eat. He would look for her first as their doors opened. He paced her in the obstacle course, silent encouragement, and even on occasion, called out to her. Noah lost track of the number of times Solomon would brush against Seth as he tried to comfort her.

Jonah seemed angry all the time. She spoke in condescending tones even to Smith, she lashed out in combat practice, and she glared at everyone, especially Seth. The cloud of anger settled over them all and spread, seeping into everything they did.

Boaz was angrier at Jonah than she was at Smith and whenever they faced each other in hand-to-hand fighting, the combat would be brutal. Noah and Adam often had to intervene to force them apart, dodging their share of blows to do so.

When the missions restarted, Noah was more than happy to see the sun again, to feel it on his face and taste the wind. Elation rose within him, an unknown and startling emotion. He stood in a meadow in the middle of a forest, crushed grass and wildflowers beneath his boots, and ignored the incessant beeping of the bag beside him to raise his face to the sun. Butterflies and birds, all manner of flying bugs and floating seeds hung in the air. There was a peace within the meadow he couldn't find in the Institute.

His training kicked in. Shaking himself from his self-indulgent moment, he opened the bag. It contained the usual: cap, sunglasses to combat the glare and diminish color, map, water and food, a folder with photos and instructions, whatever camouflage gear was necessary, and weaponry.

The note and accompanying arsenal startled him. *Rendezvous with your partner here. Kill everyone within the target area.*

A partnered mission? A partnered mission with a kill-all order and no timer. Noah lowered the folder and sat on his haunches to stare at the bag. An assortment of weapons including a sniper rifle, throwing knives, ammunition secured in a bandolier, and a gun holster with an extra slot for a long blade. Moving quickly, Noah strapped the blade to his thigh and the holster around his waist, threw the bandolier across his chest and secured the guns. Adjusting the cap, he grabbed the bag and was off in the direction the map directed.

He hesitated as he reached the rendezvous destination, pausing to hide in the protection of underbrush. Using his sniper rifle, he scouted his lush surroundings as he looked for his partner, only to discover another rifle already pointed at him. As he watched, Elijah pulled her head away from the scope long enough to identify herself. Noah dropped the barrel, lifting his head so she could see who he was.

Satisfied, they both left their cover and approached.

"Elijah," Noah greeted, lifting his cap so she could see his face better.

Equipped with similar gear to his and her rifle shouldered, she picked her way around a fallen log. "Noah."

"We are to partner."

She tilted her head. "That was obvious."

He watched himself in the reflection of her sunglasses. "Have you ever partnered before? Especially on a kill-all order?"

She dropped her gaze to fuss with her gun. "No."

"Neither have I. Judging by these weapons, we may need to engage in hand-to-hand combat."

She considered. "It is…"

"Significant," Noah supplied.

She shuffled. "Yes."

The silence between them stretched, as both lacked the social graces to start a conversation. Spotting a small bundle of wildflowers growing among rocks, Noah dropped down beside them and cupped the prettiest in his palm. Using his thumbnail, he severed the stem of the flower and tucked it into his sock.

Elijah tilted her head. "Why did you do that?"

"For Seth," he replied. "It makes her smile."

"I see." With a sharp nod, Elijah said, "Good."

After making sure the flower remained hidden, Noah stood. "Have you been outside before?" It seemed wasteful not to speak with her now they were without scrutiny.

Elijah stared at him. "We should scout."

"Yes. Of course," Noah said with a nervous twitch and a small shake of his head.

Elijah took a step backward and about-faced to head in the direction of the kill circle. She glanced over her shoulder at him, her expression as though she wasn't sure what to make of him.

Noah inclined his head and pulled his cap down. "Lead on."

They traveled low and fast through the forest. Noah noted Elijah wasn't as competent as he was at stealth, and he reasoned she may not have had as much exposure to the wilderness as he had.

The ground began to grow rocky, as moss-covered stones jutted from the dirt. They stopped at the top of a large rock cliff to check their map and Noah saw something flashing in the trees in the distance below them.

He grabbed Elijah's arm and pulled her down toward the ground to make them less conspicuous. Lying flat on his stomach at the top of the cliff, he angled his pack off his back and pulled his rifle into position to use the scope. Beside him Elijah did the same, although she watched him instead of the forest to gauge where he looked.

Peering through the scope, he whispered, "Light, two o'clock, three hundred feet."

He scanned the forest, looking for gaps in the tree line or other lights. He could tell something was there; a glimpse of what appeared to be netting, another flash of cut wood.

"A tent?" Elijah whispered after a moment. She lifted herself to peer down the slope, then rechecked her scope.

Noah caught a glimpse of a moving figure and tried to follow their path, only to be blocked by foliage. "There is movement."

"We are too high."

"Agreed."

Elijah shuffled forward to peer over the edge. "There appears to be a small ledge halfway down."

Noah refocused his search on the woodlands closer to them. "It appears clear. Go."

Elijah hesitated. "They are within our target location. It is logical that they—"

"Agreed," Noah said, turning his head to meet Elijah's gaze. "However, we need to determine numbers. That ledge might be a good vantage point for ranged assault. If it is suitable, I shall get closer to scout."

Elijah nodded. Returning her gun to her shoulder, she scrambled over the edge of the cliff.

It didn't take her long to clamber down, set up her rifle, and peer through the scope. Twisting so she could look up at him, she signaled she'd stay there. After securing his rifle, Noah cut some small, leafed twigs from close trees and dropped then down to Elijah.

"I count six at present but several tents are closed," she told him as she secured the twigs around herself to act as extra cover. She rummaged in her bag, extracting a suppressor and fixed it in place. "I see no evidence of other encampments. They are armed."

Noah nodded. "Watch for me. I shall get as close as I am able. Swiftness and silence."

Elijah returned her sight to the scope. "Will you engage in hand-to-hand?"

"If I am able."

"I shall cover you."

While Elijah was scaling the cliff, Noah had plotted his route to the camp. One that would take him close while maintaining a reasonable level of cover. Staying low and quiet, Noah darted from cover to cover, keeping a constant watch on his surroundings. Aware of his position in relation to Elijah's hiding spot, he maintained line-of-sight with her at all times so she could provide support.

Since this was a precision, militaristic strike, Noah expected the camp to have some form of lookouts or scouts. What he didn't expect was to find only one. He circled the encampment twice to verify. The lookout was a young man, propped up against the trunk of a tree with his gun by his side and safety on, and a hat over his face as he slept. He paid for the momentary inattention with his life, and then Noah slipped along the edges of the camp.

Three tents were set about in a triangle with a low burning fire positioned in the middle. Several camping chairs were strewn around the area and a table sat beside the fire. A rope strung between two of the tents had several pieces of clothing pegged on it. There were a few random plastic boxes and Noah surmised they were for food or other equipment. Since there were no vehicles, everything had to have been carried to this location. Several rifles lay on the ground beside the chairs, but they were not within easy reach of any of the six people who sat by the campfire talking and laughing.

Recalling Elijah's warning about closed tents, Noah knew he would need to be fast. He positioned himself so he could rush into the camp with the least number of obstacles. He completed a quick check of his gear and, pulling out his long knife, he nodded toward Elijah's hiding place. A knife attack with Elijah's ranged support would dispatch them efficiently while allowing for any more that appeared from within the tents.

Elijah chose her first target well: the man at the opposite side of the camp from where Noah hid. As the back of the man's head burst after Elijah's bullet entered his forehead, Noah sprang from his hiding place and rushed the closest person. Noah's blade sank into the back of the man's neck with ease as he rose in surprise from the folding chair.

Yanking out his blade, Noah shoved the man forward and used the man's back to leap for the next man, slicing his neck as Elijah gunned down her next target. With only two left, it took little effort for Noah to jump on one of the remaining men and sink his blade under his chin. Elijah took out the last.

Standing in the middle of the dead and dying men, he scanned the area, double checking the wounds he'd made would be fatal. The last thing he wanted was for one of them to reach for a gun. One of the men was still gasping, clutching at his neck and staring straight at him.

Something was wrong with the man. With his eyes. With his body. Noah moved closer, staring at the man's face. The eyes were wrong; smaller, squinty. The nose, too, it was straight, large. His face was round, his lips were small, and there was hair on the upper one.

Noah hooked a finger onto his sunglasses so he could peer over the top of them. The scales of his enemy were the wrong color. Sort of brown whereas Noah's scales were the color of ash. On closer inspection, Noah realized the man had skin, not scales. The irises of his eyes were a strange, brown color while Noah and his siblings' eyes were so pale a gray they almost blended with the white.

Noah shook his head and took a step back, convinced it was some sort of deformity. As he glanced at the other dead in the camp, the same deformity was replicated again and again. Skin tones of a variety; brown, black, pink. Was this the reason Smith had never allowed them to have face-to-face contact with the enemy? If their faces and skin revealed who they were, shouldn't it make eliminating them easier?

The harsh grating sound of a zipper cut through his musing. Noah turned and found himself staring at Ruth. The tent flap fluttered closed behind Ruth and he stepped clear of the tent, with his gaze locked on Noah. He wore garments similar to the dead men: khaki pants, white top and boots. Noah noticed several tufts of brown hair protruding from the back of Ruth's cap.

Noah stepped back, unnerved in more ways than one.

Ruth was wrong too. His eyes were a darker blue, set in a light brown face. His nose was bumpy and his lips were narrower and had more color. The bones on his face were more defined. There was a fire to Ruth's expression Noah hadn't seen before. A fire directed at Noah.

"What did you do?" Ruth snarled. He ducked down, grabbing a machete from beside the tent door before he stalked toward Noah.

Noah retreated. Emotions ran through him so fast he couldn't tell exactly how he felt. "You are dead."

"Do I appear dead?" Ruth scoffed.

Noah blinked and pointed his bloodied knife at Ruth. "What is wrong with you?"

"Nothing," Ruth said. "We're the ones who are wrong."

Noah frowned at the strangeness in Ruth's words. How was he to wear the ones who were wrong? Or was it a strange colloquialism he hadn't heard before? "I do not—"

"We are wrong, Noah," Ruth said, waving his machete as he circled Noah. "The Institute is wrong. I have been shown the truth behind the lie they feed us, and we are on the wrong side."

Noah's throat filled with bile. "You betrayed us."

Ruth spat on the ground as though he'd eaten something distasteful. "*Smith* betrayed us. Feeding us lies, omitting the truth, training us until we bled. The world is not like he tells it."

Noah gripped his knife and kept his eyes on Ruth, moving in the opposite direction Ruth circled. Was Elijah already on the move or could she see what occurred? He had to keep Ruth's attention so Elijah could... what? Kill Ruth? Ruth was their brother.

"Join me," Ruth said. He stood still, the machete pointed toward the ground as he extended his other hand toward Noah. "Join *us*."

Stalling for time, Noah asked, "Us?"

"Noah."

Noah extracted his gun from its holster and pointed at the new voice before he had even registered who spoke. "Boaz?" he blurted as he saw who it was. A sinking feeling buried itself in his stomach, making his knees weak. "But... I do not understand."

Standing on the outskirts of the camp, she gave him a somber look, thrust her hands into her khaki pants and ignored the gun. She was unchanged; her scales ash and eyes a light gray. "They lied to us. The world is very different."

Noah shook his head, keeping the gun trained on Boaz and his knife on Ruth. "How— I do not... You are not even—"

"My mission," Boaz murmured, understanding Noah's confusion, "resulted in locating Ruth. He showed me how the Institute has been lying to us. When I decided not to return, Ruth aided me in removing the ankle tracker."

"I guess not quick enough," Ruth said. "They still found us. I should have anticipated this and we should have moved farther."

Noah didn't like how they were on opposite sides of him, it kept his attention diverted. He knew that was why they maintained this position. "So, you would abandon us?"

Boaz shook her head. "Never."

Ruth rested his blade on his shoulder. "We do not know the location of the Institute. How are we to rescue you? Now, if we had someone on the inside…" He pointed the blade at Noah again as an indicative gesture. "Like you, for example, we could—"

"How is the world different?" Noah interrupted. "When Smith has not explained *anything* about this war we fight?"

"We followed with blind obedience," Ruth said.

Noah shook his head. "We *gave* ourselves to the Institute!"

"That is what they would have us believe," Ruth replied.

"They give us targets," Boaz said. "But they do not explain why we must follow orders." She gestured to the men around them. "Why did they have to die? What was their crime?"

Uneasy, Noah shuffled. His weapons were slick with sweat from his palms but he still trained them on Ruth and Boaz. "I had orders."

"We are witless pawns in a war we did not start." Ruth lunged forward. Noah took several rapid steps backward but Ruth had lunged for one of the dead men on the ground, grabbing a handful of cloth and hoisting him up. "The eyes, Noah. The face. The *skin*. Why does it startle you?"

Noah's gaze swung from Ruth to the void of the dead man's eyes. "It is wrong."

Ruth spoke, "What if I told you that every person I have encountered since leaving is as such. *Every* person. It is not them who are wrong. It is us."

The tip of Noah's blade dripped toward the ground. "What?"

"There *is* a war," Ruth explained. "What we are is at the heart of it." Ruth's blade pointed to his eyes and Noah watched in amazement as Ruth changed. His skin lost color, changing from brown to scaly gray. "Our scales and our lack of features are unnatural but we have them for a reason. They are a brand."

"A brand?"

"To mark us. To keep us complacent. They have us gender specific names based on something called a bible. Ruth is meant to be a female name while Boaz is male! They mix and match and twist us to their own devices. There is a reason why we are never allowed to see Smith. Because if we knew the truth, we would never allow them to use us the way they do." Ruth laughed and Noah felt a chill trickle down his spine. "Noah, we have this fantastic ability to blend in. To change—" Ruth paused, examining the man he held. "He was shot. Sniper round." Dropping the man, Ruth ducked closer toward the ground. "They sent two!"

Boaz hunkered down behind a tent, taking what little cover it offered and drew out a gun. "Who?" she demanded, scoping what she could see. "Who is your second?"

"See, Noah?" Ruth spat as he tried to see where Elijah was. "We are that much of a threat they must send two to keep us quiet."

"Why have we not already been dealt with?" Boaz asked, her voice rising in pitch. "Perhaps they mean to capture us?"

"We did not even know you were here," Noah said, not sure why he said it.

"What were your orders?" Boaz asked.

With regret, he met her glare. "Kill all."

"Do you intend to enact that order?" Ruth asked, his voice sharp.

His blade outstretched in one hand and his gun in his other, Noah turned his head to look at Ruth.

Ruth demanded, "What do you plan to do, brother?"

Uncertain, Noah looked toward where Elijah hid. As he did so, someone punched from behind. A spider web traced its delicate pattern across his chest and back. A pulse later, liquid lightning surged along the strands and stole his breath and his legs. Ruth and Boaz's horror-struck faces swam at him through a maelstrom of tilting lights.

"Noah!" Boaz screeched.

"Stay back!" Ruth yelled.

Noah pressed his hand to his chest and felt sticky, flowing warmth and missing flesh. Pulling his hand away, he stared at the blood coating his fingers.

His heart shuddered as it thumped, magnifying the pain. Pitching forward, he fell uncaring into the dirt and his next ragged breath was clogged with forest debris. Bubbles built in his throat.

"Noah!" Boaz screeched again.

Noah felt himself grabbed and yanked. Boaz's frantic face swam into view and her hands pushed against his chest to stem the flow of blood. "Hold on!"

He groaned at the pressure and fought to remain conscious. Above him, painted before the endless sky, Boaz jerked and her fierce expression went vacant.

She fell. Blood trickled from a hole in her forehead.

"Boaz!" Ruth bellowed, anguish twisting his tone.

Noah turned his head, staring into the vacant eyes of his sister and fought for his next breath. The world seemed to swim in and out of focus.

"What are you doing?"

"Ruth! Stay down!"

He didn't want to die. He'd barely begun to live. He didn't want to go the way of his sister, didn't want the next corpse to be his.

"Elijah! What are you—?"

"It is not me! *Stay down*!"

Deep within himself, he could feel the wound. The tears against the edges of his scales. The shredded blood vessels and muscle. The heart which could barely sustain the beat. He could feel the firing nerve endings racing away toward his brain as they relayed the damage and could feel his brain respond. He could feel the tiny parts of himself trying to mend the hurt as the army of his immune system battled to save him.

Pain gave way to clarity. All his body needed was help. Preferably before his poor heart gave out.

If the edges of the wound were closer together, if the flesh reached for each other and his army worked faster, the damage could be mended. If the flesh could be shifted closer...

Something shuddered through him, the pain fired on all fronts and he felt sick to his stomach. A headache bloomed —white hot fire which eclipsed the pain in his chest— but his flesh *reached*. It grew, knitted and meshed and as the pain in his head magnified, the frantic beating of his heart dimmed.

The world beyond the torrent of pain of his body and his head diminished until he wasn't aware it existed. Few scattered words drifted in, but he could make little sense of them.

"Ruth, you need to go."

"But—"

"You are dead to them, stay that way."

A pain in his head too vast to bear. The black beckoned and Noah went willingly.

"Noah, hold on, help is coming."

Two messages were sent within moments of each other. Both to different parties, both detailed a strange occurrence. Two messages that would ignite a change no one was prepared for:

Darcy,

Echo Seven accessed regeneration. No projected ability was deemed possible but I theorize, if they have regenerative capabilities, they can access the shift with greater ability than previous groups. I recommend we exploit this as soon as possible.

–Lacy

Rex,

Additional "Faceless" creatures have emerged and were attacked by, I believe, Welcher. Ruth is currently MIA, along with his newest recruit. We hope to make contact with him soon.

These Faceless show greater signs of ability. We need to find out which faction they're from. A breach like this should not be ignored.
—Shawn

CHAPTER 4

"Uhhh-gaaaaaaah."

"Didn't go so well?" Aly asked as she altered the strap of her backpack. She scratched the back of her leg with her shoe and looked out into the crowd of students on their way home.

Del thumped his forehead against the lockers in defeat. "Uggh."

"Guess not." She was tired, irritated because of last period's quiz, hungry and not willing to put up with Del's complaining today. "Least today's over, right?"

"I literally *hate* math," Del whined and stopped beating his head against the locker. "When are we ever going to use it again? Seriously."

"Grocery shopping," Aly pointed out and did a quick inspection of her fingernails. She found a snag-nail on her littlest finger and chewed it off.

"Taxes," Grace included as she typed on her tablet. A glance told Aly that Grace was jotting down some notes on her sheet music app. It wasn't uncommon for her to compose at school when inspired.

"Calculating the trajectory of a .338 Lapua Magnum," Fletcher said, sorting through his books in his locker.

"What?" Aly asked, confused and sure she'd misheard him.

Fletcher blinked, raised his head and looked at her. "Huh?"

"What's a..." she frowned as she struggled to remember. "Lap magnum?"

"Lapua Magnum?" Fletcher asked, returning her confused look. "Sniper ammo." He shook his head in disbelief. "Why?"

She shrugged. "You were the one who said it."

The disbelief turned to surprise. "I did?"

"Yup," Grace included.

"I guess I'm kind of distracted today," he said, closing his locker with a bang.

"No kidding," Del said with a frown. "You didn't even do most of that quiz. How can I copy answers if you don't even do them?"

"You could do your own work." Fletcher yanked the zipper on his backpack up and threw his arm through the strap.

"You didn't do the quiz?" Aly asked, surprised. Fletcher always aced all the math quizzes and did poorly on all tests that made him write essays. He said he got the structure of math; right and wrong rather than opinions.

He shrugged. "I guess not."

Aly rested her hand on his arm in concern. "What's wrong?"

Fletcher shook his head. "Nothing. I'm fine."

Aly could tell he was lying. Something had been off all day, starting with him not coming for breakfast, then being so late for school he'd missed homeroom. He'd barely said two words to her today. She'd hoped to catch him alone so she could ask him about it but he had been avoiding her. Transferring her weight from foot to foot, she plucked at his sleeve. "Fletch, you know I can tell—"

Fletcher took her elbow and tugged her into a walk, then released her. "C'mon. Home time."

"Yeah," Del said, dragging his feet as he moped beside Fletcher. "I need food after that quiz." He turned around to walk backward and look at Grace and Aly as they fell in behind the boys. "Y'all wanna grab a burger?"

"You just want food, not need." Grace poked him. "You're getting a gut."

Del warded away her hands with shooing motions and bounced so he could turn around again. "Pure muscle, girl. You're literally trippin'."

Aly glanced at Fletcher waiting for the reprimand about abusing the word "literally". It didn't appear Fletcher had noticed.

"Pure muscle, right," Grace mocked. "You should really join my gym."

"No thanks," Del said, feigning an over-the-top shudder. "Exercise. Sweating. Yuk."

"It'll be good for you," Grace said, then brightened. "I can be your gym partner."

"Yeah, like that's going to happen," Del scoffed. "I'm not having a *girl* show me up—"

Grace shoved him. "Sexist asshole."

"Hey," Del complained.

"If you're going to talk crap, she's going to call you on it," Aly pointed out.

"But Aly-cat," Del whined. "It was a joke!"

They passed by a cluster of giggling girls at their lockers, a normal thing in the hallways of the school, but Aly saw Fletcher hunch his shoulders. The group of boys they walked by next invoked the same reaction from Fletcher. Odd because they weren't talking about anything.

She grabbed Fletcher's backpack and tugged, intending to ask him what was wrong. "Fl—"

He whirled and grabbed her wrist, yanking her off balance. She couldn't read the expression on his face. It seemed so unlike him she didn't know what to think. Twisted and snarled, he saw something else, not her. As a sudden flurry of goose bumps flickered across her skin, she flinched.

He flexed his fingers on her wrist and caught her shoulder to help her balance, then jerked his hands away. "Aly."

"What's wrong?" His grip had hurt and she rubbed her wrist without looking at it.

Looking at the ground, he turned away and ran his hand through his hair. "You startled me."

She frowned. "But—"

"I'm on edge, that's all," he said, without allowing her to even get a question out. He glanced sideways at her, his gaze lingering on her wrist.

That wasn't an explanation, so Aly decided to push, "Fletch—"

Another haunted glance at her. "I gotta go."

"Are you okay?" Del asked Aly, standing close as he watched Fletcher retreat.

"Yeah."

"That was literally the weirdest shit—"

"Not now, Del," Grace said, chewing on a nail.

"I was just—"

She glared. "Not now."

"Spoilsport," he muttered. He thrust his hands into the pockets of his jeans and shuffled his weight from side to side.

Fletcher turned a corner in silence and Aly shared an uneasy glance with Grace. His reaction was strange. Aly wanted to know why he was so on edge and what she could do to help him.

"Aly?" Grace touched Aly's shoulder.

Aly dismissed Grace's concern. "Something's wrong. Look, I'll see you later, okay?" Without waiting for an answer, she hurried after Fletcher.

The first place she checked was the parking lot in case he'd left, but his bike was still in the bay. There weren't many places he could hide in the school and she knew all the hangouts he might go to be alone. She found him at the track, which was no surprise. Fletcher was on the school athletics team, so he could use the track and had his own locker in the change rooms.

As she watched him run, it was clear there was something troubling him. He pushed himself hard, his long legs stretching for each step. He'd changed into his track uniform, so he intended to run for a while, though she could tell his speed wasn't maintainable. After watching for a moment, Aly walked to the bleachers to wait.

The football team ran sprints while the quarterbacks threw the ball to each other from opposite ends of the field. Cheerleaders practiced their routines in a corner. A group of friends sat up the top of one of the bleachers and listened to music. Going to an empty bleacher, Aly sat on the fourth row and put her feet on the seat below so she could use her knees as a table. Reaching into her backpack, she pulled out her sketchbook and a pencil.

She alternated between watching Fletcher run and sketching. Her sketchbook was filled with anatomy practice, everything from hands and eyes, to expressions and gestures. Today she practiced feet, concentrating on the different moods she could create by the position of the toes and ankles.

The bleachers creaked as someone strode up to them, then a shadow fell over her. "Hey, sexy."

Keeping her eyes fixed on her sketchbook, she said, "Don't call me that."

"Looking mighty fine there today," Carter drawled. He put one foot up on the lower bleacher seat and then leaned on his knee. "Did you come to watch me play?"

Her skin crawled from his stance. "Does it really look like I'm watching you?" she muttered and gave a feminine foot hairy toes in the hope he'd get grossed out and leave.

"I've been meaning to corner you," he said, taking no notice of the daggers in her voice. "Prom's coming up."

Aly's stomach sank. "Oh, really? Hadn't noticed."

"And you're going with me."

"That's really not how you ask someone," she snapped. "I already have plans."

"No, you don't," Carter said. "I made sure no one asked you."

"That's really creepy of you." She folded her arms across her sketchpad and looked past him to Fletcher, who was on the other side of the field. Once she'd been enamored by Carter's blue eyes, blond hair and good looks, then the toxic nature of his personality had seeped through and all allure faded. He still couldn't take the hint. "I'm going with Fletcher."

"No, you're not," he scoffed.

"He asked me; I said yes. End of story."

Carter snorted. "He's gay."

"What's that got to do with anything?"

He looked bewildered. "A gay guy can't show a girl a good time."

"Oh, please," she scoffed. Slapping her sketchpad closed, she illustrated her displeasure with her actions as she shoved the pad into her bag and yanked up the zipper. As much as Fletcher didn't want to talk, she'd be stepping in his path the next time he came around. Knowing Carter, Fletcher would understand. Standing, she hooked her arms through the straps of her backpack.

"Carter! Head's up!" Ethan bellowed from the field below.

Carter, taking the rogue ball as a chance to show off, leaped for it. Having no trouble with the catch, he failed in the landing, crashing onto Aly. Within the tangle of limbs, Aly hit the bleacher wrong and a jarring pain shot through her left wrist and up her arm. Her head collided with a bench and she fell into the space between seats, her arm twisted beneath her. Carter's weight crushed her.

She gasped and mewed, struggling to breathe as she pushed against his bulk but her reach was awkward. "Get off me!"

"Not exactly how I wanted to end up on top—"

She squirmed. Her backpack had caught on something which held her in place and she couldn't move her arms to unhook it. "Move!"

"Relax, I'm moving—"

Wanting people around her to notice the predicament she was in, she made a fuss. She didn't care they were tangled. There were hands in places she didn't want them. "Stop touching me!"

"Stop wriggling, you're making this—"

"*Get off!*"

"I'm trying—"

Cloth tore as Carter was yanked from her. "Get off her!" Fletcher interposed himself between Carter and Aly then manhandled Carter away.

The force caused Carter to stumble for his footing. "What the hell?! Get off me, man!"

Fletcher turned away and hastened to her. "Aly—"

From her tangled position wedged between the bleachers, she managed an, "Ow."

"You tore my uniform!" Carter said, holding onto his ripped shirt. "You prick!"

Fletcher ignored Carter to reach down and help untangle her. He looked windswept, sweaty and unfairly gorgeous as his brown eyes filled with concern. Aly felt a familiar tug in her chest as he took her hand.

Livid, Carter charged. "Don't you turn your back on me!"

Releasing her, Fletcher swiveled to meet Carter. Fear ran rampant through Aly, covered her skin in goose bumps and stole her breath. A charging Carter was a force to be reckoned with as he was one of the best defenders on their school team.

Ducking beneath the wild swing, Fletcher planted two hands on Carter's chest and shoved. The reverberations of the hit and Carter's staggering footsteps jolted through the metallic bench. "Back off!"

Carter staggered back with an almost comical look of

disbelief on his face before it twisted with rage. "I will end you!"

Fletcher dodged the next swinging hit and the two of them clashed.

Panicked, Aly flailed, kicked her legs and squirmed. She managed to extract her arms from the straps, then yanked the backpack loose. Ignoring the bolt of pain surging through her hand, she pulled herself to her feet.

By then, footballers and cheerleaders had crowded around the two teens scuffling on the ground at the base of the bleachers. Grunts and the sounds of flesh impacts; Aly could hear the fight but couldn't see it well. She thundered down the bleachers. "Leave him alone!"

People jostled her, refusing to move. As she forced her way to the center, she could see Carter and Fletcher wrestling. With the tangle of limbs, it was hard to tell which one had the upper hand. "Fletcher!"

He heard her and his head turned in her direction. A mistake as it allowed Carter to get a grip on him and heave. In a deft move, Carter flipped them so he was on top and began laying into Fletcher's face and upper body. In an act of desperation, Aly darted into the fray and swung her backpack for Carter's back. Her bag thumped against his back and she winced, wondering how much stuff she'd broken in the connection. It might not have hurt him but it distracted Carter.

Releasing her bag, she didn't stop with the hit and slammed her shoulder into Carter's side. It was like hitting a brick wall and the shock of the hit jarred her. He retaliated, an elbow planted in her stomach, knocking the wind out of her and then Carter had her in a headlock. Crying out in pain, she felt off balance and tried to brace her right hand on the ground. Her left wrist was in agony as she tried to grip Carter's forearm. "Let go!"

Carter's grip loosened as he realized it was her. "Shit, Aly—"

Fletcher unfurled. His hand snapped up and he

slammed the side of it into the bridge of Carter's nose. The blow was followed by a jab to the stomach and a knee in the back. Carter toppled, dragging Aly with him and she sprawled sideways onto Fletcher before Carter let go.

Both of Carter's hands clutched his nose as he scrambled along the grass on his elbows and knees in an attempt to get away from them. Aly knew they had to stand up before Carter came for them again. Frightened, angry and pumped full of adrenaline, Aly grit her teeth. The chorus of chanting people around them pressed against her. So many faces and excited people with their cells and not a friendly among them. In that moment, she hated them all.

Fletcher bunched beneath her, flesh once soft turned rigid with straining muscle. Pressing her palm flat against his stomach, she tried to push herself upright only to be stalled by Fletcher's containing arms. He wrapped them around her and hoisted them both to their feet in one quick movement, then kept moving them away from Carter until the crowd didn't allow him to retreat any farther. Aly's back to Fletcher's chest, she hunched over, her heart pounding. She felt dizzy, so Fletcher steadying her seemed prudent.

On his knees, Carter checked his hands for blood then glowered at Fletcher. "Bastard. Do you know how much these jerseys cost?!"

"Keep your fucking hands to yourself next time!"

"Carter, you're an ass," Aly spat. Fletcher's encircling arms made it impossible to move but she still wanted to have a go at Carter, even with her wrist throbbing like it was.

Carter pointed at Fletcher. "He hit me first!"

"You wouldn't get off her!" Fletcher snapped. A drop of his blood splattered on Aly's forearm. She went still, zeroing in on the blood. For a moment, it seemed to glisten and she wondered how much Carter had hurt her. Even the tingling of her skin seemed to heighten. Fletcher moved them, circling the opposite direction of Carter, and Aly lost the moment.

"Everyone knows he's just using her to hide what he really is," Carter told the crowd of people. "Look at him using her a shield!"

Fletcher tensed.

"He's just trying to provoke you," Aly murmured.

Carter smirked at him. "You're just a big girl, aren't you? Does she do your hair and paint your nails?"

Ignoring her previous statement, Aly narrowed her eyes at Carter. "Oh, it's my turn to punch him."

"I so don't need this shit today," Fletcher grumbled and glanced down at Aly. "Are you okay?"

"I'm okay," she said, an automatic response even though she wasn't. The adrenaline in her system would crash soon and leave her shaky. She tilted her head up to look at Fletcher. A cut to his temple, a darkening eye and a split lip seemed to be the worst of it. The shirt, however, with its ripped collar, would end up in the trash.

Stiffening, he gripped her arm. "Your wrist."

Aly glanced down at her left wrist. She hadn't been aware she was gripping it, and now she didn't want to release it. It ached, a throbbing pain that heightened with every twitch.

"Carter, you shit! You broke her wrist!"

Derailing, Carter took a step back. "I—What?"

"She's left-handed, you complete prick, and you broke it! We have exams coming and—"

"No way! I can't help it if she's a clumsy b—"

Fletcher released Aly and took a step toward Carter. "Finish that sentence. I dare you."

"Back your squirrelly ass up," Carter yelled, backing away. "Before I make you—"

"All right," a voice boomed and Aly recognized Coach Hawkins' commanding tone. The crowd of students parted to allow him through. "Break it up."

A surge of relief passed through Aly and left her weak

at the knees. She staggered and Fletcher grabbed her again. "Aly?"

"A fist fight?" Coach said, eyeing the boys. "Really? I thought you knew better. This is really stupid of you both, fighting on school grounds."

"Wasn't my idea," Fletcher murmured.

"It wasn't Fletcher's fault," Aly intervened and took several steps toward Coach to illustrate her sincerity. "Carter started it. Fletcher was defending me."

"Carter had Aly in a headlock," someone called.

"No way. Fletcher threw the first punch!"

"Carter charged him and Fletcher blocked it!"

"Did anyone else see this?" Coach asked. Several students weighed in, adding their own embellishments.

"I *never* touched her!" Carter denied. He scrubbed at his nose again, glaring. "They're lying."

"I got it on my cell!" a student called, raising his device.

"Me too!" another called.

"Stand still, Mr. Johnson," Coach snarled and started herding people away. "I'll get to you in a moment. Everyone not involved, clear the area! I want all footage handed over to the Principal and if I find *any* of it up on YouTube, it'll be detentions for all of you! I'm especially disappointed in my football players for not intervening."

Fletcher pried Aly's hand away from her wrist and cupped her elbow to support her arm.

"No, don't—" she whined, shifting her weight onto her heels as she prepared to snatch her arm away.

"Shh. It's okay," he soothed as he ran the tips of his fingers over her skin.

"I'm fine," she protested. "It's probably just a sprain."

"It's a break," Fletcher said.

"Better not be," Aly muttered, thinking about all the work she had to do.

Still running his fingers lightly over her wrist, Fletcher raised his voice, "Sir, she needs a doctor."

Coach turned from disbanding the students and

nodded in acknowledgment. "I'm coming."

"I'm fine," Aly repeated.

"I didn't touch her," Carter protested, his voice muffled because he held his nose. "And he broke my nose!"

"No, I didn't," Fletcher said. He seemed absent, detached, and Aly grew concerned he might be more hurt than she expected. "Don't move your hand." Concentrating, he traced the same area of her wrist over and over again. His touch was gentle enough it didn't add any extra pain, but she didn't understand why he did it.

"I know," Aly said, nodding. "Are you all right?"

He met her gaze only briefly and she saw the lie in them. "I'm fine."

Coach approached Aly, wincing at Fletcher's face. "What's this about a doctor?"

"I'm in serious pain here," Carter complained.

"Her wrist's broken," Fletcher said.

Coach fixed his eyes on Aly's wrist. "How?"

Aly explained, "Carter was being an ass and knocked us both into the bleachers. Then he wouldn't get off me. I landed wrong."

Coach scowled at Carter as he complained about the pain again. "You're in serious trouble. Sit down."

Carter huffed and flopped down on the bleachers.

"Can you move your fingers?" Coach touched Aly on the shoulder as he inspected her wrist.

She tried, agony splashed up her arm as she wriggled her fingers. Tears pricked in response.

"Hmm." Coach gave her a reproachable look. "I never expected you to be in the middle of a fight, Ms. Gale."

"I never expected it either," she mumbled.

Fletcher pressed, "Sir, she really needs—"

"Right, the three of you, nurse's office." He snapped his fingers and pointed to the closest lingering student. "You, report to the office and have Principal Boyd paged to the nurse's office please."

Supporting Aly's arm so she wouldn't move it, Fletcher herded her toward school.

CHAPTER 5

By the time they reached the nurse's office, Aly's wrist showed signs of swelling. She couldn't feel bone scraping when she moved, so she settled on thinking it could be a fracture. Being left-handed, the prospect of being in a cast for a few weeks sucked. She'd need to apply for extensions on her art projects.

The school nurse gave her ice and recommended the hospital, which meant Roger would be the one to patch her up, pulling family rank on the other doctors, even if technically he wasn't allowed to. Roger would also take care of Fletcher, although she wasn't certain Fletcher wanted it. The cuts Fletcher received had stopped bleeding and while Carter's face and nose had begun to swell, Fletcher's had no sign of swelling yet.

Principal Boyd was livid. Rather than listen to his words, Aly resorted to watching the veins on his neck pulse and counted how many times a globule of spittle flew from his mouth. He spoke of maturity and college and how they had undermined the authority of the school by being so blatant in their disrespect for each other. In pain, she really didn't care, she wanted him to shut up so she could leave.

When Aly and Fletcher arrived at the hospital, Roger was waiting for them. Judging by his expression, Penelope wasn't far away. He ushered Aly and Fletcher into a private consulting room and sat Aly on the bed. Aly thought a private room was best, especially since she'd spotted Carter entering the waiting room.

"So, what happened?" Roger asked, lifting the ice-pack from Aly's wrist so he could inspect it. "A fist fight doesn't sound like either of you."

"Walked into a door," Fletcher said, blasé.

Roger raised his eyebrow. "While I appreciate the sentiment, what I really want to know is should I call the police and lodge this as assault."

Fletcher paused, then grew concerned. "Really?"

"Done that and more in my time in the ER," Roger said as he returned the ice-pack to Aly's wrist. "I'll order an X-ray, but I think Fletcher's right."

Aly looked to Fletcher. "As much as I'd like to see Carter charged, this was an unfortunate accident," she said, indicating her wrist, then pointed at Fletcher's face. "That wasn't."

"I'm fine," Fletcher responded without hesitation. "Flesh wound."

Roger reached over the gap between them and took Fletcher's chin, angling his face so he could see Fletcher's temple. "Looks like more than that to me. Glue or stitches?"

"Neither," Fletcher said, shooing Roger away. "It looks worse than it is."

"You should report this—"

Fletcher shook his head. "It's more trouble and attention than I want right now."

Annoyed, Roger said, "Fletcher, I'm obligated to—"

"I wasn't assaulted. I don't want to press charges. It was a stupid fight. Which I started."

Roger narrowed his eyes, picked up his clipboard with Aly's patient notes, and continued to fill them in. "You sound like you're listing reasons why I shouldn't."

"I am. I've got more. Doctor-patient confidentiality. Principal Boyd didn't see the need to get the police involved. Besides, I don't actually need patching up," Fletcher insisted. "So you don't have to report anything."

"And what if the other guy reports you?"

Fletcher shrugged, uncaring. "Then he does."

Aly watched Fletcher closely. She wasn't sure of the legal obligations Roger had, whether he told the truth or acted like an enraged father figure trying to protect his family. "Roger, do you have to?"

Roger sighed and tapped the clipboard he carried with the base of his pen. "No, but I still think you should."

"It'd probably cause more problems than it's worth," Aly said, rearranging the ice-pack.

"I wouldn't even be here if Aly hadn't gotten hurt." Fletcher turned to scowl at her. "You shouldn't have gotten involved."

Aly arched an eyebrow at him. "Excuse me?"

"I had everything under control—"

Aly frowned. "Carter was *sitting* on you—"

"I didn't ask for your help. I certainly didn't ask you to follow me to the track!"

"I was worried—"

"I was fine!"

"You've been so weird today—"

Roger frowned at the quarreling pair and chided, "Time and place."

Fletcher didn't seem to hear him. "I have been in worse scrapes, it's not—"

Aly was bewildered and hurt by his anger. "Why are you taking this out on me?"

Not looking at her, he snarled, "If you'd just left it alone you wouldn't have gotten hurt! Seriously, what were you thinking?"

"I was thinking about you!" she snapped. "You *punched* Carter! You, of all people, were going for it with him. He's the size of a truck and he was sitting on you. Did you expect me to watch?"

"He threw the first punch," Fletcher dismissed. "I just threw the first one that connected."

As hurt as she was, she forced her voice soft. "Fletch, c'mon. This isn't you. What's going on?"

Fletcher's jaw clicked as he shut his mouth. He stared at her, his face going blank. Spinning, he flopped down on the guest chair and made a huffy noise.

Looking between them, Roger said, "Why don't we get the X-ray done, then worry about the rest of this?"

"Can I have some painkillers?" Aly asked, sullen.

Roger raised his eyebrows. "You haven't taken anything?"

"Not yet."

Roger turned and headed for the door. "I'll be right back."

Fletcher leaned forward, rested his arms on his knees and hung his head. Aly swung her feet up on the bed and shuffled backward until she could rest her back against the head. Wincing, she adjusted her ice-pack then returned to ignoring Fletcher out of spite. Most of the ice was water and her wrist was numb from the cold, but every time she removed the pack she could feel the pain seeping in.

"I never wanted you to get hurt," Fletcher said meekly.

Aly nodded and refused to make eye contact with him. It was petty, she knew, but she couldn't help it.

"If I'd known—" Fletcher gestured the room and sighed. "I should've ditched today."

She pressed her lips together.

"Aly… I…"

She grunted at him.

He eyed her. "You're going to milk this, aren't you?"

"For everything it's worth," she said, with false grandeur.

He groaned. "Great."

"You deserve it."

"I guess."

She tossed her head and cast him a glare. "You shouldn't have yelled at me." Fletcher ducked his head. "It wasn't my fault."

He slid down in his chair. "I know."

"I was trying to help."

"I know."

Since he was so agreeable, Aly said, "You're a bumble-butt."

He flashed a smile. "I know."

She snorted, then jerked her head to beckon him over. "Get over here."

He bounded up from his chair and she shuffled over to give him space on the bed. Gangly legs up on the bed beside her, he threw his arm behind her back and pulled her in for a side hug. Aly sighed and rested her head on his chest. "You're buying pizza tonight."

"Done."

"With pineapple."

Fletcher heaved a dramatic sigh. "Fine."

"And you're not allowed to pick it off."

"*Alllleeeeeeee,*" he whined and jostled her to voice his disapproval.

"Maybe two pizzas would be better," she mused, teasing him.

"One pizza," Fletcher bargained. "A couple of Snickers, new release movie and you let me pick the pineapple off."

Aly closed her eyes and snuggled into him. "And you let Roger take a look at your face."

"I don't need—"

"I need," she said, her voice quiet as she plucked at his shirt at the waist with her good hand. "Please."

Fletcher was silent, then, with another heavy sigh, he said, "You drive a hard bargain."

"You only have yourself to blame for that."

"Yeah." Fletcher pressed his mouth against the top of

her head. "Thanks for being so patient with me," he muttered before tilting his head to rest it against hers.

"Anytime. Now, cough it up. What's going on?"

He sighed and ran his hand through his hair. "Noth—"

"Whatever it is, it's not nothing."

He shuffled. Looked up at the ceiling. He rolled his eyes and ran his hand through his hair again before he decided to answer. "Had some bad news, that's all."

Aly's brow furrowed as she tried to think what it could be. Anything she could think of wouldn't have provoked a reaction from him. Money worries made him defensive. School made him hide behind humor. What would make him depressed? "What bad news?"

Fletcher's eyes dropped to the floor. "Cousin of sorts... I got word he died."

"Oh, Fletch," Aly murmured as her heart gave a painful twang. Tears pricked in sympathy. "I'm so sorry."

He didn't say anything but his arm tightened around her.

She chewed on her bottom lip. "Why didn't you say anything?"

"I'm fine," he insisted.

"You're not. I know how hard this must be but you don't have to go through it alone."

Fletcher's thumb brushed against her forearm. "See, that's the thing. It's not hard," he murmured.

"What?"

"It's not that... I'm not..." He sighed. "I'm not *sad*, Aly," he admitted in low tones.

That was a surprise. "You're not?"

He looked at the white, tiled floor. "I haven't seen him in years. Not since... I feel..." He rubbed his neck. "I feel relieved more than anything."

"I know you're not close to your family... but relieved?"

"Yeah. I know." He looked at her, seeking reassurance. "Is it bad of me?"

She gave him honesty. "I don't know."

"See…" He sighed and scrubbed his hand through his hair again. Parts of it remained sticking up as he'd done it so much the past few minutes. "It's over for him."

She tried to be soothing. "That kind of happens when—"

"Not what I mean," he interrupted. "I just… he…" Fletcher raised his hand and stared at his palm. "I can't explain."

"You could try."

"No." He shook his head. "I don't even know where to begin. There's so much… but it's over. He won't have to worry anymore."

Since it didn't look like he would elaborate, Aly placed her uninjured hand over his upraised one. "You know I'm here for you. I can help." She paused. "I can help more than picking a fight with one of the linebackers and getting yourself beat up can."

He snorted and curled his fingers around hers. "Would've hurt less."

"Exactly. I understand why you did that, though. You're a mess. It probably didn't take much to provoke you into doing something stupid."

"I usually have more restraint than that."

"Everyone loses it sometimes."

"Thanks, Als. You're my favorite person."

Why did he make that sound so sad? Snuggling closer, she muttered, "Bumble-butt."

The X-ray revealed an extra-articular, non-displaced, distal radius fracture, which didn't mean much to Aly. She could have done without the medical jargon, but as Roger continued to explain, it was a simple fracture, the bone hadn't moved, surgery wasn't required, but a cast would be applied once her swelling had decreased. For now, she had to wear a splint.

By the time the tests were complete, Grace and Del arrived and Penelope had delivered an animated speech about what she thought of the situation. As Aly and Fletcher listened, Aly was glad Carter wasn't at the hospital anymore. He'd been sent home with ice packs and a few painkillers for his not-broken nose.

Penelope wasn't angry at them, just about the situation, and Aly was sure she'd ring Principal Boyd. Aly could barely listen to Penelope complain to Roger about it, who nodded carefully every time it was expected. Painkillers always made Aly drowsy and this time was no different.

Fletcher, who'd washed the blood from his face and allowed Roger to butterfly clip his temple, sat beside her with his arm around her again and let her doze on his chest. Outside their room, Penelope dialed up the Principal to give him a piece of her mind.

"Wow, your mom's scary," Del said, watching as Penelope paced up and down the hallway.

Aly watched with a wilted gaze. "Yup."

"Your mom's like that too," Grace pointed out. "Except she'd be quoting legal stuff at the same time and threatening to sue."

Del nodded. "True."

"Best let her get it out of her system," Roger said, tucking a small paper bag into Aly's backpack. "Painkillers, you know the drill. No driving. No more than two every four hours, no more than eight in a twenty-four-hour period."

Aly said, "Uh-huh."

Roger patted her leg affectionately. "Love you, honey." To Fletcher, he said, "Call me if you have lingering headaches, Fletcher. Don't try and soldier through the pain."

"Gotcha."

Aly said, "Uh-huh."

"We should get you home," Fletcher said, as Aly listened to the reverberations in his chest.

Aly said, "Uh-huh."

"Are you high?" Del teased, grinning.

Aly sighed. "Uh-huh."

"Think she'll have crazy dreams again?" Grace asked, giggling.

"Probably," Del replied with a light laugh. "Her whacked out dreams are the best." He side-glanced Grace with his best shit-eating smile. "'Member that time she sliced her knee at the lake? What was the dream that time?"

"Potato sacks and unicorns," Grace teased and squeezed Aly's leg.

"Oh yeah! That's right. Throwing themselves over cliffs!" Del announced and launched into an embellished retelling of the story.

Del's voice and Fletcher's heartbeat lulled Aly toward sleep.

"Pizza tomorrow?" Fletcher suggested.

"Nope," Aly said, stirring. "Not getting out."

"She'll be fine in a few hours," Roger told Fletcher. "I gave her a stronger dose to start with while we checked things out."

"Okay. I'll be over…" Fletcher's chest rumbled again and she drifted away to the sound of his voice.

Later, when she'd woken, groggily rousing from her bed because the desert in her mouth craved fluids, Aly headed for the kitchen. She found it odd there didn't seem to be any lights on, despite it being dark outside. She'd slept longer than she'd anticipated.

Switching on the light in the kitchen, Aly jumped in surprise when she saw Penelope and Roger sitting at the kitchen table. "What are you doing with the lights off?"

Penelope blinked, looking like she'd been woken from sleep herself. "It's later than I expected," she said, her voice husky.

"Man," Aly said as she headed for the fridge. "Those painkillers are trippy, Roger. I had the strangest dream.

Fletcher was telling me to trust the Snickers, like he was some sort of Yoda." She put on a mock Yoda voice. "Trust the Snickers, Aly, *mmmm*." Returning to her own voice she continued, "It was hilarious; he's going to make so much fun of me when he hears." She grabbed a bottle of water with the wrong hand, winced and switched hands. "This is going to take some getting used to." Kicking the door closed, she wrestled with the lid. "Little help?" she implored since she couldn't get her fingers on the broken hand to grip.

"Aly." Roger rose to his feet.

"Yeah? Wait, I got it," she said, then used her teeth to open the lid. "What time is it? Is Fletcher here yet?"

"Aly."

Aly swallowed her mouthful of water as she studied her parents. Something in Roger's voice. A warning. Something wrong. Penelope struggled to keep her composure. A wad of used tissues in the middle of the table. Roger was pale. Nerves and panic flared in her belly. "What's wrong? Where's Tim?"

"Tim's fine. He's at Ryan's place for the night," Roger said, placing his hand on Penelope's shoulder. Steeling himself, he said, "Aly, honey… there's been an accident."

Penelope burst into tears and covered her face with her hands.

Stunned by her mother's reaction, Aly's heart began to pound. "What?" she squeaked.

"Fletcher… he… he was…" Roger's voice cracked.

Her mind jumped to conclusions as she took in the subtle clues her parents presented. Shock bolted through her and she shook her head in denial. "No," she said, all her breath whooshing from her.

"His bike… it rammed into the barrier on the bridge. We don't know why yet…"

The bottle dropped from limp fingers and spilled onto the floor by her feet. Hot tears flooded her eyes, terror burst within her torso and she felt the world spin out of control. "Dad, no. *Please.*"

Roger struggled with his words, then choked on them. "Honey, I'm sorry. He's gone."

CHAPTER 6

The room was too white. The brightness of it sliced at his eyes as he tried to open them. After the incredible amount of concentration it had taken to open his eyes in the first place, he was loathe to open them again. The blinding light only worsened the headache pounding behind his eyes and made the want to sink back into unconsciousness greater.

"Noah."

He knew that voice. The sound of it scraped along his spine like a chilly finger and unbidden prickles danced along his sensitive flesh.

Eyelashes fluttered against his cheeks before his eyes tested the world again. Still bright, but he could make out vague shapes swimming above him. A bright light with a circular shadow behind it, beyond that was something white and humanoid. The figure moved away and vanished out of his line of sight.

"Noah."

Smith.

Training forced his eyes open and his shoulders off the bed before pain overwhelmed and forced him flat. Groaning, he tried to move at a more sedate pace only to find his wrists and ankles strapped to the bed. Even though it was futile, he still tried to pull at them. "Wha—?"

"Explain yourself."

Blinking, he alternated between opening each eye to snatch a view of the overly bright room. "I do not understand."

"Explain."

Giving his wrists another experimental tug, he asked, "Explain what?"

"The bullet should have killed you, and yet, here you are."

In his haze caused by a pounding headache, he said, "I told my body to fix the damage."

Silence filled the room, bringing with it a score of other sounds. The buzz of electrical equipment, the hum of the air-conditioner and a hypnotic, rhythmic beeping, all of which lulled Noah. By the time Smith spoke again, Noah was almost asleep. "And it did?"

Rousing through the headache was hard and he couldn't manage anything more than "Yes."

"Can you do it again?"

"I do not know."

"What's wrong?" Another voice, feminine, one he hadn't heard before. Their words seemed to slur together in his ears but he thought he heard a tone beneath, something that didn't exist in Smith. Compassion.

"Headache."

"I see," the female said.

A sharp pain in his arm and then, to Noah's relief, nothing.

Upon waking the next time, Noah stumbled through his morning routine without being fully aware. Toilet. Shower. Dress. Stand to attention. He didn't wake up completely until a small figure barreled into his chest and held on. He froze, arms held up and away from his sides, while he tried to determine what had occurred. With sudden focus, he saw all his siblings staring at him in shock from their respective doors. All except one.

"Seth?" Noah asked, startled.

Her face buried in his chest, she squeezed him and he felt a flare of pain to the left of his sternum. "I th-thought you were d-dead too."

"What?" he blurted, watching his siblings close in around him. Lowering his arms, he rested his hands on Seth's back and fixed his gaze on Adam and Moses as they approached.

"Two weeks," Elijah said, her voice catching. Noah's eyes flashed toward her, startled to discover the pained expression on her face and unshed tears in her eyes.

"Elijah?" Noah coaxed. His eyes drifted over everyone's concerned faces to register their emotions. They lingered on Jonah as she held her position away from them.

Elijah took a deep breath to steady herself, blinked, and raised her chin. "You have been absent for two weeks. Boaz is also missing."

"Two weeks?" Noah echoed, stupefied. "Boaz?"

"We do not know," Moses supplied.

"When we returned from our mission, you were barely breathing," Elijah continued. "Smith would not tell—" Her voice cracked and she threw herself at Noah as well, wrapping herself over the top of Seth so her mouth was strategically by his ear. "Do not mention Ruth or Boaz. They do not know and neither does Smith," she whispered, then hid the action with a muffled sob in his neck.

He remained stiff. Why would Elijah want him to lie? A lie was alien to him, what need did he have for doing so? What gain could lying give him? Something wet dripped against his neck and he realized not all Elijah's emotion was feigned. He pulled one of his arms out from between Elijah and Seth to include Elijah in the hug.

"What happened?" Adam asked, his hand on Noah's shoulder. They all seemed to need physical contact with him and Noah wasn't sure why. It unnerved and comforted him in ways he couldn't explain.

He blinked at Adam's question, then frowned. "I do not... I remember..." He struggled with the particulars. He didn't know how much they knew, how much Elijah had told them, or even if his memories of the situation were true. "The mission. We were..."

"We were finished," Elijah mumbled and then pulled away. She sighed and shoved her hands into her pockets. "They gave us a kill circle and we completed the circle. But there was another sniper. Long distance. Neither of us saw him—"

"Noah was lucky," Smith interjected. "Next time he may not be as fortunate. Return to your places."

Sliding his arms from her back, Noah clasped Seth's upper arms to tug the small woman away from his chest. "Seth?"

She smiled and wiped her eyes with the back of her hand. "I am h-hap-py you live."

He returned her smile. "As am I."

She lingered beside him for a moment, happier than he'd seen her, before she returned to her position. As Noah took his place to stand at ease, the movement of his hands as he clasped them behind his back pulled at his chest. He barely managed to stave off the wince it caused but it did serve as a reminder to examine himself more thoroughly when he had the chance.

Their morning routine was normal. They ate breakfast and then ran on the treadmills with their heart rates monitored. His siblings seemed happier than usual, Seth had a bounce in her step that seemed to permeate through all of them, even Jonah. The mood caused Noah to wonder what it must have been like for them while he was gone.

The missing two weeks gnawed at him with every step he took. He couldn't fathom why Smith had separated him for so long. Added to that was Elijah's request for him to withhold information. He recalled Ruth and Elijah's voices as he fought the pain of the bullet wound, but had they continued to speak after he succumbed to the darkness? Was Elijah now a traitor? Or had Smith really betrayed them as Ruth had said?

The longer he spent on the treadmill, step after step, the more he thought upon what Ruth had said and what Noah had done to his body to survive. Somehow, he'd increased his capacity for healing. He didn't know what that meant, but he was certain it wasn't natural.

Smith called them to a halt much sooner than Noah expected but he was glad for the chance to stop. The accident had left him more aware of the inner workings of his body. He could feel how hard his heart was working to keep the pace and how lacking his lungs were in processing oxygen. The workout had taken more from him than he had expected. Deep in thought, he rubbed the heel of his palm across the spot on his chest in an attempt to alleviate the pain. Slumping against the wall, Noah wondered what he could do to increase the capacity of both his heart and lungs as well as ease the pain in his chest.

"You had a joint mission?" Jonah asked.

Noah looked up, startled from his thoughts.

"Yes," Elijah answered for him. "We did."

"What sort of enemy could warrant two?" Jonah said. "Especially the two of you."

Elijah shot to her feet and faced Jonah. "What does that mean?"

Jonah's eyebrows rose, then her eyes narrowed in response to Elijah's anger. "Your skills are complementary. I imagine you would have fulfilled the sniper role, while Noah was close combat. Or did they have you both sniper?"

Seeing it wasn't a criticism but a musing, Elijah relaxed. "We both had choices for weapons. You are correct in your role assumption."

Jonah grew pensive. "Odd. They have never allowed

me to get close to my target."

"Nor me," Moses added.

Adam commented, "Mostly it is specialized testing."

Noah exchanged a startled glance with Elijah. Why had they all risked speaking and why was Smith allowing them this moment to communicate? More importantly, why did it sound like the others had only ever had *one* target?

Jonah's eyes narrowed as she caught the exchange. "How many targets have you had?"

"Including the mission with Elijah?" Noah asked, then continued with Jonah's nod. "Twenty-two."

"Seventeen," Elijah said.

The stares of his siblings alarmed Noah, so he stared back in defiance. It was not his fault Smith chose to give him and Elijah more targeted missions.

"That many?" Solomon asked.

"Multi-kill targets," Noah said. "One was a convoy car of five occupants."

"It is not possible," Jonah said with open-mouth astonishment.

"Are you h-hurt?" Seth asked.

Noah realized he was still rubbing his chest. "It is where the bullet struck me." He let his hand drop to his lap. "It aches."

"It hit you *there*?" Moses asked, crouching down beside Noah. "How did you survive?"

"I do not know," Noah replied, his voice low. He still could not describe the feeling of making his body twist to his will and heal the damage done.

"It is one of the tools of our enemy," Smith intruded, his voice so sudden they all jolted at the interruption.

Noah felt a bolt of panic. Did Smith believe *he* was part of this enemy? Swallowing, he tried to contain the nerves that settled in his belly.

"It is?" Solomon asked.

"One that I have deemed time to teach you. Sit."

Noah sat up straighter while the others sat on the floor

around him.

"Our enemy calls it 'the shift'. They have the ability to create an illusion that allows them to take the appearance of another. This shift is undetectable with current technology and allows them to remain among the general population and avoid detection."

"Who is our enemy?" Jonah asked, clasping her hands behind her back.

"You have told us nothing about them," Adam noted.

Smith appeared to ignore the question. "It is my belief you have the ability to mimic them."

Moses put his hands on the floor behind him, leaning back to ask, "How?"

"Our enemy is not human," Smith continued. "We believe they are the first wave of an intergalactic war, sent to Earth to take control of key positions and make a hostile takeover more successful. The Institute intercepted and have even managed to merge alien DNA with human. It is part of the reason why you have no memories beyond this place, as the process was particularly painful. We were not aware access to the shift would be contained within the genetic structure we used, but it seems Noah may have inherited it. Since you all have similar genes, the probability of all of you being able to access the shift is high."

Noah frowned as he listened. Something was wrong with Smith's explanation and he wasn't sure what that was.

"All of us?" Elijah asked. There was a tone of eagerness in her voice.

"This is why you had us study anatomy," Solomon said with a wary glance at Seth. "In preparation."

"I always felt like I was *remembering* instead of learning," Jonah muttered and Noah's eyes flashed to hers, sharing her feeling. It seemed most of them felt the same. Perhaps their previous lives, whatever they were, explained that.

"The ability to change appearance may not be the only thing you have inherited. Noah has the ability to regenerate his cells. I am very interested in how he does this as we were not aware it was possible."

Gazes fell on him. Noah shrank back and changed the subject. "Explain the physical differences."

"Differences?" Jonah tilted her head in question.

Elijah nodded, addressing Smith. "Their eyes were odd."

"As was their flesh," Noah added.

Sitting beside Noah, Adam bent his knees and draped his arms across them as he asked, "Different how?"

Elijah frowned as she thought. "Much more diverse in their color than we are."

"Brown eyes. Various shades of skin," Noah said, thinking back. "Pinks and browns and blacks. Skin, not scales."

"Skin?" Adam blurted and looked at his arm. "How?"

"It was not only that. Their face was also different. Their bones were more defined. Smaller lips and eyes. Larger nose. The general shape of the face seemed rounder."

Smith went silent, so Noah turned his attention to his memories, specifically Ruth's appearance. In his mind's eye, he watched Ruth's skin change from brown to ash gray scales. Ruth had said everyone was like that and it was theirs that was wrong. He'd also called them a "brand". Like their names.

A brand. Ruth's companions had been so diverse in their appearances, while Noah and his siblings looked similar. But were they really similar, or was it only their scales they had in common? Were they genetically siblings? Or was that another lie?

"Does our appearance reflect the alien heritage?" Noah asked.

"Indeed."

Noah nodded and studied his boots as he thought, rubbing the heel of his palm against his aching chest. Ruth's eyes, before he'd changed them back to gray, had been blue. The color of his skin had washed away like water as it faded back to ash. Noah lifted his arm and studied it.

Uniform. That was the only way he could describe his arm. The unbroken crisscrossing of tiny scales. Ruth's skin had appeared so vibrant. Exposure to sunlight had allowed for variances in color. *Tanned*, Noah's brain supplied. Freckles. Moles. Impurities on the surface.

Illusion? Healing himself had not been an illusion. Regeneration was not a passive ability. He'd fought the desire to die to escape the pain, and had forced his body to heal. The regeneration was a part of the shift itself, only Smith didn't understand. Or had lied to them; something that Noah increasingly believed to be probable.

Skin was an organ, the largest organ in the body; Noah knew that from his anatomy lessons. Pigmentation, melanin, of which there were certain types that affected certain appearances. Change the type and/or abundance of the type, and the skin would change. The genetics alone involved...

Noah shook his head. The ability to shift wasn't in the knowledge of genetics. There was no genetic predisposition for his flesh to reach and heal. That had come from him. While the ability to shift involved the genetic structure, Noah didn't believe a complete dissection was necessary. Willpower, however, was a key component.

"What is concerning you?" Elijah asked.

Noah flicked his gaze to her and declined to answer. Skin color was connected to melanin. Dependent almost. Flood the skin with melanin and it would change color. Join the scales instead of leaving them defined. Make them wrinkles and divots and textures.

That was the plan. Reality might differ.

Once Noah had an image, loosely based on Ruth, he searched for the spark inside him. The spark that had ignited when he lay dying to change his body, *mend* his body, and pull flesh together to make it whole. He wasn't sure what he was looking for, or what would happen when he found it, but it didn't stop him from searching. Ruth could do this. Boaz hadn't, but maybe she hadn't had the chance to learn. Noah had already used the shift to save his life. Surely he could find that spark.

So much unlocked potential. He knew it was possible. He'd seen it happen. He knew he could do it.

So he did.

Pain gripped him and Noah jerked in response. Hands clamped down on his legs. Stiff-backed and teeth gritted, Noah exhaled a groan.

Elijah gasped, taking Noah by the shoulders to keep him still. "Noah!"

The others closed around him. His field of vision narrowed until all he saw was Elijah haloed by white. Her mouth moved with words of encouragement or terror but he couldn't make it out, not with the ringing inside his head. Spots began to appear in the haze and Noah realized he wasn't breathing. Snatching in a gasp, he concentrated on forcing through the pain. He wouldn't deny it hurt, but he could also *feel* his skin rewriting itself. He could feel the shift inside and he *knew*.

It wasn't an illusion. It was a physical change.

Smith was wrong.

Then it was over, the pain dissipating to a dull ache in his head and his siblings were all staring at him in wonder. He panted to catch his breath; harsh, ragged breaths that soon faded as he sat back and lifted his arm to study the changed skin.

Breaking the silence that followed, Smith spoke. "Congratulations, Noah. You have accessed the shift."

CHAPTER 7

The world swam. She saw Fletcher's face drifting on the tides of focus, his mouth moving to mismatched words without sense. Sound echoed from far away, washed away by the ocean in her ears. She fought against the fog but it wouldn't allow her to find him. He was out of reach and she couldn't get to him no matter how hard she tried.

Trust the Snickers.

A snatch of a voice, an echoed whisper on the wind and the fog cleared a fraction. She was in the forest where they played paintball. Fletcher taunted her in a game of hide and seek that had no end.

You won't ever see me again—

She whirled. His voice had come from behind her. When she turned, she was met with nothing but endless green.

If you find yourself lost—

Clouds gathered above her head, turning the forest to dusk. Shadows scattered among the green, obstructing and growing, changing with time. A dark shape moved through the woodlands and she still couldn't see him.

You won't understand and I'll be gone—

The forest swirled, the shape of the trees blurring. She

couldn't see as dizziness swept her away. All she could hear was Fletcher's voice echoing through the wilderness. "Fletcher?" she called, desperate to find him, desperate to stop the torrent of the spiraling woods.

Trust the Snickers.

"Fletcher, please!" she called, as the sky opened up and drenched her. Water steamed from her skin and burned her through.

Don't believe—

She yelped, brushing at her skin to sweep away the pinpricks of pain as the rain splattered against her. The forest was burning, the green lost to a torrent of red and orange. Heat pressed against her, held her down, and suffocated her.

Then he was there, emerging from the dark as fire and pain. His face twisted and obscured by flame and his mouth an open hollow of a scream as he burned alive.

Hurt you—

Aly woke to a wet pillow and her blanket tangled around her legs. Staring at the early morning light staining the ceiling, she was gifted with a moment of undeserved peace before she remembered. Fletcher was gone. Covering her face with her hands, a painful sob tore through her chest.

Her tears, like they had been over the past few days, were a flood that ended as fast as they came and left her weak. She found it difficult to do anything. Eating drained her, as did seeing people who came to give condolences. Fletcher's death was thrown in her face over and over as they offered up their regrets. Grace's persistent presence, while appreciated, was also hard. Aly felt so crowded, so many people around her all the time and yet, when they vanished she felt so alone. Grief and exhaustion took its toll. She couldn't sleep most nights, staying up late to watch the stars with tear-filled eyes.

When she could sleep, her dreams were growing ever worse. A crisped, black and smoking Fletcher haunted the woodlands as he tried to give her a message she couldn't make sense of.

She blamed herself. Fletcher had been coming to see her. She'd overheard her parents talking to Grace's dad, Jonathan, about Fletcher's last moves. Jonathan was part of the team investigating Fletcher's death. The local pizzeria reported him picking up a pizza and that was the last anyone saw of him.

She'd never see him again.

She'd never forgive herself. Knowing he died because he planned to uphold her silly little promise was too much to bear. She'd lost him because she'd been petty.

All her hopes and dreams had been obliterated in a moment. The thought of him being interwoven with her life—gone. No traveling across the countryside. No parties, or graduation, or college, or partners, weddings and children. He'd never get to see any of it. Never share, never have his own experiences. Trapped in an eternal moment and forever young, taken before his time.

She stared at the black dress hanging on her door and wished the world would stop. Tomorrow would be the worst day she'd ever endure. Fletcher's funeral.

Her parents were paying for it. Fletcher had no family who cared. Aly didn't even know how to contact any of them to inform them. That thought alone grated at her. Did he really have no family who cared enough to miss him?

Penelope said Fletcher was like a son and Roger had pulled out his credit card without a thought. It wasn't a big affair. Fletcher wouldn't have wanted the trouble. A simple ceremony, a mahogany coffin. Closed casket because she'd overheard Jonathan mention "burned beyond recognition", but the bike had definitely been Fletcher's.

The door creaked open and a pajama-clad Tim poked his head through. "Aly?"

Staring at the wall, she couldn't bring herself to smile. "Hey."

Tim's bottom lip quivered. "I miss Fletcher."

Hot tears dripped down over her cheek to join the mess on the pillow. "I do too," she murmured and opened her arms.

Tim rushed across the room and dove into Aly's bed with her. A little rearranging and Tim's back pressed against her chest as she hugged him.

Tim sighed and snuggled closer, then, with his thumb in his mouth, he murmured, "Tell me a story?"

"What would you like to hear?"

"Tell me how Fletcher got his bike."

Aly pressed her lips together. She couldn't get angry with him. As hard as it was for her to talk about Fletcher, it wasn't Tim's fault. He was too young to process death properly. Remembering the better days would help them both. Kissing the back of his head, Aly whispered, "It was the ricketiest, most broken down thing I'd ever seen, but Fletcher looked at it like he was in love— "

Aly stared at the blank page on her laptop, her mind wandering. She sat on her window seat bathed in sunlight, and yet she felt cold. Beside her was an untouched sandwich and half-empty glass of juice; her mother's attempt to get her to eat something. If it was like any of her other attempts, it would go stale before she thought to eat it.

She rested her chin on her knees and listened to the music playing from Fletcher's iPod. Roger had gone to Fletcher's place to retrieve it because Aly hadn't been able to face it yet. She and Fletcher had different tastes in music but shared a few favorite musicians, like Grace's piano compositions. Listening to Fletcher's playlist made her feel closer to him.

In her mind, she drew, while the page before her remained blank. Swirls and patterns that made no sense, and colors dreary and drab. Darkened clouds, a crying heart, thorns and petal-torn roses. Depressing images full of pain and anger. Things Fletcher wouldn't have wanted. He was light and color and freedom and she needed to represent that.

It was impossible to settle on one image. So many things she wanted to draw, so many favorite images, but as she stared, one picture formed above the rest. Hard to do while she still had a broken wrist and she'd have to do the basic outline with her non-dominant hand—but she had to do something. She needed to draw if only to escape for a while.

Taking a bite of the sandwich, Aly repositioned the tablet on her thigh and began to sketch.

Lingering outside the funeral home, Aly hid in the shade of one of the thick willow trees in the corner of the garden. She didn't want to go in. Didn't want to say goodbye, didn't like the finality of it all. If she didn't do this, she could pretend he'd gone on a long trip and maybe he'd be back again. But time remained an unforgiving partner and it kept ticking on. People were taking their seats for the ceremony and she owed it to Fletcher to be there for him.

As she watched those attending his funeral enter the mortuary, Aly realized she could name every single one of them. Dean, Tyrell, and all the members of the paintball team. Everyone in their year at school and a few teachers and Principal Boyd to represent. A few of Fletcher's co-workers and some of the nurses. Barry and Miguel from Dirk's Diner, where Aly worked and Fletcher frequented.

Aly hadn't realized how intertwined their lives were.

Now, she'd have to face the rest of hers without him.

"Hey," Grace murmured, as she parted some of the wispy hanging branches of the willow tree.

Aly kept her head resting on the trunk of the tree and tried to smile. "Hi."

Grace didn't say anything as she walked to the other

side of the trunk and copied Aly's position. Her misery echoed Aly's.

"White?" Aly asked, indicating Grace's dress. She kept her tone neutral, not meaning it as a criticism, just curiosity.

"My grandmother," Grace replied. She plucked a leaf from the tree to twirl in her hand. "She says it's respectful."

"Is it?"

Grace shrugged. "It's not Fletcher's culture, though, so I can't help thinking he wouldn't find it very respectful. I … couldn't bring myself to argue."

Aly smiled more naturally. "Fletcher would prefer us in flannel and cut up jeans."

Grace made a noise that might have passed for a laugh if the circumstances weren't so somber. "He would."

"He'd have a good laugh at me," Del murmured as he approached. "Literally."

Aly turned her head, then pushed away from the tree. "Del… you look respectable."

Del ran a hand over his cornrows, then tugged feebly at his tie to loosen it. "Mom made me. Thought…" he shrugged and pulled the white shirt out of his black pants so he didn't look so pristine. "Fletcher'd get a kick out of it at least."

Aly smiled because Del was right. "He would."

"How're you doing?" Del asked.

She shrugged. "You?"

"'Bout the same." Del sighed. "It's all… so…"

"Surreal," Grace supplied.

"Wrong," Aly added.

"Unfair," Grace said, and plucked another leaf from the tree to shred.

"Yeah," Del muttered. He thrust his hands into his pockets and rocked back and forward from heel to toe.

Aly saw Penelope appear at the door to the funeral home. She paused at the foot of the stairs and waited, watching her and Aly knew why. The ceremony was ready to begin. Her heart ached in her chest and she sighed. "I don't want to do this."

"Me neither," Grace said as she took Aly's hand.

"The three of us," Del said, offering his elbow to Grace. "We can do it together."

Aly struggled to blink away tears. "There's supposed to be four," she murmured and allowed herself to be led to despair.

Roger waited by the podium at the front, with Fletcher's coffin behind him. He'd offered to do most of the speaking and since Aly couldn't find the words she wanted to say, she let him. After all, she guessed this was mostly for her since Fletcher wouldn't have wanted this.

She sat at the front, between Grace and Del, gripping both their hands as she anchored herself and was, in turn, an anchor for them.

Roger cleared his throat, his voice husky but gaining strength as he spoke. "We're here today to celebrate the life of Fletcher Norman—"

Detached, Aly heard Roger talk but she didn't listen. She knew Fletcher's life; why listen to someone retell it? She stared at the screen behind Roger as it played photographs from his life, and lost herself in her memories. It came as surprise when Grace squeezed her hand and then bumped her shoulder. "Aly… did you want to speak?"

She blinked at Grace, then turned her eyes to Roger.

"Aly?" Roger asked, and gestured the podium. "You don't have to but I thought…"

Swallowing, Aly rose to her feet. She'd tried to think of what to say, really she had, but in the week before the funeral, she'd been unable to think of what Fletcher would have wanted. Standing at the podium, the words didn't come easily, but they did come.

"I met Fletcher when I was eight. I was reading in the park—Harry Potter of all things—and I'd climbed a tree to sit in its branches to read. I wasn't expecting to make a friend, just be alone. But this boy climbs up and starts annoying me about my book. He was covered in dirt and grinning madly, and the first thing I did was quote Hermione and said, 'You have dirt on your face'. I thought I was being really clever, but he just laughed and asked me if I wanted to hear the ending. He teased me and then offered me a bite of a Snickers bar…" She smiled at the memory. "And I stole it. Ate the whole thing and laughed when he complained."

Del laughed from the front row.

"Since then, Snickers have been our thing." Aly scanned the audience. Tamara, with Lloyd at her side, was crying. Kate dabbed at her face. Ezekiel might've been praying. Ethan had his arm around a tearful Madison-Lee. Even Carter looked somber. Her eyes brushed over them and Aly decided it was easier to look at the bouquet of flowers at the back of the hall. It didn't cry. It didn't do much of anything at all.

"Whenever I was angry at him, he got me Snickers. When he failed a test, I got him one. When things were rough at home, I always had one handy to help perk him up. There were 'just cause Snickers' and 'felt like it Snickers' and 'you're grumpy, here's some chocolate Snickers'. It was part of us. That's what best friends do, you know? We rib and tease and taunt and wrestle, and have each other's back no matter what."

She sighed, hating the feeling of the sympathetic gaze of so many people fixed on her. "So many things I could mention. Fishing trips we took; the summer camp we spent the entire time mucking around and playing pranks on the other campers. The carnival in Redding when we were thirteen. We ate ourselves sick on corndogs and went on all the fast rides." She caught a memory she wanted to mention. "Fletcher's face as he taunted me and bet he could eat more than I could." She smiled. "He could. He could also throw up more than I could."

There was a brief presence of laughter in the room and she thought he would've appreciated that.

Aly continued, "The Friday movie-slash-games night. We still do that, staying up for as late as we can, playing Xbox in our rumpus room." She swallowed. "For a while, it was just the two of us. Then Grace's family came to town and it was three. Fletcher was happy because now I had someone to do the 'girly things' with. I didn't know anything I did was particularly girly, but Fletch never did like having his nails done."

Grace's smile was watery.

"Then Del turned up six months later and clicked with Fletch." Her lips twitched upward of their own volition. "I was so jealous of Del because he could do things I couldn't and I thought he would ruin our friendship. Only it didn't. It made us four. We're a team..." Aly swallowed. "We were a team."

Del stretched out his hand and took Grace's to offer her solidarity. "We're still a team, Aly-cat," she said.

Aly smiled. "Yeah. We are." She sniffled and blinked rapidly before looking up at the ceiling. It was hard to talk with the lump in her throat but she struggled through. "I can't imagine life without you, Fletch. You've always been there. A part of my life I took for granted. It's funny how things can change in a moment. Two weeks ago, we were looking at colleges and planning to go to parties and avoiding life decisions and now..." She reached into her pocket and fisted the chocolate bar she'd stashed there, lifting it out. "I'm gonna miss you so much." Tears spilled over and she left the podium to place the Snickers on the coffin. "Bye Fletch."

Through the haze of tears, Aly caught a glimpse of a girl sitting on the far right of the last row of seats. Even though her features were mostly shrouded by the Yankee's cap on her head, Aly had thought she'd known all of Fletcher's friends and she didn't recognize the girl. The torment on the mystery girl's face was clear but that wasn't why she stood out. There was a flare of recognition, an ache of familiarity. Aly *knew* the girl, except she couldn't say how, and she hated herself because she felt like she should. She felt by not recognizing this girl, she was letting Fletcher down.

The girl's expression changed as their eyes connected, from anguish to something Aly couldn't name. It was bewildering, this strange déjà vu feeling cradled in the palm of grief.

Grace's arms enveloped her, closely followed by Penelope, and Aly succumbed.

CHAPTER 8

"You will hold until instructed otherwise."

The seven of them stood in a straight line, several feet apart. Stiff-backed and arms by their sides, there was no respite from their position even when they were not under instruction.

Now Noah knew how he found the shift simple. Intense pain as the process began, but as it neared completion there was little discomfort. He theorized that pain was part of the process, especially since he rewrote nerve endings. He wished he could illustrate the method to the others, but communication remained banned. Each time they tried to speak, Smith brought them back in line.

Smith seemed to believe Noah should be having trouble with accessing the shift. The first time Noah was successful, Smith's questions had been so extensive and invasive that Noah decided to pretend the process was more difficult. He copied the others in their efforts, not wishing to stand out. He grit his teeth and clenched his hands and made appropriate noises to indicate a pain he didn't feel. And because it was easy, he could study the photographs Smith provided longer and concentrate on particulars, like skin blemishes and scarring. But not only that, there were details within the shift that could change—moles and freckles and wrinkles, for example—but it went deeper than that. There were parts of his body that didn't feel like they reached their full potential and could be changed.

Noah stared straight ahead, using his peripheral vision to check on the others and their progress. Jonah was as stony-faced as ever but a slight shake in her clenched fists illustrated her pain. Adam's panting sounded overly loud in the silence of the room. Seth's face was streaked with tears. Moses seemed to be doing better than Seth, but was coated in a fine sheen of sweat. Elijah... she displayed the same tells he did; the handshake, the clenched teeth, but it all looked deliberate. Even so, there were times she lost her shift too.

Solomon... Noah knew he was racked with pain each time until Smith finally allowed them to relax to their natural forms. Most of the time, Solomon couldn't remain standing. Falling to his knees would result in punishment. Crying out in pain would result in punishment. Failure to complete instruction would result in punishment. Solomon couldn't avoid it. He wasn't built for the shift and Smith didn't believe him.

This time, as expected, Solomon groaned and fell to his knees.

"On your feet," Smith commanded.

As he lost his shift, Solomon folded forward and used his knuckles to brace on the floor.

"On your feet," Smith repeated, stressing each word.

Solomon's breath sounded harsh and heavy. "I cannot."

"You will."

"Hurts."

"*Stand.*" Smith's voice rang out, echoing through the room.

Noah knew a command when he heard it. If Solomon failed to comply he would be punished. Noah twitched as he willed Solomon to rise. Training kept Noah in line, a single-minded obedience, but why did he obey? He wasn't rewarded, only punished for non-compliance.

They were all punished. It ranged from unending klaxons in their bedrooms to the deprivation of food and water, to being forced to run the obstacle course until they collapsed, or even sometimes to pain. They had all woken to the taste of the gas in their mouths and a pain that could not be explained flooding their bodies.

Noah wondered at the change in Smith, the sudden demands that they *must* access the shift—and so fast. Even if the war went poorly, rushing them to shift when some of them were not as capable as others was a bad strategy. Especially since both he and Elijah could be in the field right now.

Solomon pressed his palms flat to the floor, then lowered his head down until the top rested against it too. "I cannot."

"Non-compliance will result in—"

"Punishment," Solomon interrupted. "I know." He pushed back, rocking to sit on his feet. "You ask too much. I cannot comply."

"Then—"

With quiet dignity, Seth stepped out of her light and crossed the space to Solomon's side. Crouching down, she placed a hand on Solomon's back, another on his knee and smiled at him.

"What?" he asked, aghast.

She turned her head to the speaker through Smith's voice came. "I-i-if you p-punish hi-m, then you p-p-punish me too."

"No, Seth," Solomon said. Taking her by the upper arms he tried to push her away. "No."

"F-f-amily," she told him with a smile.

"Get back in line," Smith demanded.

"N-no," she said, firm.

"If you will not comply then you will share his

punishment," Smith said.

Adam broke the line. His boots clipped against the floor as he strode to Solomon. "I will share it too."

"Get back in line," Smith told him.

Without further thought, Noah moved from his allotted place and joined the others in Solomon's cone of light, standing beside Adam. A fleeting glance and Adam nodded his approval. Elijah came next, followed by Moses, standing slightly in front of Noah and Adam respectively. They had much smaller forms, while Noah and Adam were the tallest, but they surrounded Seth and Solomon like a shield.

"What are you doing?" Smith asked.

"He is our brother," Elijah said.

"We have a kinship," Adam said. "A loyalty to each other because of the bonds of family. You said we were siblings, that we share genes. Yet you question when we cannot stand to see one of our family hurt?"

"Get back in line," Smith commanded again.

"You will not allow us to communicate with each other and yet you keep us together," Moses said. "You expect us to stand firm and witness as you torture our brother?"

"You will cease this idiocy and return to your designated areas." Smith's voice, still toneless, included language Noah had never heard from him before. It was a break in expected character and another nugget of information.

"What are you afraid of?" Noah asked. "Are you afraid of what will happen if we stand together?"

"You do not stand together."

It was true. Jonah still stood in her beam of light, ignoring what occurred.

Concerned, Noah asked her, "Are you afraid?"

She glanced at him out of the corner of her eye and said nothing.

"Stand with us," Elijah said.

"What does obedience get?" Adam asked. "Nothing

but more pain and questions. We are not even able to speak to each other. This is no way to live."

"You delude yourselves into thinking you deserve life," Smith said. "I have no more patience for games. You have five seconds to get back in line."

No one moved. There was no point. They would be punished now whether they complied or not. Adam reached out and put one hand on Moses' shoulder and one on Noah's shoulder. Noah offered the same comfort to Elijah, placing his hand on her shoulder and she placed her hand on Solomon.

Noah counted to five in his head and then heard the tell-tale sounds of dart guns and a sting on his shoulder.

Seth went first, collapsing into Solomon's arms he held her close, curling around her when he passed out.

Elijah's knees buckled and Noah grabbed her with both hands. He pulled her against his chest, giving Smith the impression he was helping her to stand, while using the sound of his sibling's protests to mask what he whispered in her ear. "Study the shift. There are subtleties to the change."

"What?" she croaked.

Adam groaned and sunk to his knees. Moses wilted straight to the ground. Noah knew he had little time left to make Elijah understand.

"The shift," he murmured, struggling against the tranquilizer, "it is easier for you and me. Study it as much as you can."

Elijah tilted her head until it rested on his shoulder so she could stare at him. "For what purpose?"

"I do not yet know. I do know the method Smith has us using is *wrong*. The shift cannot be forced."

Elijah nodded. "I sense that too," she whispered, slurring. "I will—"

Elijah slumped and Noah allowed them both to sink to the ground, no longer having the strength to stand.

When he woke, Noah had no concept of how much

time had passed. He was groggy and his limbs felt heavy and weak. His mouth felt like it had a fine layer of fuzz inside it and he licked his lips to remove some of the taste. With a groan, he allowed his legs to fall over the edge of his bed and used it to lever himself up.

Something was out of place. Missing.

Another groan and he placed his elbows on his knees, hunching over so he could rest his face in his hands. It was hard to get moving. Smith must have increased the dosage of gas to contain them. Or perhaps Smith had kept him under longer than usual.

Rubbing his hands over his face, he continued upward until he could run them over his head and was startled to discover the prickle of hair. It was longer than they ever allowed him to have. Noah wondered what color it would be.

There was an ache in his arm and as he checked, he saw needle marks. Quite a few of them, his left elbow looked like it had a rash as it was covered in little red marks, some several days old. There was also some flesh missing, he could see a square mark on his inner elbow. He sighed and heaved himself up so he could shower and be rid of the icky, unwashed feel.

He was halfway through his shower when he realized what he missed. He raised his head, water trickling down into his ears at the revelation.

Smith hadn't spoken a word. Nothing. No directions. No command. No inane voice telling him which activity to complete next for even the simplest of tasks, such as dressing.

Noah wasn't sure if he felt relieved or concerned.

He dressed as fast as he could, eyeing the door as he did so. Would it open when he went close, or was he stuck in this room? He needn't have worried, the door slid open as he approached and Noah cautiously walked into the adjoining hallway.

Seth stared at him from the doorway of her room,

standing in the spot where Smith always instructed her to stand. There was a small amount of light-colored fuzz growing from her head and Noah thought she might have red hair if allowed to grow. He offered her a tiny, reassuring smile and took his spot.

Adam came out of his room next, a similar hesitance in his step. He seemed relieved as he saw them both and he took his place without a word. Jonah exited her room without looking around, going straight to her designated area and stood at ease.

Elijah walked out of her door and locked eyes with Noah. "Hello."

They all jolted, Elijah included. By the startled expression on her face, she hadn't meant to speak. Since she did, Noah responded, "Hello."

No reprimand. Nothing from Smith. They waited for one, even as Moses and Solomon joined them, they waited in silence. Almost silence. The air-conditioning had a slight hum and one of the fluorescent lights sang. Noah could hear himself breathing and his ears, having nothing better to hear, rang.

Bored, Noah concentrated on the shift. He probed out with his senses and studied the structure, looking at what could be modified. The ear, for example, so intricate and so flawed. Designed to filter out certain frequencies, but if he could determine the shift needed to allow the ear to access those frequencies... the possibilities were endless.

"Are you w-well?"

Noah blinked and looked at Seth, whose gaze was fixed on Solomon.

Solomon nodded. "I am."

A smile bloomed on Seth's face and did not fade as they dropped into silence. Noah was tense as he waited to see if the conversation would be chastised.

"Thank you for standing with me," Solomon said after a short time.

"I c-could not—not s-stand and w-aatch," Seth replied.

"It was a kindness," Solomon replied, genuinely touched. "Thank you."

Seth's smile brightened her entire demeanor.

"What do you think they are waiting for?" Adam asked.

"I am not certain," Moses murmured.

Elijah broke her position and walked over to one of the bench tables they usually ate at. "If I am forced to wait, I shall at least be comfortable."

They watched her sit and waited for the reprimand. When nothing came, Noah broke his position and joined Elijah. "Hello," he said, sitting opposite her.

"Hello, Noah," she replied, smiling. She extended her hand across the table. "This is the traditional greeting, I believe."

Noah took her hand and a smile burst from his face. "I believe so."

Seth and Solomon joined them, offering their hands to shake as they were allowed to greet each other. Adam and Moses were quick to follow and the six of them sat at the table, while Jonah remained where she was.

"What do you make of this?" Moses asked.

"Perhaps it is another experiment," Elijah offered as she glanced around the room. "To see what we would do when given the chance to interact?"

"I find I do not care," Noah said. "Smith can analyze our behaviors as he may, but I will take the chance to speak of my own free will."

"I agree, brother," Adam said, thumping his hand on Noah's shoulder. "It is a new and interesting development and I care not what Smith thinks."

"Unless this is what he wants," Solomon pointed out.

"I fail to see what gain Smith foresees in allowing us to speak," Moses said.

"I would assume we know nothing of Smith's true intentions," Adam mentioned.

"Perhaps it is a chance for us to aid our siblings," Noah said.

"What do you mean?" Elijah asked.

Noah clasped his hands beneath the table and lowered his voice. "The shift."

Varied reactions from his siblings. Contemplation from Elijah, consideration from Adam, shock from Moses, concern from Seth and denial from Solomon.

Solomon warned, "You shall be punished."

"Then so be it," Noah said. "If Smith will not punish us now for speaking to one another, then he will not punish us for something that will aid him in achieving his goal. He wishes for us to learn to hold the shift."

"And we all have varying degrees of talent," Elijah included.

"Exactly," Noah continued. "Different insights to the shift. We should be able to help each other gain better access to it."

"I doubt that is possible," Solomon said, dejected. "It is a task I fear I cannot complete."

"T-try," Seth said, placing her hand on Solomon's arm.

"I am certain I can aid you," Noah said.

"How?" Jonah questioned from her position.

Noah turned his head and gestured an empty seat. "Join us."

Jonah hesitated, then briskly took a place. She leaned forward, palms flat on the table as she stared at Noah. "How can you aid him?"

"There are subtleties I have not yet determined," Noah explained, unnerved by her intensity. "Variances beyond what they tell us. I am certain, given time, I can unravel the shift." He hesitated, then purposely glanced at the camera in the corner. "Although, I am not sure I trust this silence. It is not something I wish to share with them. I do not know how much they can hear."

Adam nodded. "I understand."

"Until I can," Noah continued, looking at Solomon, "I would suggest you try the shift more slowly. In sections, perhaps. It does cause the least amount of pain. I believe you try to change too much at once; focus on one area at a time."

His face creased with thought, Solomon nodded. "I believe that could work."

Noah chewed on the inside of his mouth, then said, "Also you need to accept the shift. It is not an illusion; it is a physical change that you *must* allow."

"A physical change?" Jonah blurted, her eyes wide.

Noah nodded. "You all work so hard to maintain the shift whereas I allow it to happen. When it does, there is no pain. I *become* the image rather than projecting an illusion. You teeter on the edge when you should allow it to occur."

Elijah's face changed to one of understanding. "That makes so much sense."

"They should have allowed us to speak sooner," Moses muttered.

"I agree," Solomon said. "It would save so much effort."

"I... I-I-I do," Seth swallowed and closed her eyes in concentration. "-n-not under-und... der...stand-"

"You should not speak," Jonah said, and Seth flinched. "You waste our time."

Solomon scowled. "She has as much right to speak as you do."

"And it is a question we have all posed," Adam said, also adding to Seth's defense. "It is not a waste of time."

"I disagree," Jonah said, brisk and with no remorse for Seth's hurt feelings. "We are at war. I believe we should complete our tasks and be done so we can aid—"

"Then what is this?" Elijah argued, waving her hand. "This silence Smith now offers; it is not a task to be completed."

Jonah dropped her defiance. "I am unsure."

"Perhaps it is you who wastes time," Adam chided.

Noah studied Jonah through narrowed eyes as he gained a better sense of her personality.

Jonah bared her teeth in anger. "I will not—"

"Do not," Elijah said, interposing her hands between Adam and Jonah. "We are new at interacting and social ineptitude is something we each carry. We should allow each other a certain freedom to speak our minds before we worry about politeness."

Jonah stared at her. "Politeness? You worry about being polite?"

Noah nodded. "Seth's affliction is not her fault. She should have a voice. Calling attention and denying her a chance to speak is rude."

Jonah's eyes widened. "Rude. I am not *rude*."

"You are," Noah said. "As Seth is too kind. Adam is quick to judge. We all have our own faults."

"What is yours?" Jonah snarled.

"I am wary of the trust we can place in you," he replied and Jonah rocked back in horror. "I am wary of the trust I place in any of you," he continued, looking at each of them. "I do not know what occurs with you while I sleep. I do not know if you receive anything I do not, and as I know I received things you did not, the opposite is logical. I do not trust anything at present."

"It is good to be wary," Adam said, nodding.

"But…" Elijah looked confused. "You…" She hesitated and pressed her lips together.

"I told you to study the shift," Noah said with a nod. "As I tell *all* of you to study the shift. Beyond that… I do not know if I shall share my findings. Trust should not be something that comes easily."

"It must be earned," Moses said.

Noah nodded.

"N-no," Seth whispered and Noah looked over at her. "F-family. We *must* trust."

Elijah answered, her voice kind, "Seth, we do not even truly know each other yet."

"And how are we to manage that?" Jonah asked. "We are trapped in here and—"

A door clicked and swung open a fraction. The eleventh door. The one they were never allowed near.

Noah looked at the door, then at Jonah, thinking it was entirely too convenient. By the look on her face, she thought something similar.

Adam was first to his feet and moving toward the door.

"You do not know what is out there!" Elijah protested, rising to her feet.

"It will be better than here," Adam said as he thrust the door open. Beyond him, Noah could see a short hallway, then something green.

Green.

Noah hurried to follow. Something clattered behind him as the rest of them rushed for the door.

The hallway led outside to a small, fenced courtyard. Short trees tied against sticks to aid their trunks. A mulched garden bed of flowers planted around the inside of the fence line. Several heavy concrete seats sat in the middle of square paving. Everything seemed so new, pristine, and Noah wondered if everything had just been planted.

The sun. The sky. The scent of fresh dirt and mulch.

Noah blinked and raised his hand, staring at the light filtering down through the wire.

Seth took several steps forward and dropped to her knees, cupping a small purple flower in the palm of her hand. "Beautiful," she murmured as she traced the petals.

"Have you never been outside?" Solomon blinked, looking around.

"No," she replied, entranced by the flower.

Noah felt a stab of guilt. He'd been in the sun so many times and Seth had never had the privilege. Looking at Elijah, Noah guessed she felt the same as he did.

"What is this?" Elijah murmured as her shoulder brushed against Noah's.

"I do not know," he replied. His fingers touched the rough leaf of a sapling.

Surrounding the fenced courtyard was another building, two stories if he judged it correctly. A massive, one-way glass window and a single door, but they would have to breach the fence before they could get to the door. Noah doubted he could reach the glass window through the fence.

Despair settled in his chest as he realized what this was.

A cage.

A cage with sunlight and gardens and the feeling of freedom was still a cage. It was—

"Incentive," came Smith's voice.

CHAPTER 9

Incentive, as Noah and his siblings soon discovered, had a lot of criteria that needed to be fulfilled before the door outside opened. They all had to do every task assigned to them, including the shift, and if one of them failed, none of them would go.

As a direct result of their conversation—and now Noah knew how much Smith overheard— their required depth of shift had changed. Noah and Elijah's instructions included complex shifts with skin tone, scars, facial structure and changes to body dynamics. Solomon's images were close to his own and the rest's instructions were somewhere in the middle. When they had advanced enough, Smith started issuing rudimentary roles to act. Personas to be. People to replace.

What surprised Noah the most was that he was able to tell his siblings apart, even in their shifted form. Smith ran tests, giving them identities to shift into while separated from each other and Noah could still tell them apart when they met up in their alternate forms.

They started spending longer with their eyes, faces and skin shifted. Choosing his own form, Noah rarely returned to the faceless, gray appearance of before. As their hair continued to grow, dark for Noah, Adam and Elijah, blond for Solomon and Jonah, light brown for Moses and red for Seth, they grew used to the rounded look in each other's new faces and the variances of the colors of their skin.

Activities became more personalized. Elijah received more tutelage in ranged combat, while Adam, Moses, Seth and Noah were issued with more complicated physical maneuvers. Jonah was allotted more time to strategize, given scenario after complicated scenario to resolve. Lessons also started to include socialization skills, slang and other variables which they hadn't learned before, and Noah found the world outside their walls fascinating.

Every day they were given time to socialize with each other. Offer insights into lessons. Laugh. Solomon had a particularly vibrant sense of humor and Noah loved to listen to his jokes. Tasks allowed them to work as a team, or in pairs, including mock combat scenarios. When Noah and Jonah were paired, there was little the others could do to thwart them. Jonah's quickness of mind and Noah's speed of body and ability to grasp what Jonah planned made for a terrifying duo. In any combat situation, whether it was capture-the-flag or a dummy rescue/assassination, Noah and Jonah would win each time.

It seemed to Noah that whatever Smith's ultimate plan was for them, it had become more refined, even if Noah couldn't unravel what that plan was. Smith didn't give them any clues, but it didn't stop Noah from forming theories.

Now their daily lessons included information about what existed outside the walls, Noah often wondered about it. What the society was like. What was the war and how did they fit into it? What would it be like to live as an ordinary person, not confined like he was?

Sometimes, Noah would even fantasize about being rescued from this place by people who claimed they were his parents. They'd discovered what parents were when learning biology and genetics and it always made him wonder. Seth tried to ask during the lesson but was ignored. Elijah was similarly ignored. When Moses asked, Smith said they had no parents, they belonged to the Institute, and it was their choice to give themselves to the Institute and to cease asking.

Smith kept saying they chose this, but Noah began to have trouble believing it. What had he been like to choose this? To live like this? Trapped in a room with other people, every action witnessed, every word recorded when everyone else on this planet, including the alien invaders, were free-roaming. So many questions and no answers. It plagued his thoughts every day. Theories and possibilities, sometimes they shared thoughts from the outrageous to the mundane but were never any closer to learning anything more about Smith's alien invasion.

Alone in his room one night, he accessed the shift without being subjected to Smith's watchful eye. His intent was not to shift into a new form but to change *this* form. Augment it.

It went horribly wrong.

He thrashed in his bed, overcome by noises. A buzz in the air-conditioning vent above his bed. Water moving in pipes within the walls. A fly and its incessant hum. Some sort of tearing sound, with something struggling; was that the fly? His blood rushing, the sound of digesting food. The sound of his body growing, all the intricate inner processes that the ear normally doesn't pay attention to, crashed against his senses all at once. He was hyper-aware of things he'd never noticed before and he didn't know— couldn't tell—what was the most important thing to listen to. It was all important. It all had to be listened to. He couldn't differentiate.

It was too much.

A headache exploded. A sudden, blinding pain settled right behind his eyes, his vision tunneling toward darkness as a result.

Then, within the shadows his eyes forced on him, he heard voices.

"Echo Seven's heartbeat is unstable. What's going on?"

"He's going the same as Echo Ten. We've seen the sevens go before."

"The implant isn't registering the same breakdown in chemistry. Call Darcy."

Implant? What implant? Noah tried to concentrate on the voices, seek them out within the mess of sound.

"Ma'am? It's Lacy. Echo Seven's having an unknown reaction, permission to... but ma'am, he could die... I understand...Yes ma'am. Monitoring only... Should we have the Smith unit interact? ... Very well."

Their voices dipped away, lost to the swirling maelstrom occurring in his ears. He must have changed the wrong section. Removing all the changes he made, he struggled to return to his original form. It took more concentration than usual and Noah fought against the pain in his head and the urge to pass out. Gradually noise dimmed, but the remaining headache throbbed.

He panted, eyes closed and hands limp as he waited for the exhaustion to pass. Eventually, he dropped into fitful sleep.

Left with a lingering headache in the morning, Noah couldn't eat breakfast. He stared at his tray, nauseated by the sight of food and yet unwilling to look into the chaos of the overly bright room.

"Are you w-well?" Seth asked, and he flinched away from the boom of her normally quiet voice, the movement causing him more pain.

He blinked slowly. "Headache." Pounding and blinding, he'd never experienced this before. His vision tunneled, colors seemed strange and definition was fuzzy.

"You are almost the same color as our scales," Moses noted.

Noah sighed and clasped his head with both hands.

Elijah studied him. "You attempted something."

He closed his eyes. "Perhaps."

She leaned in close and rested her hand on his shoulder so she could whisper, "What did you try?"

"Augmentation," Noah replied as quietly as he could to prevent being heard. "To the ear. I shifted incorrectly. Heard too much and could not control the volume."

Elijah's eyes widened but she managed to school her expression.

"Smith is a program," he whispered.

"What?" she said.

Noah pushed his tray away from him, folded his arms on the table and buried his face in his elbow. "I overheard them speaking."

Elijah rested her hand on the base of his neck. "You *overheard?*" She glanced around. "Solomon, did you not want to show Seth something?"

Noah winced but said nothing.

"Oh, yes!" Solomon announced without questioning and Noah heard him bound to his feet. "Dance with me!"

"I b-beg your p-pardon?" Seth asked, astounded. Noah peeked out to see Solomon standing with his hand extended to Seth and his back bent at the waist.

"Like we saw on the screen yesterday. Dance. Adam can do drums."

Excited, Adam surged from his seat and crossed to the practice mat and began to drum against it. "How is that?"

The distance was sufficient that the noise didn't make Noah's head pound any more than it already was.

"Perfect!" Solomon announced, happy.

Jonah clicked her tongue in distaste as Solomon dragged Seth over to the mat. One hand clasping hers, Solomon put his other hand on the small of her back and began pulling her around the mat in a semblance of a dance. Noah smiled to himself as Seth started giggling, especially when Solomon began to hum off-key.

"This is pointless," Jonah announced.

"Only you could think so," Adam told her.

"Augmentation?" Elijah whispered once Solomon's distraction was underway. "Is it even possible?"

Noah nodded. "Indeed. I have not perfected it, but I was able to do it."

"Really?" Elijah said, excited. "That is amazing. I never would have—"

Noah interrupted, "Smith is a program designed to interact with us. The person in charge is 'Darcy'. They called her ma'am and did her bidding."

Elijah's hand on the back of his neck toyed with the hair at the nape. "I see."

"They have numbered us," Noah continued, wondering why Elijah's hair play soothed his headache. "I am Echo Seven."

"Echo? That implies other groups."

"It does. They also spoke of an Echo Ten."

"There are only nine of us." Elijah looked toward the bedrooms. "The tenth room."

"Echo Ten is gone," Noah said, saddened by the loss of a sibling they weren't aware of. "There is more. They seemed to know I had a reaction to the augmentation."

"Hmm."

"They also mentioned implants."

Elijah's fingers paused in Noah's hair. "Implants?"

"I can only imagine it would be in or close to our brains," Noah continued and twitched his head to get her to move her fingers again. The brain was the only part of him that didn't change with a shift. He thought he would have noticed a foreign body otherwise, but perhaps not. He would have to have a closer look now he knew.

Elijah nodded. "I agree."

"I will attempt the augmentation again," Noah said. "I believe I know what I did wrong."

"I will attempt it also if you tell me what sections you changed and how."

"I would suggest you wait. Since they monitor us, if you show the same symptoms I do, they will know we are attempting something."

Elijah chewed her lip. She looked like she wanted to argue but saw the wisdom in his words. "Agreed."

"I will inform you once I have knowledge."

That pleased her. "Thank you."

Noah snorted. "Also, they use most informal speech."

Elijah raised an eyebrow at him and her lips curled upward. "Indeed?"

He grinned. "We have been learning their slang."

She smiled more freely. "We should try to use it more as practice. Your color has returned."

He looked at her sheepishly. "Your administrations have helped."

Elijah gave a light laugh, then rubbed his back between the shoulder blades. "I shall inform the others, especially about the shift. Rest."

Noah nodded and obeyed.

Smith's voice permeated through his skull a short time later, ending Solomon's revelry and Noah's retreat.

To Noah, the lessons that day didn't seem as hard as normal and he wondered if it was a deliberate choice to allow him to recuperate, or if the ease was by chance. The only physical activity for the day was by choice, so Noah sat against the wall with his eyes half-lidded, watching as Jonah and Moses sparred and Seth and Solomon talked, and planned his next shift.

Noah's headache vanished just as their dinner arrived in the dumbwaiters, so he ate with gusto. He was ravenous and didn't turn down Jonah's leftovers.

That night, he tried again. The shift went better, now he knew what to expect and what he did wrong. The sharp, fiery pain reduced to nothing more than a dull ache, something that was easily endured. Over the next few nights, he slowly increased the shift, changing the eardrum in increments to reduce the risk of overwhelming his hearing. With each augmentation, he could hear farther and more clearly. Soon, he was able to hear conversations beyond the walls he and his siblings existed in.

Most of the conversations were about families or sport. Something called "football". Sometimes they discussed results of the day's activities. Mostly, night time seemed reserved for quiet work, the clacking of a keyboard was a frequent sound.

There were only a few consistent voices behind the walls. A female called Lacy and three males, Diego, Wade, and a third, unnamed voice that only appeared along with cleaning machines, and never said much beyond a greeting and generic questioning about family health.

No one mentioned the war. Conflicts were mentioned, Iraq or Afghanistan, but they were never talked about as though they mattered. "A shame about the death toll." Not like the war Smith spoke of. Smith spoke of devastating losses. Enemies at the gate, every day they lost to training increased the death toll. They were on the brink of losing the planet. So why did those people beyond the wall never speak of it?

And who was Darcy?

Noah found it unfair that those who contained them were allowed to venture from this place to their homes and families. Resentment had begun to unfurl inside him and his siblings as more and more it seemed they were being lied to.

He did overhear one conversation of note. It was late and there were only snatches of conversation because an industrial cleaning device was nearby.

Wade asked, "Has Echo Two given us any more insight?"

"No," Lacy replied. "Echo Two believes Echo Seven is close to a breakthrough. We're not sure what that is. Echo Two believes it has something to do with last Wednesday's readings. I suspect Echo Seven will inform Echo Four of any progress he has made since Echo Four is almost his equal in the shift."

"I don't understand what Darcy's thinking. This group

has been given so much more freedom than our other subjects," said Diego.

"Look at the raw data we get from this group about shifting," Lacy said. "Even Solomon's data has increased—"

Wade interrupted, "We're not supposed to call them by name."

"It's hard to think of them as subjects when they have such defined personalities now," Lacy replied, apologetic. "Why did Darcy give the group names if we weren't supposed to use them?"

"Lacy—"

"All I'm saying, giving them freedom to talk to each other and go outside on a regular basis has improved their abilities."

"I agree, but I can't see her allowing the same freedoms to the others. There's something special about Echo group."

Echo Four was Elijah, Noah was sure, but which one of them was Echo Two? Not necessarily a traitor, but certainly untrustworthy to learn his secrets. But what of these other groups? There were more?

He did not dare try to shift during the day to learn the identity of Echo Two or discover more about the other groups. Not since the augments made other sounds enhanced as well—he didn't wish to be deafened by an overzealous Adam in his ear when least expected.

Noah tried other augmentations. Muscle to make himself stronger and faster. Bone density. Enhanced sight. After watching a documentary on porpoises and their ability to use ultrasonic sound to communicate, he began experimenting with his vocal chords so he could speak within different frequencies. He hoped the Institute didn't have ultrasonic detectors. The initial pain of a shift soon dimmed as he grew more confident in his skills and more aware of his own limits.

By day, he would endure Smith's mind-numbingly

boring skin shift, taking on the outward appearance of another being; by night, he would experiment.

Within a month, he decided he should share his findings. He devised a way to tell his siblings of the augmentations he could do. He started with Elijah because he knew that of the other six, she'd be the most likely to achieve it. Skin pigmentation on the back of his hand showed Elijah a close-up of the inner workings of the ear, then, when he knew he had her attention, he changed the skin pigmentation to show her what she needed to shift. A detailed shift since it was an image, but also easy since it was only one section he changed.

She grabbed his hand, her breathing stifled, her eyes riveted on the image.

"Careful," he whispered. "They see."

"You achieved it," she breathed.

He smiled. "I did. Do this tonight, then whisper my name when you are done and I will tell you the rest."

"How?"

His grin grew wider. "You shall see." He dropped his smile. "It will hurt."

Elijah's elation died. "Much?"

"I do not know. For me, it is bearable, but if you do it wrong—"

She nodded. "The headache."

"Also, there is something else you should know—"

"What are you two whispering about?" Jonah demanded.

Noah wiped his hand clean of the image. "Nothing." Jonah had brought attention on them, which meant the attention of those watching them would also be focusing and he couldn't afford for them to find out. One of the others was Echo Two and he didn't know which one.

Elijah seemed surprised at his answer but said nothing.

Jonah stared at them a moment too long before she returned to her food.

That night, Noah lay on his bed with his eyes closed

and listened to the world with his augmented hearing. Adam was snoring. Seth made little snuffling noises. His other siblings all murmured in their sleep. Keyboards clacked and other voices murmured beyond their walls. Lacy was quiet tonight.

Elijah whispered, "Noah?"

Noah smiled. Rolling onto his side, he covered his mouth to hide his words. *"Well done. Do not speak, I do not know if they have microphones in our rooms and it would not do to be overheard. I am currently speaking ultrasonically. The image I showed you allows you to hear that high and I do not think they track high frequencies."* He outlined the process to change vocal chords so Elijah would be able to speak to him. *"Make sure you cover your mouth,"* he advised, *"to prevent them from reading lips."*

Elijah made a noise of agreement.

Dropping into silence, he waited again. Elijah was good; he had no doubt she'd achieve the augmentation. It was only a matter of time and Noah was practiced with patience.

"That was more difficult than I anticipated," Elijah murmured finally.

"You have done well," Noah said, pleased.

"Only because you have already done the hard experimentation. I do not believe I would have been able to discover this as quickly as you have."

"Do not discount yourself," Noah said.

"What else have you learned?" Elijah asked.

"Many things. Like our eyesight can also be augmented. As can our muscles and bones."

"Intriguing. We must teach our siblings this as soon as we can, it will be good to discuss things freely and I believe it would aid Solomon greatly."

"I am unsure if that is wise. It is possible one of us reports to the Institute and shares secrets."

Elijah was silent for a moment. *"How do you know?"*

"I overheard one of them talking about Echo Two's reports. I am

aware I am Echo Seven. They also mentioned Echo Four being nearly my equal in the shift, so I believe that would be you."

"That leaves the others."

"What do you think we should do?"

Elijah considered for a time. *"We teach them anyway. We tell them we know one of them reports to those who hold us. We leave it up to them."*

"That is a dangerous decision."

"They are our siblings. We have to trust they will do the right thing."

"They are our siblings because we were told they were. What if there is no truth to that?"

"We have to believe there is truth."

"We do not share enough of the same genetic markers to be—"

"Does that matter? Siblings of blood or heart, this involves all of us."

He pulled a face. *"You are more trusting than I am."*

"We have nothing else, Noah. Nothing but each other. I am not willing to believe one of us voluntarily shares information. If someone gives the augmentations to Darcy, then they do, and we shall not share any other discoveries. We will give them enough augmentations that we can escape this place. We shall inform the others of that, as well."

Surprised, Noah asked, *"Escape?"*

"I do not wish to remain here," Elijah said. *"Do you?"*

He considered. *"I do not know anything else."*

"We can learn. I want to be able to make my own choices, Noah. I do not like being told what to do, how to train, what to wear, who to kill. This is no life."

"And the war?"

"We deserve freedom too. Why fight in a war when we do not know what we fight for? We see what life could be on the screens; do you not want that?"

"Very well," Noah replied. *"I trust your judgment."*

They worked quickly to spread the word between their siblings. Adam received the ear instruction via a wrestling match between him and Noah. Seth received it on the back of Elijah's neck while Seth brushed her growing hair. Moses got the message during lessons when Elijah aided his aim. Jonah got it during a scenario brainstorming session as Noah sketched a picture. Solomon was given the message by Seth.

It took them varying lengths of time to accomplish the necessary augments to the ear, with Solomon being the last to hear them converse. It would take him longer to make the modifications to speak without fear of being overheard, but in the meantime, he was able to listen as Noah outlined what he'd heard from those who worked beyond their walls.

"It is not me!" Adam protested upon hearing of Echo Two.

Peacemaker, Elijah said, *"We do not accuse anyone."*

"But you believe one of us betrays the rest!" Moses said.

"Yes," Noah said. *"And we have decided we do not care."*

"Why?" Jonah asked. *"Why would you risk giving us the knowledge of augmentation when you know one of us is this Echo Two?"*

"What else can we do?" Elijah said. *"It is us against them. One of you may give them information, yes, but the others do not. We are strongest as a group."*

"United," Noah said.

"We can escape together. Surely that must be better incentive."

"Besides," Noah continued. *"What I have given you is not all I can do. If Echo Two informs, Elijah and I will withhold our discoveries."*

Silence.

"You would blackmail us?" Adam said carefully.

"Yes," Elijah said.

"I accept these terms," Adam replied.

"As do I," Moses added.

"Can y-you aid S-s-Sol-omon?" Seth asked.

"Yes," Noah replied.

"I accept."

"Yes," Solomon whispered, his voice as low as

possible.

"*It would seem I have no choice*," Jonah replied.

"*Between us*," Elijah said. "*There is always a choice. That is what will set us apart from the Institute.*"

"*Also*," Noah said, swallowing. "*There is something you need to know about Boaz… and Ruth.*"

CHAPTER 10

Mondays were hard for Aly. Fresh off a playful, mostly relaxing weekend, she trudged into the dark recesses of learning, worrying about the future and studying for finals that would determine the rest of her life. She'd never minded Mondays in the past. With Fletcher by her side, she always felt she could survive anything.

Except Fletcher wasn't by her side.

She was only here because she had to get out of the house. Penelope's mothering, Roger's quiet compassion, and Tim's confused grief; it was too much for her to handle.

Staring at the school from the safety of her car, Aly sighed. People and their emotions would be just as bad here. Talking behind their hands or bouncing up to her to offer their condolences. Couldn't people leave her alone? With another sigh, she reached for the key.

The passenger door opened and Del slipped into the seat. "Hey."

Aly dropped her hand away from the key and let the car run. "Hey."

Del closed the door, then rested his elbow on the frame and his head in his palm. "It feels like it should be raining."

"Yeah." Aly didn't bother to ask how he felt, it was written all over his face. "Been back at school long?"

Del shrugged. "Dax flew in on Wednesday. Mom seemed to think I needed cheering up. Kind of sick of his version of being coddled." Del's brother, Daxton, was in his first year of law school. Aly didn't have much to do with him since he was mid-twenties, but he was a pretty cool guy whenever he visited.

"Which is?" She scratched the edges of her yellow cast, imagining she reached the itch which tickled deep inside.

Del's eyes flicked down to her wrist, then shied away as though he didn't want to be reminded. "Literally attempting to beat me in every single computer game in the house."

"And failing."

Del shrugged and gave her the ghost of a grin. "He never stood a chance." The grin faded. "Victory isn't half as fun without Fletcher."

The barb of grief sunk deeper into her heart, but Aly knew she was in the same place as Del. If they couldn't talk to each other, there wasn't any hope for them. "He would have kicked Dax's ass."

The ghostly grin returned. "Definitely."

She gave a semi-dramatic sigh. "Though his 'I win' dance left a lot to be desired."

Now Del laughed. "It did! I think it was the butt wiggle."

Aly felt a smile creep across her face as Fletcher's dance appeared in her mind. "It was!"

They shared a moment of memory before the smiles began to fade and melancholy slid back into place. She hated talking about Fletcher in past tense. It didn't feel right.

With a sigh, Del lifted his head from his hand. "There's Grace. Ready to brave the school?"

"I don't have much of a choice."

"We can ditch. Go for fries 'n' shakes. I'm sure Grace'd go for that."

Aly pulled a face. "I'm supposed to report to the counselor first. Mom'll know if I don't go."

Del scrunched up his nose. "Ick. That'll be an absolute blast."

"Yup." She reached for the key and yanked it out of the slot. The car engine sputtered and died and without the noise of it, the sound of the schoolyard was more prominent. Talking, laughter, happiness that was out of place with Aly's current world.

"I'll walk with you."

Aly opened the car door and prepared to face the day. "Thanks."

Mr. Saxon was a stern-faced man. A beard with scattered with white and gray hair. His eyes mostly hidden beneath a massive, unkempt brow that ran straight across his forehead without pause. The air-conditioner clattered away in the vent above her head. The room always felt too cold. He was overweight with hyperhidrosis, so even as she was freezing, he wiped a bead of sweat away from his brow with a stained cloth.

Aly always thought his eyes were like two penetrating icicles, but she'd never had much to do with him. Fletcher had been in and out of this room since his uncle had died, mostly for the state's check-up and records but occasionally for his attitude.

She tucked her good hand under her thigh to keep it warm, while her casted hand rested on her lap. Walking through the school had been a trial, even with Del's escort. People stared and whispered. Too much sympathy in their gaze. She just wanted everything to stop.

"So, Alyson, how are you—"

"Aly," she corrected.

Mr. Saxon glanced down at the folder that contained her student notes. "Aly," he corrected in such a way she got the feeling he didn't like to be interrupted, "how are you feeling?"

"Fine." She kept her tone short and clipped and hoped he'd take the hint.

"I know this must have been hard for you—" he began.

"Look," she interrupted. "I know my mom asked you to check my stability and such, but I don't need my head shrunk right now. I just want to get through today and go home."

"All students are entitled to one mandatory session," he said, clasping his sweaty hands together in front of him and resting them on the desk. Aly wondered if his arms would stick to her folder.

"Entitled?" she asked. "If it's mandatory, how is that entitled?"

He ignored that. "Especially with a death of this nature. You were his best friend," he continued, glancing at the notes. "In fact, there has been speculation you were more than just best friends, even if he was—"

"What *nature*?" She zeroed in on that and ignoring the speculation.

Something on Mr. Saxon's face made her skin crawl. When he spoke, his tone felt belittling. "Fletcher was gay. Being ostracized is still very real and must have been so detrimental to his mental health."

Aly felt an icy fist settle in her stomach. "What?"

"You must've heard the rumors, whether there is any substantiating—"

"*Rumors*?" she shrilled. "Are you implying—" She rose from her seat with such force she banged her cast against the table. The pain and the reminder only served to make her angrier. "Fletcher didn't commit suicide! It was an *accident*!"

"Nevertheless, Mr. Boyd has asked me to make sure all students are aware—"

"Fletcher was in an *accident* and you've been counseling on suicide?" she shrilled, throwing up her hands. "No wonder there are rumors!"

"Ms. Gale, please sit down."

She slammed her good fist against the table. "He was coming to see me!" she yelled, glaring at Mr. Saxon. "He'd bought pizza and he was coming to see me—" she waved around her broken wrist. "Because of this— this *thing*. It's *my* fault he's dead. And now you're adding unfounded rumors of *suicide* to that? It had *nothing* to do with the fact he was gay!"

Mr. Saxon honed in. "You believe it's your fault?"

She stared at him, her chest heaving. The whole world seemed off-kilter and she couldn't find her feet. "You know what? Screw this. I'm out." Snatching up her bag, she stalked to the door. She shoved it open too hard as she made her grand exit and the glass rattled in the window as it crashed against the wall. For a moment, she thought it might break and was strangely pleased by the prospect.

She stormed through the halls, glaring at anyone who dared make eye contact. She avoided Grace and Del, not wanting to take it out on them or explain her fury. The pair of them watched with wide eyes and frozen stances as she kicked open the main doors of the school.

Mr. Jenkins stood at the base of the stairs, ushering in the straggling students. He turned at the noise ready to yell at whoever was damaging school property. The angry look softened as he saw her. "Ms. Gale."

She stomped down the stairs and strode past him, managing to keep her voice contained to a low growl. "Sir."

"Can't stomach school?"

She kept walking. "No." Reaching her car, she threw her bag on the back seat and yanked open the driver's door.

Mr. Jenkins' hand closed over the top of the door. "Aly."

Out of respect, she gritted her teeth, clenched her fists and tried to contain her anger. With eyes fixed on the inside of her car, she grumbled, "What?"

"I understand you don't want to be here right now. That's fine."

Aly's eyes rose to meet Mr. Jenkins' dark ones. "Sir?"

Holding her gaze, he said, "Don't drive angry."

She nodded, mollified. "Okay."

"It doesn't—" Mr. Jenkins began.

She pursed her lips. "Don't you dare tell me it gets easier. I've had enough of that line. Especially when Mr. Saxon has decided—" she broke off and wiped her cheek.

"It doesn't get easier, Aly," he said, his voice gentle. "It gets different. Eventually, different will be okay, but that's a long way off. Until then, take the advice of those who've lived this. Grief has its own timetable. Let yourself follow it. There's no rush. Fletcher was important to you in ways only you know. It's okay to take time to come to terms with his passing."

Aly swallowed and said nothing.

"You know where I am if you need talk." He released her door and headed toward the front doors.

Following Mr. Jenkins' retreat with her eyes, Aly noticed Grace standing at the base of the stairs. Seeing she had Aly's attention, Grace pulled out her phone and a moment later, Aly's beeped.

> **How clef-er:** [Are you okay?]
>
> **Aly:** [No.]

Mr. Jenkins reached Grace, glanced over his shoulder, and then said something to her. Aly imagined he reminded Grace of the school rule which said phones needed to be off during class.

> **How clef-er:** [Wait for me. I'll ditch.]
>
> **Aly:** [I'm fine. You have finals to study for.]
>
> **How clef-er:** [You're more important.]
>
> **Aly:** [I need alone time.]

Grace watched her for a minute then nodded and turned to head up the stairs and back into school. Aly slid into the driver's seat and rested her head on the steering wheel.

Her phone beeped and Aly squinted at Grace's message.

How clef-er: [Mom's doing her monthly dumpling cook this afternoon. Want to come? No talking, just food.]

Aly studied her phone for a minute. She enjoyed Lan's dumplings and listening to Lan talk about her adventures on MasterChef as she cooked. The want for something normal, and not associated with Fletcher, made her ache.

Aly: [Yeah, I'll be there. I have to work at five.]

How clef-er: [You're going?]

Aly: [Monotonous normality.]

How clef-er: [Love you. Be safe.]

Aly: [I will. Love you too.]

Tossing her phone onto the seat beside her, she jammed her key in the ignition and cranked up her tunes. Thinking better of it, she grabbed her phone again and sent a text through to her mother.

Aly: [Can't stomach school. Saxon has decided to counsel on suicide. Going to Grace's this afternoon then the diner. Be home after nine-thirty.]

With a smirk, Aly imagined the angry phone call her mother would make to the school and it almost made her feel better.

At first, all she wanted to do was drive; head out of town and hit the open road and just go, but as she turned a corner, she realized where she'd been heading. Fletcher's rickety place.

He'd done the best he could with the little he had. He rented an apartment at the back of a house that belonged to a retired man, with reduced rent in exchange for garden and general maintenance duties. The four of them repainted the outside about a year ago, laughing and having water fights. Del and Fletcher had fixed the brick fence in the front yard. Aly and Grace had planted the few neglected yet sturdy plants beneath the windowsill. The lawn could be cut, but it didn't look unkempt yet.

She parked on the road and turned off her engine. Taking a deep breath, she grabbed her phone and her backpack and headed for the front door.

The place was a tiny box. Half of the box was taken up by a bedroom and a bathroom/utility and the rest of the box was a small kitchenette and living space. Roger said he'd pay rent on it until Aly could bear to sort through Fletcher's things. It wasn't much per month, but enough so Fletcher had to work hard to afford it.

Fletcher didn't have much. Aly was amazed by how much junk she collected every time she cleaned out her room, but Fletcher's place always looked sparse. He had few personal items, but he had the "normal" things: a small flat-screen TV he'd spent ages saving for; an Xbox that had been a "you can have it, I got a new one for my birthday" hand-me-down from Del; a lumpy, old, and what was considered brown about a decade ago sofa they'd found at a yard sale, littered with several throw pillows Aly and Fletcher had made in art class when they were twelve; and a small table with mismatched plastic chairs.

The only new and colorful things in the room were the paintings on the wall, which Aly had done for Fletcher. One of them was a self-portrait she'd done when she was fifteen for an art project at school. She'd wanted to throw it out but Fletcher decided he wanted it and stole it. Another one was a sunset on the beach and a third was the cartoon bee she liked to draw. Nothing special, she'd always thought, but she'd been proud when he'd put them on his walls.

Every birthday and Christmas, ever since she'd been old enough to know it would make a difference, Aly had given him two presents. Something he wanted and something he needed. New curtains. Matching dishware. She'd bought him printed sheets of Batman and Robin one year. Things he'd always accepted with a roll of his eyes and a subdued look but couldn't return because they were a gift. And she always felt bad for the presents he got her, which he must have done without for months to buy.

Now, as she stood in the center of his home, his life didn't seem to amount to much.

It didn't reek, to her surprise. She'd thought a few weeks of dishes in the sink and unemptied trash would saturate the house with the smell of decaying food. Being practical, she checked the sink and the bin, surprised to discover both were empty. So was the bar fridge, she noted as she checked it. Maybe Penelope had been here.

She wandered over to the couch and saw one of Fletcher's red flannel shirts draped over the arm. Without thinking, she picked it up and pressed her face to it to breathe in his scent. It was still strong. Memories of him coursed through her, particularly memories of him wearing this shirt.

There were things of Fletcher's Aly wanted. Things she wanted no one else to know she had.

His laptop; she knew the password. And his pillows. A couple of his shirts. Pictures. A few keepsakes of things she'd given him over the years. Things that were meant to give her a lifetime of reminders, instead of having him there.

Lifting her face away from the shirt, she shoved her arms through the sleeves and headed toward his bedroom.

Del always joked Fletcher was a neat freak and teenagers were not supposed to have clean bedrooms, but Fletcher liked things tidy. Everything had a place. Even his desk was cleaner than hers. His bed was rumpled because he hated making it in the morning and did nothing more than throw a duvet over it, but the sheets were clean.

Aly wondered if Fletcher would have minded her rummaging through his bedroom. Did he have certain stashes he wanted to hide? Would he have that one folder in his laptop for more nefarious things, or a box of magazines hidden under his bed?

No, she discovered as she looked. The only thing under his bed was a book that had fallen from the nightstand. As she picked the book up and returned it to his nightstand, she noticed that the framed picture taken of the four of them at the lake last summer was missing.

Turning to survey the room, Aly noticed several things out of place. Fletcher's beaten sneakers, the only pair she'd thought he owned, were thrown at the base of his wardrobe. The sneakers had odd black marks on the soles and as she examined them closer, she could have sworn they were burn marks.

Fletcher's laptop was gone. She couldn't find it. Fletcher never took it anywhere. A gaming laptop, it stayed on his desk. There was even a cleared space where it was supposed to be. Its carry case was gone as well.

Upon opening the cupboard, Aly was surprised to discover the bag Penelope had given Fletcher for summer camp was gone. Some of his favorite shirts were missing as well, ones she'd wanted to take.

"What's going on?" Her voice sounded loud in the stillness of his room, yet voicing her question aloud made it seem real to her. Had someone been here? Some of his family, perhaps?

Taking a step back from the wardrobe, she turned to survey the room again and caught the tail end of a memory or dream. She couldn't be sure of what it was but Fletcher's voice whispered about the corner. Her gaze lingered on each corner of his bedroom before she noticed the tiny scratch marks on the floor where the feet of his bed were, as if his bed had been moved repeatedly. She pulled the bed away from the wall, following the direction and length of the scratch marks, then lay across the bed to see the corner.

One of the wooden floorboards was raised. She hadn't even been aware they could lift up. She'd always heard stories, and seen in the movies, about things hidden beneath floorboards. Why would Fletcher have the need for such a hiding place?

Squeezing into the gap between the bed and the wall,

she pried it up with the fingers of her good hand. Inside the dark space was a blank envelope. With her heart pounding hard, she lifted the envelope out and tore it open. Inside was a scrap of paper with a single line.

Go to the place we kissed.

Heat flooded through her at the memory of how stupid her thirteen-year-old self had been; brand new hormones and thinking she'd been in love with him. They'd been down by the lake with her family and snuck off to the small boat dock there, and she'd practically launched herself at him. Mashed lips and confused hearts and he'd told her while he loved her, he couldn't love her the way she wanted. When she'd pushed about the why, he elaborated. It had been an awkward time for both of them and here he was, asking her to go to the lake.

He would be one to tease her even after death.

It didn't make any sense. Why would he send her there? The envelope looked new; had he known something would happen? And if he'd known, why hadn't he warned her? Or tried to get away? Or something—anything—other than dying.

She didn't have any answers, only more questions, and sitting here doing nothing wasn't any way to find the truth. "Damn it," she muttered, and rose to her feet.

CHAPTER 11

Noah didn't know when the decision to escape the Institute switched from discussion to doing. It felt as though they were always building up to it. It was a combination of things: the utter disdain in Diego's voice when talking about them; being treated as subjects, not people; the grueling training when others beyond their rooms got to go home; and the knowledge that somewhere out there, Ruth was free. That was a major part, Ruth being free. They wanted to experience it too, wanted to live like those beyond the walls did with homes and families. They wanted to find Ruth and ask him why and how Smith lied. Knowing Smith was a program made the decision easier for them. If the Institute couldn't be truthful, why should loyalty be demanded?

When they overheard Wade talking about a breeding program for Noah and Elijah to pass on their regenerative capabilities, something no one else had managed to replicate, they knew they had to leave.

The Institute had a plan involving long-term infiltration. Even though Noah didn't know details, he and his siblings were all given identities to learn. Training increased as they were educated in culture, computers and internet usage, and the concept of money. Jonah theorized they were going to replace known aliens and try to gain information.

As each identity was located in different cities and the maps they were given showed those cities to be a great distance from each other, they decided they would have to escape before they were sent out into the world. Elijah wouldn't leave anyone behind or even entertain the idea of escaping in twos. After much discussion, even Jonah agreed the best course of action was for them all to leave as a unit. Escaping together, they could help each other and protect the group.

Their first problem was the implant. While they weren't certain it contained a GPS tracking locator, they couldn't risk it. As they learned more and more about human culture, they discovered hospitals and the equipment there. A device might discover the location of the implants and surgical implements could aid in removing them.

Then Elijah was taught about X-rays, specifically about them being part of the electromagnetic spectrum just as visible light was. Noah thought since human eyes could see visible light naturally, they could be augmented to see in the X-ray spectrum as well. He tested out several theories. That discovery changed everything.

Now, he could not only see the implant, nestled in the lining at the top of their nasal cavity in a place that didn't shift, he could also see beyond the walls and into the next room before objects became indistinguishable from each other. The overlap of objects gave him a headache but he could identify hallways and monitoring rooms above the courtyard. He could follow the dumbwaiter down until the track became lost to ambiguity.

Although the others found they couldn't duplicate the finesse required for a shift like that, just as they also couldn't manage regeneration, Elijah could copy his instructions. The two of them spent several days mapping the rooms beyond the hangar as subtly as they could. The walls were too thick to get a clear view and there was a lot of object noise, but there seemed to be a large, open space on one side and offices on the other.

While the others practiced augmentation, such as making their muscles stronger or their lung capacity greater, Elijah and Noah worked out new augmentations as well as studying the implant. Noah thought he could shift it out, or at least move the flesh away from it so it could fall into his nasal cavity and be sneezed out, but he couldn't practice in case Smith was alerted. Knowing the others wouldn't be able to shift it out, Elijah thought she could remove it before they escaped the Institute if they could find the right tools. Removing it before they escaped would mean, if there was a tracker, they could get farther away before their movements were discovered.

Elijah and Noah also worked closely with Solomon every night, talking through every shift and augmentation, so he would be ready when they made their escape. They would have to move fast and far the first night, putting as much distance between them and the Institute as possible.

Jonah raised an unforeseen problem: currency and their lack of. It was a conundrum; they knew the world outside operated on it. Adam suggested they raid as much as they could from the Institute before they left, not just money, but things to sell. Computers and technology seemed to be the only option.

Solomon hit on the idea to steal tools that wouldn't be missed. A screwdriver each so they could open their doors. Weapons were stashed around their main hangar. Not guns because they were sure to be noticed, but knives and other blades. It wasn't much, but they hoped it would be enough to get them out the door. In the days before they were ready to depart, Seth hid a few wire cutters at various points beneath the compost in their small courtyard, hoping they would not be missed.

In their rooms, on the night of their breakout, they

feigned sleep as they waited for the world beyond their rooms to quieten. Solomon started his shift a full hour before the rest of them to ensure he'd have every advantage he could available to him.

Noah was anxious as he listened to the world beyond his wall, waiting for the moment the voices and sounds of movement disappeared. His throat felt dry, his stomach knotted and his legs twitched restlessly as he worried they would be discovered before they'd even made the attempt. With every voice, he listened and waited until they drifted away and there was nothing left to listen to.

"*Are you ready?*" Elijah murmured into the darkness.

Noah swallowed and squashed the churning in his belly. "*Yes.*"

"*Let us away,*" Jonah commanded.

Noah sprang from his bed. Having already determined the clothes drawers were not alarmed, he threw on his clothes and boots faster than he ever had before, then went to the door.

The sliding door took a bit of maneuvering to open. With his palms flat against the door, a deftly jammed screwdriver got the door open enough to dig his fingers into the gap and apply more muscle to force the door open. Holding it was another matter, the door groaned as it tried to close. Noah squeezed through the gap he'd made, pushing against the door and holding his breath to make himself as skinny as possible. Once through, the door closed immediately.

No alarms that he could hear, he noted, as he hurried to Seth's door to aid her. She flashed him a wide grin as she squeezed through the door while he held it open. "Thank you."

"Shh," he reminded her, returning her grin.

Her eyes widened and crinkled at the corners as she covered her mouth with her hand, the apology clear on her face. Noah squeezed her arm and went to help Adam with his door.

It wasn't long before they were all free and running toward the courtyard with Jonah and Adam staying behind to pry open the weapons locker. Once there, Elijah and Noah used their shifted eyes to survey the surrounding rooms while Moses and Solomon cut a hole in the wire fence.

Elijah signaled to Noah she'd found a window which didn't appear to be latched that they could use as their entry into the Institute.

Moses made a soft noise and moved aside to hold the wire up. Elijah and Noah ducked through first. Taking up a position beside the wall, Noah cupped his hands before him and braced so he could boost Elijah up. Using him as a ladder, she stepped onto his shoulders and he clasped her ankles to hold her steady as she worked the window open while Seth darted down the corridor to warn Adam and Jonah they had a way out.

A soft click told Noah that Elijah had the window open and he flattened his palms and held them up higher so she could use them as stairs. Once she was through, Moses went next. Solomon cast a wary look down the hallway and then gave Noah a worried expression. Trying to be sympathetic and aware his brother worried about Seth, Noah gave him a small smile and cupped his hands. After a moment's hesitation, Solomon allowed Noah to boost him up to Elijah and Moses.

Seth came running down the corridor the moment Solomon was up the wall, still beaming. She crawled through the small hole in the fence and bounced on Noah so hard he was able to springboard her up to Solomon. Wiping his sweaty palms on his knees, Noah braced again as Jonah appeared, carrying several guns and closely followed by Adam.

Adam and Jonah tossed the weapons up to Moses and Seth, then scrambled up Noah. Once they were all up, Noah backed up, then ran up the wall and reached for Adam and Moses' hands. As a unit, they grabbed him and heaved him into the building.

Accepting the gun Jonah shoved at him, Noah glanced around. He'd been right when he'd thought this was an observation deck, there was little here but it was obvious to him the place was frequented. There were scuff marks from chairs on the walls and floor, and a dirty bin against the wall.

"Which way?" he whispered to Elijah, since it had been her job to scout.

She gestured down a hallway and took point. They fell in behind with Noah bringing up the rear. He shifted his eyes to include heat signatures, a trick they'd also discovered they could do when they experimented. It was a long, straight hallway, with no windows after their courtyard windows. No doors either. No adornments of any kind. No cameras they could see.

Elijah pulled up short with a gasp and Noah shifted his eyes to normal to see what startled her.

It was a window similar to the one they'd come through and its view was another, empty courtyard. Dirt, no trees, just a cage like theirs had, an open roof and one door.

"Another group?" Moses whispered as he pressed his hand against the glass.

"We knew there would be others," Jonah replied.

"What should we do?" Elijah glanced down the line to Noah.

Studying the roof, Noah suggested, "Perhaps we should exit the roof? It is clear to the top, we could manage a jump if we are careful."

Solomon cleared his throat and altered his stance. "Should we not be raiding?"

"What if there is nothing to raid?" Elijah studied the open roof now. "What if all this is purely for observation?"

"There *must* be an office close to our rooms," Adam said, taking a few steps back to peer down the way they'd come. "We have heard them working at night. We should go back and search more thoroughly. Then go through the roof outside our room."

"Agreed," Jonah said, her shoe squeaking on the floor as she turned.

"We sh-should r-r-escue them," Seth said, stumbling over her words in her rush to get them out.

Noah's eyes dropped down from the roof. Elijah fidgeted, caught between moods. Moses made an odd noise at the back of his throat. There was logic in Seth's words, but Noah couldn't see any way it could possibly work. So many variables that could go wrong. Glancing around, he could see the same hopelessness in the eyes of his siblings.

Solomon answered for them, his voice soft. "We cannot."

"We should aim to escape ourselves," Elijah agreed. "We cannot support a group we know nothing about."

Seth shook her head and her eyes shone with tears. "We cannot leave them. It is n-not fair."

Solomon stepped up to her and placed his hand on her arm. "No, it is not."

Seth looked up at Solomon and Noah could see she wanted to argue. As much as he didn't think rescuing others was a good idea, he also didn't want to upset Seth.

"They might try to prevent us from leaving," Adam reasoned.

"If they know nothing of the outside world, how do we convince them?" Jonah asked. "It is better for us to escape now, while we can, and investigate the possibility of returning for them at a later date." She reached for Seth, stalling in the middle of the action and dropped her hand. Noah wondered if her intent had been to comfort or to force her moving. "We need to go."

Jonah ran down the corridor the way they'd come as soon as the words had left her mouth. With a sympathetic glance at Seth, Noah followed. Once they returned to their courtyard, Jonah had them split up. There were three more corridors, one for each wall surrounding their rooms and while Elijah had picked the longest corridor, Noah could see the ends of two of them and several doors leading off the edge of one of the hallways.

"They were locked," she explained as he glanced at her.

Noah nodded. "We break them."

"And the alarm?" Solomon asked.

Adam flashed him a smile. "So we be hasty."

"Five minutes," Jonah commanded. "No more. Take what you can."

"Then through the roof," Elijah said. "If we can find rope it will make it easier."

Noah went to the door at the far end of the hall and his siblings each picked another door. A shoulder and a fierce shove broke the flimsy lock and he was inside. A small, windowless room filled with cleaning items, boxes of paper, and stationary supplies. A quick search netted him a few box cutters, a pair of scissors and a flashlight.

The next room contained a single desk with two chairs either side of it and a computer terminal. Noah crossed the room so he could rummage through the drawers of the desk, hoping to find something. As he opened the first drawer, the monitor flicked on.

If the text on the screen had said "login", Noah would have ignored it but someone had forgotten to log out. Instead, it opened an email program, and one of the subject headings caught his eye. "Echo Group".

Sitting in the chair, Noah opened the email.

Darcy,

Echo group has shown an alarming increase in unity unseen in the other groups and this unity outweighs their progress. I believe it stems from your lax restrictions and their ability to communicate. It is detrimental to the program to continue to allow them such freedoms or to consider allowing the other groups the same freedoms. These creatures should not be afforded basic human rights. Giving them names was unwise, as there are staff members who are beginning to feel affection toward the group.

Allowing them to replace known natural shifters will backfire. Their personalities are becoming more distinct and their trust in Smith is dwindling. How long do you think it will take for them to realize everything they know is a lie? We have no way to control them once they start interacting with real people. There is also concern that they will stand out because they will not be able to integrate correctly, especially with such prominent roles.

I am concerned about the mayhem they would invoke on the program if the media were alerted to its existence. Cloning and genetic manipulation on such a scale would see all of us imprisoned, regardless of our involvement in the program.

We must terminate Echo group immediately. Harvest Echo Seven and Echo Four for future generations and start afresh. The Smith program must be rewritten. Foxtrot is almost full grown; we should focus on them. We have all the necessary data we need; Echo's usefulness is at an end. Perhaps engage in more detailed explorations of Echo Seven's regenerative abilities. Imagine the possibilities if he could regrow organs for harvest.

—Wade

Words rattled Noah's brain. Clone. Genetic manipulation. They hadn't given themselves to the Institute like they had been led to believe. They were *grown*.

He let out a bitter laugh. Lie after lie, had there been *any* truth to what Smith had told them? Was there a war? Were there even others who had the capabilities to change their bodies like they could?

Did he even care anymore?

Noah scrubbed a hand over his head and then searched the computer deeper. What he found shook him to the core. Vats of growing people in various stages of development. DNA structures. Countless experimentations and disposals. An ongoing circle.

They even used "recruits" to take care of escapees. Some of those people he'd killed had been like him. If only there was a way to ensure future generations wouldn't be subjected to the same horrors he and the others had been.

"Did you find anything?"

Noah flicked his gaze up to Elijah and closed the screen he was on. "No," he said with a heavy heart and stood. "Box cutter and a flashlight. You?"

"These," she said with a sympathetic look as she held them up. A long, slim, dual-pronged device and Noah knew what it was to be used for.

His nose twitched. "Oh."

"You are the last. It is quick," she assured him.

He grimaced. The idea of having that up his nose wasn't appealing but he tilted his head back and held still as Elijah inserted the tweezers up his left nostril, blinked so she could shift her eyes, then clamped on the implant. There was a little pain as it was removed, enough to make his eyes water, and then the infernal thing was dropped on the ground and crushed beneath a heel.

"Nicely done," Noah commented, grateful. He sniffed then pulled on his nose to help ebb the pain. "Do you need—"

"I was able to locate a mirror," Elijah said with a wry smile. "In the same room I found these."

He nodded. "We should leave."

"Agreed." She frowned, peering down the hallway. "What is going on?"

Seth and Solomon came toward them with broad grins and holding hands. Noah's gaze dropped down to their joined hands then back up. "We found a map," Solomon exclaimed, walking with hurried step while pointing the opposite direction. "The exit is not far."

Elijah gasped and grabbed Noah's arm. "A map?"

"It was on the wall," Solomon said, excited. "Emergency exit."

"Fortunate," Noah said.

Solomon nodded. "They are scouting the exit, we need to—"

Solomon's words were interrupted by a high-pitched

squeal and the four of them drew weapons in response and looked around, primed for attack.

"An alarm?" Elijah suggested.

"Then we need to leave," Noah blurted, looking to Solomon. "Which way?"

Leading the way, Solomon darted down the corridor with the other three right behind him. As they skidded around a corner, Noah could see Adam holding a door open farther down.

"Alarm!" he yelled as he saw them approaching. "Jonah and Moses ran for the fence!"

"Go!" Elijah bellowed at him, her boots thumping against the floor.

"We will catch up!" Noah called.

Adam vanished through the door and seconds later, Jonah roared ultrasonically, "*Shooters*!" followed closely by three loud bangs.

Noah and Elijah sped up, passing Seth and Solomon with ease as they sprinted ahead to catch the door Adam exited. Before they reached it, Adam barreled through, clutching one arm and staggering. He hit the opposite wall with his shoulder and left a smear of blood.

"Adam!"

"I am fine," he ground out through gritted teeth and bent over to clutch his leg.

Noah got to him first, gripping his upper arms. "How bad?"

"Two," Adam muttered, and broke out into a sweat. Blood coated his fingers as he pressed them against his wounds. "Shoulder, calf." He gasped in a breath. "They are on the roof."

"This roof?" Noah questioned.

"Yes. Above us."

"Can you heal?" Elijah's voice was tight. She pressed one hand over the top of Adam's wounds, the other reaching for the tweezers so she could extract the bullets.

Adam slid down to the floor, Elijah going with him.

"Perhaps with the pain as motivation, I will have some success this time."

"We shall stay with him," Solomon said as he and Seth reached them. Seth tore up her jacket to use as a bandage and Solomon held out his hand for Elijah's tweezers.

Noah shucked off his jacket, tearing off the arms and handing them to Seth to use. "Elijah and I shall clear the way."

"Be ready to run," Elijah said and, as she stood, she looked to Noah. "Through the middle?"

Noah nodded. "They will not expect that."

A predatory grin spread across Elijah's face. "Let us go."

Sprinting toward their cage and the gap which headed to the roof, Noah steeled himself for what he needed to do to get his siblings free. It didn't matter their guards might be innocents. *They* were innocents, held against their will and it was time for them to be free and anyone who stood in the way of that was an enemy. What price would he pay for freedom?

Elijah's expression was set in fierce determination, her pace matching his.

Pausing at the window, they looked up. Elijah hummed. "How do you propose—"

"Brace on the walls." Tucking the gun into his belt, Noah climbed up onto the frame of the window. "Follow me." He leaped for the corner, bracing one foot against each wall and using his fingers to dig into the small cracks between cement panels. Bending his knees, he braced and sighted the next crack, then propelled himself upward. Catching it with his fingers, he slammed his feet against the two walls again to brace, and repeated the action. A quick glance down saw Elijah copying.

It took three jumps to reach the roof. When he was there, he hung onto the edge and inched out of the way so Elijah could come up beside him. He pulled himself up long enough to get a glimpse of what was on the roof before dropping back down.

"Two shooters, nine o'clock," he told Elijah as she reached him. "About thirty yards. I cannot see any others but there appear to be several vents and various machines and piping."

Elijah nodded. "Take out the shooters then worry about what else there is."

"Agreed. Silent." He paused to consider. "Deadly force only if necessary. Perhaps we can knock them out."

She looked skeptical. "Noah..."

"There already has been unnecessary death. If we kill their guards, are we any better?"

She considered for a moment. "I see your argument."

Elijah readied herself on the wall and Noah did the same as they prepared to spring from the hole. Hoping Adam was ready and able to run, Noah took a deep breath and nodded to Elijah. As quietly as he could, he pulled himself up onto the roof and made for the nearest vent as cover. Elijah darted for another vent close to him.

Keeping part of his attention on Elijah's location, he peeked around the edge of the metal vent, cataloging all he saw. Two shooters with their backs to them knelt at the edge of the roof, scanning below with their weapons. As he looked every direction, he couldn't see any other people on the roof—but he knew there was a possibility of them.

Another nod to Elijah and they left their hiding places.

It was easier than expected to subdue the two shooters on the roof. They were not expecting an attack from behind. Two quick kicks to the head had them both dazzled enough they could be bound with their own handcuffs and their weapons and communication devices removed.

Noah scanned the rooftops while Elijah secured the men. "I cannot see any more."

"I do not think they would fire on us," she said, her voice filled with scorn. "They want us for breeding purposes."

Noah considered as he continued to scan. "No."

Elijah glanced at him in surprise. "No?"

"I discovered an email," he said, deciding she needed to know. "While it appears we have outlived our usefulness… they apparently want to harvest us both for future generations."

She stopped and stared at him. "Wouldn't they need us alive for that?"

"I do not know and I do not think we should test that theory."

Adam's voice echoed ultrasonically, *"Noah, Elijah, are you in the building?"*

Elijah and Noah exchanged glances. *"No."*

Solomon said, *"We hear footsteps."*

Noah's chest tightened and Elijah went pale.

Jonah commanded, *"Run!"*

Seth and Solomon, aiding Adam, burst from the building down below and charged for the fence. They had barely left the safety of the doorway when the gunfire started.

All three fell.

CHAPTER 12

Aly,

I don't know how many times I've written this letter. I can't seem to find the right words. I guess it's too late now. I don't know what's led to you finding this letter, but whatever's happened, it's hurt you. I never wanted you to get hurt, as much as that was probably inevitable.

I hope it's not because I died. I really hope it didn't come to that. I hope I was able to run, even though that means leaving you behind and I don't know that I could have done that anymore. If I did die, believe me, I would have done everything I could before succumbing. If there was a way to live, I would've found it.

Not that going missing would have been any better. Maybe if I were dead, that would at least give you closure. I refuse to believe it would have been an accident; that's not my style. You would never have found this letter if it was something as simple as an accident. This is something I will only ever give you if they come.

I'm probably confusing you.

There's a war raging. It's been raging for years. An underground war between factions you've never heard of and will never hear of. I don't even know how many sides there are; it's all a complete, blurry mess now. Lies and half-truths all wrapped up in mythology and religion and torn apart by those who should know better.

I didn't want to fight anymore. I chose to run. I ran very, very far. Changed everything about myself. I left them behind, but they didn't leave me. That's why I've always been so tight-lipped because there was nothing to tell. I lied to you about everything: my family, myself, even my name. I didn't know which side was right, or if there even was a right side. I was tired. Tired of it all. I didn't start the war. I won't finish it. I'm just a soldier, trained to follow orders from commanders I know nothing about, who went AWOL to find out why we were fighting.

I understand this won't make sense. After all, we've known each other since we were eight. We might be the same age, but I've seen so much. This war is older than me, it's older than memory and it does not protect its children. Age is just a number; it says nothing about experience.

I suppose my past caught up with me. It was about time, I guess. I lasted longer in Bellhollow than I did anywhere else. I had a chance to grow up normally. I was even hoping... well... I wanted to stay. I hoped that by integrating so much, they'd never notice me. I guess they did.

I know you're confused but I can't tell you more. Not even now. I don't know what happened and I don't want you at risk. It is better that you don't know—they can't make you talk then. I don't even want them to have an inkling you might know something you shouldn't. I was just some boy you knew in school, nothing more.

Whatever happens, or has happened, there is something I need to say. Thank you. Thank you for your time, for your friendship and most of all, for your love. You have given me more than you could possibly imagine and I can't repay you.

I hope you'll be happy. I hope you'll live your dreams. I want that for you, but I know it'll be hard. I never meant for this. You're my best friend and my favorite person in this world and I didn't want to hurt you.

If people come, if they look for me, don't believe what they say. Don't go with them. Trust your gut, you've always had good instincts. When we first met, you knew something was different about me, I could tell by the way you looked at me. You judged me, it was like you could see through... you could see into me and you chose to trust

148

me. You said… do you remember? It was so weird, such a kid thing to say, but you said, "You don't fit your face," and then laughed it off and complained it was the dirt on my nose.

No one has ever seen me like you do. You were right. I don't fit this face. Yet, it's a better one than all the others because it got to see you.

Those prickling sensations you get around me sometimes and probably ignore, I want you to stop ignoring. I can see when you get goose bumps; it just took me a while to figure out why. If you ever feel it again, trust it. Be wary around whomever you get it from. If something is off, if you feel something is wrong, then it probably is.

If you ever find yourself lost, trust the Snickers. I know it's a joke between us, but if you ever need a sign, that'll be it.

One last thing. Burn this. Forget you know. Plausible deniability.

Stay beautiful. Keep smiling. Live long and be happy and forget me.

Love,
Fletcher.

"Are you all right, honey?"

Aly looked up from the order pad she'd been staring at to the aged women she should be serving. Shaking herself mentally, she tried to smile. "Yes. Sorry, Ms. Fitzgerald. What was that last order?"

Sally Fitzgerald's smile contained the all too familiar kindness of someone who knew things weren't right. "Apple pie, please."

Aly shook her head; Sally always ordered pie and Aly felt like an idiot. "Right, yes, of course," she said, scribbling down the order. "It shouldn't be too long."

Sally touched Aly's broken wrist. "I was sorry to hear about your young man."

A common misconception from her customers, though Aly had done nothing to dissuade them. Technically, he had been hers. Her best friend. Fletcher had been a semicommon customer and most regulars knew of him. She plastered the same brave smile on her face she'd shown to all the rest. "Thank you."

"He was always so nice to everyone," Sally continued. "And he was so in love with you."

Aly blinked several times, then shook her head. "No, he—"

"He couldn't take his eyes off you every time he was here," Sally said. "And the way he said your name... even these old bones can still swoon."

Her voice caught in her throat. "What?"

"Oh, yes," Esme, one of Sally's friends, included. "The way someone who loves you says your name is always so different than the way anyone else says it. He always spoke yours with such reverence."

Startled, Aly had to blink back the sudden influx of tears. "Oh."

Sally grew concerned and her friends exchanged troubled glances. "I'm sorry, dear. I didn't mean to upset you."

"Take it from us, dear," Esme said, trying to be soothing and failing. "It'll get better."

"Thanks," Aly said, wanting to get away as soon as she could. "I'll bring your drinks in a minute. Let me know if you need anything else."

Tearing the order from the notepad, she clipped it to Liam's order rack, reciting it off to Liam inside the kitchen, then headed for the drinks. Barry, knowing Sally well, had pre-prepared them. He hadn't said a word when Aly had come for her shift today, although Liam had had a few ready: They weren't short; there were enough staff, and she didn't have to come back until she was ready.

Being busy helped. The routine of orders, smiles, and serving drinks kept her mind occupied. The constant condolences from customers made it harder. Aly endured because she had to. The way she felt right now, she'd never be ready, and that's why she was here. If she didn't get back on her feet soon, she never would.

Although the day had been tough, it was easier than spending the day in bed watching the hours tick by and feeling sad. After Aly had spent the day at the lake, reading Fletcher's letter over and over again and staring at the water as she tried to decipher his words, she'd gone to Grace's house. Stuffing dumplings had been therapeutic, as well as listening to Grace and Lan talk about food, cooking, boys, Lan's college days, and the future. After a few failed attempts to get her to participate in the conversation, they'd let her be silent.

Penelope had left a cryptic, "We'll talk when you get home" message on Aly's phone. Aly decided not to worry too much until later. There was only so much she could deal with at once.

"Are you okay?" Jemima, the other waitress on shift, asked as she squeezed by Aly carrying a tray of drinks for one of her tables.

Aly dabbed at her eyes with a spare napkin so she didn't ruin her makeup. "Yeah."

Jemima paused at the end of the counter. "Need a breather?"

"I'm good," she said, throwing the napkin in the trash. "Just caught off guard."

Jemima nodded. "That will happen. Those old dears," she tilted her head at Sally's table. "They mean well, but I think age has brought on a lack of tact."

Aly snorted. "Yeah, probably." Taking a deep breath, she brushed her hand over Fletcher's letter in the pocket of her apron. She fixed a smile and picked up the tray of drinks Barry had finished.

Work continued at a steady pace. Sally and her friends ate their meals and were replaced by another patron as soon as the table was clean. Jemima finished her shift at six and went off to her night classes and Miguel took over from her. Maya replaced Liam in the kitchen. Simon, the cook's helper, arrived at six-thirty to help with the dinner rush and the dishes, and Barry retired to a corner booth to do the books before heading home.

At eight-thirty, half an hour before her shift finished, Aly stopped serving tables and let Miguel take them all. She did the odd jobs, like making sure the napkin containers and salt and pepper shakers were full. She also cleaned off tables when patrons finished, restocked the straw holders and emptied the small glass washer underneath the counter.

Normally, she'd go into the kitchen and help Maya before her shift ended. Tonight, however, her skin prickled as a man arrived, stronger than the tingling sensation she occasionally felt, only this time it was sustained. He sat in the corner booth and picked up a menu.

She tried not to be obvious about studying him. Dark hair, tanned skin, he had a large nose and scruff on his chin. Shucking off his dark jacket, revealing large arms, he draped it over his knees and pulled out his cell.

Her fingers touched Fletcher's letter again. Was she only wary of the man because of Fletcher's letter? Or had she had this feeling in the past and ignored it, only choosing to take notice now? She didn't have an answer. Aly shook herself and picked up two shakers and a napkin container and walked over to his table. The closer she got, the more uncomfortable she felt.

He glanced up from his cell as she approached, gave her the once over, lingering on her name tag, and focused his gaze back down. Grimacing, he shuffled away from her and she wondered if she'd invaded his personal space.

"Evening, sir," she said, sliding the shakers onto the table. "Welcome to Dirk's. Miguel will be with you in a moment."

"Thanks."

Feeling dismissed, she continued to replace the salt and pepper shakers on the tables. Finishing her task, she passed Miguel on his way to the stranger's table. "Are you off, babe?"

"Yup," she said, smiling. "Need a cig break before I go?"

"I'm good, thanks." He tapped his upper arm. "Wearin' the patch."

Aly paused to empty her tip jar into her pocket. "Good for you."

"Yeah, well, we'll see how long it lasts this time." He flashed a toothy smile. "Can you take the dish tray on your way out?"

"Sure," she replied, heading for the tray.

"Have a good one! Hi, sir, can I—"

The bell tinkled, indicating the door opening and Aly looked up automatically. The man who'd arrived to sit in the corner hurried out, pulling on his jacket. Her eyebrows lifted in surprise and she glanced at Miguel.

"How rude," he said, dusting his hand on his pants. "Oh, well. One less customer." He glanced over at Aly and grinned. "Means I might get to finish early."

Aly lifted the tray. "Night, Miguel." Turning so she could push the door open with her back, she entered the kitchen. "Hey guys."

"Hey," they greeted, Maya from the grill and Simon from the sink.

When he saw what Aly carried, Simon lifted his hands out of the soapy water. "Here, I'll—"

"I'll stack the dishwasher on my way out," she said, carrying the tray over to an empty bench.

"Thanks, Aly," Maya said, grinning, and her copious bracelets jangled as she flipped the burger patty she cooked. "It should be just about full."

"Pretty slow tonight," Aly commented as she stacked the shelves, hoping to prompt them both into returning to whatever conversation they were having before she'd arrived.

"Yeah, there's some sort of festival in Redding," Simon said, transferring the pan he'd finished washing to the drying rack.

"Oh, really?" Maya asked, curious. "I didn't know. What sort of festival?"

"Not sure," Simon said, and picked up the next pot. "Some sort of heritage one. I'm not big on that stuff."

"Huh," Maya said as she plated up the meal she'd finished cooking. "I'll have to check it out. Gravy needs a restock."

Simon lifted his hands out of the sink again. "Right. On it."

"Thanks." Hitting the bell, Maya left the plate on the small window. "Order up!" Returning to the grill, she said, "You know, you really should get more culture, there's only so many car rallies your poor girlfriend can handle—"

Aly finished stacking the dishwasher and headed for her locker. Storing her tips for the night in her purse, she extracted her keys, slung her bag over her shoulder and headed for the door. "Night guys!"

Maya and Simon broke their conversation to echo her, then picked it up again without pause as Aly opened the back door and headed out into the night. The back of Dirk's was always neat. Each trashcan had a closed lid, the dumpster was open but only because Simon hadn't done the final trash run of the night. The air didn't have a back-alleyway smell too it, but nevertheless, Aly startled several rats as the door banged closed behind her.

Clutching the strap of her purse with both hands, Aly set off to the communal parking lot a few minutes away. She never liked this walk at night, it gave her the creeps being alone, but asking Fletcher or her mom to pick her up after every shift had seemed like it was too needy. It was mostly lit, if rather deserted.

The night felt hot and moist. She was glad of the lightness of her blue diner's uniform, although she missed the cool air of the diner the moment she left it. A soft ringing in her bag drew her attention and she rummaged through it for her phone. Looking at the face which popped up, she smiled as she answered. "Hi!"

Grace said with fake cheer, "How was work?"

Aly's smile grew wider. "Grace, you don't normally call me this late unless something's up."

"Your mom just left here," Grace said in a more resigned tone. "I'm peeking out the window; yup, she's driving off. Two guesses what the topic of discussion was."

Aly sighed and pinched the bridge of her nose with her fingers. "Frick."

"I was studying," Grace explained. "I didn't even know your mom was here until I went downstairs to get some tea. I don't... I don't think it's bad. I mean... they understand, you know. They're being moms. Mom said they want to get us both in grief counseling. Del too. Proper ones, not just the school shit. They think you'll take to the idea better if I go too."

Aly grumbled. "Great."

"I kind of think..." Grace sighed, "It's a good idea."

"Yeah," Aly said with a heavy heart, "I guess."

"Anyway, I just thought I'd give you the heads up."

"I know Mom wanted to—" Aly's skin prickled in warning and she glanced around. Her heart skipped a beat as she saw a shadow in the darkness behind her. She increased her speed. "Ahh... um... Mom wanted to talk to me anyway."

"About this morning?"

Aly glanced over her shoulder again, her eyes zeroing in on the figure behind her. The distance between them seemed the same, which meant he was following her, not just traveling in the same direction. "Probably. I mean, really, what should I have done? They've been counseling suicide."

Grace gasped. "Oh. Shit. I didn't realize."

Were those footsteps speeding up? She thought they might be. "He didn't give you—"

"I haven't been."

"Really?" She glanced over her shoulder again and used

her broken hand to rummage inside her bag for her mace. She wished she could change direction, but every other way around her led to darker places. Better to stay in the lighted area, it wouldn't be long until she was on the street and into a more populated place. "He led me to believe it was mandatory."

"Not as far as I know…" Grace sighed again. "But then, I've not really been paying much attention to the teachers lately outside class."

"Yeah, I get that…" Another glance over her shoulder and she caught a proper glimpse of the figure following her. "Um… Grace?" she said, trying not to panic.

"Yeah?"

"Someone's following me."

"What?" Grace squeaked.

"Saw the same man in the diner," her voice cracked and she increased her speed again. "Now he's creeping on me."

"Stay on the call," Grace blurted and Aly could hear her door open. "I'll get Mom to call Dad." Grace's dad was a police officer so it made Aly feel a little safer. Hopefully he was close. Even if this was a false alarm, better to be safe than sorry.

Her fingers curled around the mace, she switched hands so she could use her good hand if she needed. Trying to keep an eye on the man behind her and stay calm enough so she didn't break into a run, she continued.

"Mooom!" Grace bellowed and Aly winced and took her phone away from her ear.

A van screeched up to block the end of the alley, preventing her from accessing the parking lot without going close. Aly's stomach dropped as the door opened to reveal two black hooded figures who leaped from the van and waited by the door, clearly watching her.

She froze and the hair on her arms and the back of her neck stood on end. "Oh. God."

"Aly? Aly?"

Her throat was dry, her chest felt like all the air had been shoved out, and her heart doubled its beat. A bead of sweat trickled down her back and she shuddered. She'd seen movies like this. A follower to scare a victim, accomplices to snatch once they ran. What followed... she didn't want to think about. With a twitch of her shoulder, she knocked the strap of her bag down to her elbow which would allow her to use it as a weapon if the mace didn't get her free. Dropping her still-on phone in her bag, she turned sideways and looked down the alley. That was her best bet, mace the man and run. All she had to do was make it to Dirk's and she'd be safe.

The man who'd been following her pulled something from his pocket and pointed it at her. Hidden in shadows, she couldn't tell if it was a gun or not. "We need you to come with us."

Swallowing, she sized him up, then the two figures motionless by the van. "I'd rather not."

"You don't have a choice." His voice sounded like gravel and she wondered if he tried to disguise it.

"There's always a choice," Aly snapped, fear making her tone harsh. Her voice was the only weapon she had and she was determined to use it. "I've called the police."

The man appeared undisturbed but he stopped approaching her. "It won't matter."

"Black van, hooded figures," Aly said in a raised voice, hoping Grace could hear. "You really can't expect me—"

The man smiled and Aly shivered as the fear in her belly multiplied.

Footfalls too close behind her and Aly spun with her mace lifted. He'd been a diversion! The other men— "Stay back!"

A sharp pain stung her shoulder. A wasp? Her body kicked into flight mode. She pressed the button of her mace, spraying it into the faces of the men as much as she could. The man from the diner grabbed her in a bear hug, pinning her arms to her sides. The can of mace clattered to the ground and her purse went flying as she lost her grip on them.

Screaming in both pain and hope for a passer-by rescue, Aly struggled. She kicked her legs, squirming. She had to shake free from the man's grip. When he lifted her off the ground, she became dead weight, dropping toward the ground.

"Get her legs," he grunted, staggering.

Aly redoubled her efforts, lashing out at the men around her. She kicked for the men's ankles and swung her feet for their heads. She swung her arms. She jerked her legs. She tensed her body and strained against them. "Let me go!" she yelled. "Help!"

The man holding her changed his grip so one of his massive arms slung across her chest. He clapped his hand over her mouth to stifle the screaming. She opened her mouth as wide as she could but his hand was too awkward to bite.

Her head spun, everything was wonky and numbness spread from her shoulder. One of the men grabbed her leg and she kicked at him, losing her shoe.

"Hold still."

She beat her hands on him. With all her wriggling, she managed to get purchase with her teeth and bit down as hard as she could. The man holding her howled and shook her to break her grip. The taste of blood burst against her tongue.

A figure cleared the top of the van.

At first, Aly thought they were flying, but it wasn't possible. She could feel the weakness from her shoulder stretching and it played tricks on her. She was yanked around so much the brief glimpses she caught made it appear the figure flew. She must have imagined the speed at which the figure descended upon the men trying to take her. That was the only explanation.

One of the men around her was yanked away by the scruff of his neck. The man holding Aly retreated, moving backward and curling himself around Aly while still trying to free his hand from her mouth. Keeping her teeth clamped on his hand, Aly freed her arm enough and elbowed him in the ribs.

A yelp followed by the sound of something big crashing into the trash can and Aly spun wildly. The man's grip loosened as the figure leaped on him. The man jerked forward, ramming into Aly's back and she could feel the force of the hits through the reverberations in his chest.

"Let her go!" a deep voice said. Aly guessed it was her rescuer.

"Get off me!" the man holding her bellowed.

The world swam. She could feel her muscles relaxing without permission. Fear burrowed deeper inside her and gave her the strength to fight harder. A flash of a gloved hand and the big man holding her dumped her on the ground. Before she could bolt away, someone grabbed a fistful of the back of her dress and yanked and released her in one quick motion.

She spun and hit the ground on her side and her head smacked a wall. Her vision went wonky and the pain from the impact made the scuffling in the alleyway inconsequential. Fear disappeared as she fought to stay conscious. Reason told her it was a bad time to succumb but she didn't know how to stay awake.

Someone grabbed her upper arm. "Let's go!" he hissed and yanked her up. "We have to move."

Her knees buckled and she crumpled in a heap.

"Shit," he said, hunkering down into her distorted field of vision. Light eyes. Dark hair. A face mostly shrouded in shadows. A name bubbled up only to break on weakened lips.

With ungentle fingers he checked her eyes, then her head, then swore viciously as he yanked something from her shoulder. He pulled her forward and then she was bent over his shoulder, dangling.

As he stood, Aly lost all sense of what occurred next.

Some sort of discharge, the man holding her arched, every muscle stiff before he fell forward. Aly fell from his shoulder and came to rest in a puddle.

"Interesting," a voice crooned as the darkness enveloped her. "She had two bodyguards... bring him."

The last thing she saw before her vision faded and memory slipped away was a man reaching down for her.

CHAPTER 13

Noah dropped to a knee, jerking his stolen gun up as he searched for shooters. Beside him, Elijah stifled a gasp. One of the two bound men beside them began to wiggle and she bashed him on the head with her gun.

Below, Adam and Solomon scrambled up from the ground. Adam scooped up a ragdoll Seth and limped for cover.

"I cannot see," Noah muttered, then switched to ultrasonic. "*Jonah, clarify shooter directions.*"

"*Uncertain,*" she responded. "*Hold positions and provide cover fire.*"

"*Right,*" Elijah replied and Noah heard the slight shake in her voice. The two of them fired several shots in random directions, trying to force whoever shot into hiding.

All Noah's senses worked overtime to locate whoever lurked in the darkness. His eyes darted from location to location, using all the shifts he had discovered he could do and he couldn't see anything out of place. Where had the shot come from? It had sounded like it had come from beyond the fence line. What was out there? Nothing. Scant trees, a few dusty ditches. The little moonlight didn't betray many secrets of the grasslands around them but he could see mountains in the distance. And… was that a figure?

Elijah hummed. "Can you see anything?"

"No."

Adam and Solomon ducked for cover behind several metallic barrels that had been left near the fence. Noah dropped his eyes to them, then out beyond the fence again. Shifting his vision so he could see the infrared spectrum, he could see Jonah hiding in a ditch, Moses a fair distance away from her, also hiding. A mass of other heat signatures approached on foot.

Elijah fidgeted. "We should move—"

"Wait," Noah whispered. "Look at the fence." He switched to ultrasonic. "*Jonah, Moses. About ten bodies coming up to your right.*"

"*Acknowledged,*" Moses said.

Noah saw them both turn. Angling his gun down, he checked below. "*Adam, I cannot see anyone near you. Are they hiding in the—*"

"*Seth is dead.*"

Noah's insides twisted into knots. Elijah cried out in denial and her hand shot out to grip his shirt. Below, Moses and Jonah stilled.

"*You need to get out of here,*" Adam continued after a moment. "*Solomon is… comatose. I cannot run—*"

"*We are not leaving you,*" Elijah responded and re-sighted her gun, surveying the surroundings. "*If we—*"

"*Get out of here,*" Adam commanded. "*We will only slow you down.*"

Jonah said, "*Elijah, Noah, we cannot wait long.*"

Noah stood, throwing an arm through the strap of the gun.

Elijah stared at him. "Noah, we cannot leave—"

Noah launched himself over the side of the building. He grabbed onto the metallic piping that ran from the top of the building down the side. It wasn't much to hold onto but he was able to use it, with his feet against the wall, to shimmy down. Reaching the bottom, he glanced up to nod at Elijah and swung his gun to cover her descent. The moment she was down, the pair ran for Adam and Solomon's cover.

As he ran, Noah fired off several shots in the direction of the party approaching Jonah and Moses, then slid in behind a barrel. A pale-faced and sweaty Adam clutched at his leg as he wrapped another makeshift bandage around it. Solomon's face was devoid of expression, his eyes stared straight ahead and he cradled Seth on his lap.

A single trickle of blood slid down her forehead.

The analytical part of Noah studied the shot. Seth had been shot from ahead, which meant the shooter had been beyond the fence and not from the buildings as he'd suspected. A look at Solomon told him it would be better to stay quiet than to voice this.

Solomon didn't appear to have any injuries and he roused when Elijah touched his shoulder. "Solomon? I am so sorry." Tears filling her eyes, she reached out a shaky hand toward Seth's face.

"Do not touch her," Solomon growled, curling around Seth's body.

Elijah's tears spilled over and Noah turned his face away. "She is my sister too," Elijah whispered.

Fire flared in Solomon's face and he bared his teeth. "You will not—"

"Later," Noah said as sharp as he could. There was no time for grief. "We must flee. Solomon, are you injured?"

Solomon's gaze bored into Noah's. "I can run," he said after a long moment.

"Good," Noah said, moving so he crouched in front of Adam. "Get on."

Adam shook his head. "Noah—"

Noah reached back, grabbed the front of Adam's shirt and pulled him forward. "We do not have time to argue." He cleared his throat to change to ultrasonic. "*Jonah, meet us at the fence line. We have rifles."*

Adam tried to writhe free. "Noah—"

"Do not argue! Elijah, cover," Noah said, handing her his rifle so he could use both hands to support Adam.

Elijah gripped the guns. "Right."

As a protesting Adam settled on Noah's back, Noah looked at Solomon and tried to quieten the pain in his chest. "Solomon, your sole duty is to get Seth out of this place. We can give her that peace at least."

A fierce determination filled Solomon's face. "A place in the sun."

Elijah stifled a sob. "Yes."

Noah closed his eyes, concentrating on his body for a moment. Improved muscles in his legs and arms to be able to carry extra weight. More strength for jumping. Larger lung capacity. "Are you ready?"

They nodded. Noah focused on the fence. "Let us go."

Elijah led the charge to the fence line. With every step, Noah was sure they were going to be fired on. He could feel Adam's weight slowly decreasing and knew his brother must be shifting to make it easier on him. When Elijah reached the fence, she stopped and bent over, allowing Noah to use her back as a stepping stone to clear the barbed wire lacing at the top.

Jonah was ready to assist Noah's landing and it took him a few staggering footsteps before he steadied himself. Turning back, Noah watched Solomon clear the fence, then Elijah took a few steps back for a run up as she followed them.

"This way," Jonah murmured, accepting a gun from Elijah. "Moses found vehicles."

Noah frowned, pausing instead of following Elijah. He didn't recall seeing vehicles when he surveyed on the rooftop. Twisting to question, Noah caught Jonah standing close to Solomon. Lifting a hand, she hovered it over Seth's face but did not touch her. "Seth."

Words died in his throat before he could form them.

Sensing Noah's gaze, Jonah was indignant. "Go," she snapped at him and thrust out her hand after Elijah.

Noah didn't move, caught in his own wave of grief.

Adam squeezed his shoulders. "Noah, we can do nothing for her."

Noah forced away the avalanche. "I know." Turning back, he settled into a steady run. The direction was the opposite of where he'd seen the people approaching Jonah and Moses. Adam thudded against his back with every step and Noah struggled to find a rhythm that disturbed them the least and still made travel fast. It was hard not to look at Solomon, cradling Seth to his chest as he ran beside them.

"How far do you think the vehicle is?" Adam murmured.

Noah didn't waste his breath. "Unsure. I did not see."

"I expected it to be closer," Jonah said from a short distance ahead. "Where is Moses?"

Frowning, Noah blinked to shift his eyes into the infrared spectrum again. Counting the figures ahead of him, he could only make out Jonah. "Wait."

Jonah glanced over her shoulder. "What is wrong?"

Surveying his surroundings was hard while he carried Adam and ran. So many blind spots. "I cannot see—"

Cracks of gunfire and Noah's legs buckled. Adam was thrown from his back and tumbled to the ground. Jonah cried out as she fell.

Noah's legs were on fire. Three spots, left calf, right thigh and right calf. Two bullets had gone straight through, the third was lodged against bone. He hunched up as the bullets continued to spray, hoping he wouldn't take more. Peeking out through his arms, he tried to see Adam. He'd been on Noah's back and the bullets had come from behind. Had his brother taken hits that had been meant for him?

Noah grit his teeth and concentrated on healing his legs while he cowered. Nothing else he could do; Jonah had the rifle and if he moved, it would make him a bigger target.

The gunfire stopped as fast as it had begun and stillness filled the night air.

Noah unfurled, reaching for his handgun, only to have the ground beside him shot.

"Stay down!"

Moses' voice. Noah stilled and waited.

"I am sorry," Moses called. "They want you and Elijah alive. The rest are forfeit."

Realization dawned and Noah felt strength drain from him.

"Traitor!" Jonah spat, her voice laced with pain and Noah glanced over to see her clutching her side. Adam was still and Noah wondered if he was already dead. Noah couldn't see Elijah, even with his still-shifted eyes. They didn't have time; Noah could see the red mass of people moving in their direction in the distance.

"They are going to let me be free," Moses said, his boots crunching against the ground as he grew closer. "With money, property. I will want for nothing."

Noah's stomach clenched at the pleased tone in Moses' voice. He couldn't look at Moses, didn't want to see the truth written on his face. "In exchange for us."

"Yes. It is better than scrounging with no idea where the next meal will come from."

Noah knew they would never allow Moses to be free. Noah read from the Institute's databases that anyone in the past who had tried to escape was hunted down by one of their own as target practice. Glancing at Jonah's heat signature, he kept his mouth shut. The traitor deserved his fate.

Moses stopped a small distance away, a gun pointed at Noah, another at Jonah. "If it means anything at all, I am remorseful this is how it had to end but I had my orders."

Noah narrowed his eyes. "Did you kill Seth?"

"Death is kinder when you do not see it coming. It was all I could give. She was too precious to—"

A guttural cry and something large and misshapen charged and slammed into Moses. Arms too large for the torso, head perched upon massive shoulders, one leg bulkier than the other, two glistening fists slammed against Moses' chest and knocked him down.

The anger in the roar chilled Noah. He had to take advantage of this distraction. Moses screamed for aid and Noah ignored him. His brother had made the decision to betray them, so Solomon would extract vengeance.

Solomon shifted out of control with no concern for himself. He'd torn himself apart to be a voice of rage and grief. Noah didn't think there would be anything left once this was over.

Noah scrambled, rolling onto his belly and commando crawling through the grass and dirt in Adam's direction. He had to get to his siblings. They were too closely pursued to stay. "Jonah! Are you hit?"

She moaned, lying on her back and using the hand not applying pressure on her stomach to pull herself along. "Stomach and thigh… I cannot… Noah, I cannot…"

Noah's mind went blank.

"Please do not let me die." Jonah sounded so small.

Swallowing hard, he murmured, "Hold on. Adam?"

Another roar and a wet, ripping sound, and Moses' cries ended. Noah rolled over so he could see, then shifted his vision from the red spectrum so he didn't have to. Solomon stood with his back to all of them. His chest heaved with exertion. Skin stretched so tight over fleshy limbs it split open. With deliberate care, he reached down and picked up Seth, cradling her against his torso, then, with a grunt, turned to face them.

No return from that shift. Death haunted Solomon's face, even in the pale moonlight. How much time he had before his heart failed was only determined by Solomon's sheer will. He lurched toward Noah, the knuckles of one hand adding extra support as he moved. Noah held Solomon's gaze. The pain he saw swimming in Solomon's eyes, mental and physical, made him feel ill.

Solomon tapped Noah with the back of his hand, a comradely gesture, then touched his fingers to Noah's legs and gurgled.

"Hold." Every moment passed was another wasted, so Noah increased his regeneration as much as his tolerance level allowed. Pain tore through his legs as he forcibly repaired the damage in front of the bullet and used the healed flesh to push it out, then closed the hole. He bit the inside of his mouth to keep from crying out. A shift headache, one he had not endured since he'd shifted his ears wrong, bloomed but he shoved the pain aside. He could succumb later, right now, what was left of his siblings needed him.

The pain dimmed in his legs and Noah opened his eyes to find himself flat on his back and Solomon's misshapen face peering at him. With an experimental wriggle of his toes, Noah decided his legs were healed enough so he could help Jonah. The pain in his body dipped to a more tolerable level, but the headache would become a problem.

"Check Adam," Noah suggested, panting lightly.

Solomon grunted and heaved away, still cradling Seth.

"Solomon?" Jonah asked.

Solomon grunted again.

"I do not think he is able to talk," Noah murmured and groaned as he half sat up. Rolling onto his stomach, he used his hands to help support him as he tested his legs. Achy, but they would have to do. Glancing at where he'd seen the group of people last, he could see flashlights. "We need to go."

"Leave me," Jonah said. "I will slow them down."

He staggered to her side, flopped down on his knees, scooped her up then heaved himself up as fast as he could. The noise Jonah made was part exasperation, part pain, but she swung an arm around his neck to help steady them both.

Solomon stood with Adam, unconscious or dead,

unceremoniously draped over Solomon's shoulder. Noah didn't question. If Solomon thought he could carry both Seth and Adam, then he could.

Limping in the direction they had been heading and away from the moving flashlights, Noah continued to strengthen his legs. He glanced at Solomon, lumbering by his side, and listened to the ragged breath and creaking bones. Solomon, catching Noah's gaze, gave him a nod and nothing more.

"Elijah?" he called ultrasonically and then listened for a response.

He stumbled down a small ditch, his knees threatening to give way. Jonah moaned in pain, writhing in his arms. She clutched at the shoulder of his shirt and rested her head against his neck. "Elijah?"

"Nothing." He hesitated. "Is it bad?"

"You should have left me."

Noah said nothing, instead choosing to concentrate on walking.

"Stubborn ass."

He snorted, recognizing Wade's phrase, then his head snapped to the left as he heard an engine approaching. "Solomon!" he blurted in warning, ready to defend. "Vehicle—"

"The truck is me," Elijah transmitted, ultrasonically.

Jonah lifted her head. *"Where the hell have you been?"*

Noah raised his eyebrows in surprise at hearing Wade's vehemence pouring from Jonah's lips. A glance at Solomon told him he shared Noah's disbelief.

"I found a truck," Elijah explained as two headlights flashed in the dark. *"What has happened?"*

"Moses revealed himself as Echo Two," Noah told her and moved toward the lights. *"Jonah has a stomach wound and Solomon... he..."*

"He took care of Moses," Jonah said, proud.

Solomon gurgled and coughed.

"And Adam?"

Noah focused on Adam, still unresponsive on Solomon's shoulder. *"I do not know."*

"A-live," Solomon garbled, though it took him great effort. His voice sounded like it bubbled through water. Or blood.

"We need to get away from here," Noah said, glancing over his shoulder. *"They are coming."*

The small truck bounced into view as it drove over the top of a hill. It spun its wheels, screeching to a halt beside them. Elijah jumped out of the cabin and bolted for the cargo door. "Let us go!" she said, throwing it up. "Get in."

Noah coughed from the dust the truck kicked up and hurried to the back of the truck. He lifted Jonah up into it, allowing her to crawl in. "Elijah, Jonah needs—"

The truck's shock absorbers groaned as Solomon lurched into the cargo hold. With extra care, he removed Adam from his shoulder and laid him on the floor. Taking a step back, Solomon slumped against the side of the truck with a heavy sigh and cuddled Seth.

"Get in," Elijah said, shoving Noah to force him up into the cargo area. Jumping up, she grabbed the handle to pull the door down. "We will take care of it."

"We?" Noah dropped down to a knee to grab the door before she could close it fully. "Who is we?"

Behind the truck, there was a cracking sound and a green light appeared. Noah swiveled, drawing his weapon only to have Elijah move so she blocked his sight.

Several glow sticks were tossed into the cargo area and Noah found himself looking at the man he had been trained to replace. "Hey. I'm Rex."

CHAPTER 14

Fractured memories.

Street lamps flaring as the van passed beneath. A rhythmic thumping that vanished as quickly as it was noticed. Men's voices, watery and a long way off, washing over her and the words were lost. The constant light and dark spaces of the street lamps faded to complete darkness. It was so hard to move; her body was heavy and wouldn't obey her, and the swaying of the van rocked her back under.

The sound of tires on gravel rattled through her before the van stopped. Jostling as she was lifted allowed her to swim toward the surface, but she could only see more light and dark spaces. Footsteps echoed along paved walkways, broken windows and… was that a candy store?

More hallways closed in around her. Dark, dim and dusty. A rusty iron door creaked and then…

Black.

Cold, wet and black.

No fear; she was too far under. Fear would be there when she woke. So would awareness, but right now, she existed in a space between moments.

A space full of memories and dreams.

She sat with her feet up on the window seat in her room and hugged a pillow to her chest as she watched the rain fall outside. Everything was gray, even the rain. A monotone that surrounded her. There was only one splash of color, one thing that was an anchor and held her to the dream.

Before her, the color sat with his back to the window frame and played with a stress ball, tossing it up and down and squeezing it into different shapes.

"Guys suck," she said, wiping at her face.

"Couldn't agree more."

"Present company excluded."

He bumped his knee against hers. "I'm so glad you clarified that," he teased. "I was worried."

She rested her head against the cool glass and looked out into an out-of-focus world. She couldn't see much beyond the water on the windows. She knew she should be looking down into her garden and seeing Tim's swing set, regardless of the heaviness of the rain, but it didn't exist. "What's wrong with me?"

"Nothing," he responded. "You're gorgeous and wonderful and he's a butt slug."

She lifted her head up and looked at him. "Is that the technical term?"

He grinned. "Yep."

"Butt slug. Sounds kinda gross."

"That was the idea." He spread his legs and patted his chest. "C'mere."

With a sigh, she crawled across the gap and snuggled up on his chest. He wrapped his arms around her and said, "Don't let them bother you, Aly. It's not you. It's me they have a problem with."

"Well, they just have to deal," she said as his color spread into her. "Cause I don't know what I'd do without you."

He rested his head on the top of hers. "Yeah."

"There wasn't any other way."

"Did you say something?" she asked, rousing.

"Nope. Just sitting here. Enjoying the snuggle."

"I knew I was living on borrowed time. I'm thankful we've had as long as we've had, but I can't risk it anymore."

"It must be your turn to have a boyfriend," she muttered, ignoring the voice that seemed to float on the wind.

"They'd be as threatened by you as yours are by me."

The thought warmed her and she couldn't resist a tease. "Yeah, but think of the threesomes."

He laughed, his chest rumbling and she smiled into his shirt. "Yeah, I'll go find myself a boyfriend so we can have threesomes. Good idea."

"It's never been like this before; I've never been so entrenched... and I'm afraid."

"Everyone at school thinks we must."

He squeezed her. "Grace and Del don't and they're the ones who matter. I don't give a flying *ffff...* hoot what other people think."

"You're right," she said with a sigh.

"It's only a matter of time before they figure it out. You're the one thing in my life I need to keep safe. Keep hidden. There's a loose board in the corner of my room. Find it, Aly."

He laughed again. "Of course I'm right. I'm never wrong."

"That's crap and you know it," she said, pushing away from him to glare. "You've been wrong countless times."

"I won't ever see you again and you won't understand and I'll be gone."

"Oh, yeah." His eyes twinkled as he took up the challenge. "Name one."

She grinned. "Tomatoes, fruit or vegetable?"

"Hey," he wagged a finger at her. "That's a trick question!"

"If they find you, they'll hurt you. I have to die to protect you."

The smile dropped off her face as the phantom words finished. "I think they did find me. Whoever 'they' are."

Fletcher's smile grew melancholy. "It's okay. I'm coming."

Her chest ached as she realized what this was. Part memory, part wishful thinking. Her brain conjured up a safe place, a last moment. "How can you? You're gone. This is a stupid dream and when I wake up, you'll be gone again."

He reached out and tucked her hair behind her ear, his fingertips tracing the shell. "Trust the Snickers."

She leaned into his touch, turning her face so he cupped her cheek, determined to keep him here as long as possible. "I miss you."

"I know."

The world closed in. Everything faded and her bedroom was replaced by somewhere cold and dark and scary and a reality she didn't want to face. "I don't want to wake up."

Color seeped away from Fletcher's face and she lost him in the dark. "I know."

The mattress she woke on had a funky smell. Aly crinkled her nose in disgust as she pushed away. Her head felt like straw, her mouth was dry and her eyes were itchy. It took a while for her sight to adjust to her surroundings but when she did, her heartbeat doubled. The room she was in seemed no bigger than a janitor's closet, enough space for the mattress, a small light and nothing else. She was trapped.

She surged up and hit the door, scrambling for the handle. Locked, but that didn't stop her from jerking the handle around and putting a shoulder to the door to see if she could force it open. Kicking the door for good measure, she turned to the small room to see if there were any other means of escape she might have missed.

Nothing. No vents or holes in the ceiling, none that she could fit through.

Turning back to the door, she thumped on it screaming, "Let me out!" She then pressed her ear to the door to see if she could hear anything.

Nothing.

Dropping to the floor, she tried to peer under the door. Vague fuzziness and light. Lying down only got her dirty. She searched the pockets in her uniform dress and apron and came up empty.

Fletcher's letter was gone. She searched again. It'd been in the pocket of her apron. A stab of loss filled her, then she shook herself. She'd been kidnapped and she was lamenting over a lost letter. She needed to get a grip and figure out how to get out of here.

Something inside her cast caused an itch. She ran her finger under the edge to scratch her skin as she studied the ceiling. It was a trick she'd learned from Del; digging her fingers into the cast helped to ease the itch. As she did so, her fingers touched paper. Extending her arm, she peered into the cast, trying to get a grip on whatever was in there. Pulling out a corner, she recognized Fletcher's letter. "How did that get there?" she wondered aloud. She had no memory of shoving it there. Tucking it in again, she sat on the edge of the mattress and tried not to cry.

No weapons, unless she counted her remaining shoe and she didn't think it would do much damage if she threw it at someone. Nothing to do but wait—and waiting was the worst part. She didn't know when the door would open or *if* it would open. She didn't know what would happen if the door never opened and she shuddered to think about what would happen to her if it did. Who took her? What were their intentions? Who was the man who tried to help her? Where was she now? What had they done while she'd been asleep?

She knew someone would be looking for her. Grace had called her father. The chance of them spotting the van she was taken in was high. She had to hold out hope they'd find the van and would find her.

Every noise made her think of approaching footsteps. Every flicker of the light above her head made her think it would blow and she'd be left in the dark. Time played its tricks. Aly huddled in the corner, hugging her knees to her chest while her mind conjured up dark terrors.

When they came, they came in a rush. Two bulky men shrouded in black who burst through the door and were on her before she could scream. She recognized one of them from the diner and he made her skin crawl. Each of them taking an upper arm, they dragged her from her closet and into a dank hallway.

"What do you want?" she protested, wincing at their grip as they marched her up the hallway. "Where are we going?"

They didn't answer.

Boots splashed through small puddles of water as they traveled down the corridor. Aly's bare sock was drenched with water as they passed many chained, padlocked doors. The place seemed abandoned. Broken glass and small piles of trash were scattered along the hallway. Several rats crept along the floor, scattering as the men carting her came close.

She dug her heels in in an attempt to slow them down and delay whatever came next. "Please, I just want to go home." She struggled harder. "I haven't done anything!" When that didn't work, she opted for, "What about a bathroom? I need to pee."

They shoved her into a room so hard she couldn't keep her footing. One of them grabbed her again, hoisting her off the floor by the elbow and shoved her in a wooden chair. The other grabbed her unbroken wrist, snapped a handcuff around it, and then attached it to the spindle of the chair. "Hey!" she complained.

Both men retreated to the doorway and stood at ease with their hands behind their back on either side of the door.

Aly tugged at the handcuff, noting the chair wasn't bolted to the floor. She could pick it up and swing it at them if she had to. "Let me go!" She glared at the men.

"You have no right to—"

"Hello, Miss Braddock. So glad you could join us."

Aly jerked her head in the direction of the voice. A woman leaned against a wooden table in the middle of the room, peeling an apple with a knife. Her eyes were so dark they appeared devoid of pupils and her dark hair had tufts of white at her temples. She wore a black beater, cargo pants and boots, and Aly could see a green jacket draped across the table beside her. There were three thick scars on her left upper arm, like claw marks. Her whole appearance was carefully crafted to be intimidating. It worked; the icy hand of fear traveled down Aly's spine.

The woman cut a piece of apple and used the knife to carry it to her mouth. "Or perhaps you would prefer I call you Aly?"

Aly moistened her lips. "Um… Aly… but my last name is Gale. Not Braddock."

The woman raised a manicured eyebrow. "Really." She lifted a piece of paper from the table beside her. "Alyson Rose Braddock, born to Madeline Spenser and Rex Braddock. Birthday, April—"

"That's not me," she interrupted, hoping this was a case of mistaken identity.

The woman stopped speaking and stared at her.

Aly blurted, "My mom's maiden name was Penelope Spenser and my birth dad's name was Leon Braddock. Roger—Roger Gale adopted me when he married my mom and I took his name."

The woman placed the piece of paper on the table. "He tried *really* hard to hide you, didn't he?"

Aly tilted her head. "Who?" Swallowing and hugging her broken wrist to her chest, she continued, "Look, I really don't know what's going on here and I want to go home. I promise I won't tell anyone."

The woman toyed with her knife. "It's not that simple. We've been looking for you for a long time."

"Me?" Aly squeaked, curling in on herself. She zeroed

in on the knife and although she knew the woman used it to unnerve her, it didn't alleviate the fear.

"We want your father," the woman continued.

Seeing they brought him up, Aly knew they weren't talking about Roger. "My biological father is dead. He died when I was six months old."

"I doubt that," the woman scoffed, "given that he had two mimics guarding you."

"I don't understand," Aly said. She could feel tears of frustration forming. "Please, I just want to go home."

"Where is your father?"

"He's dead," Aly insisted. "I can show you his grave. I visit once a year. He's in Sacramento—"

"We know he's alive. Where is he?"

"I don't know what answer you want," Aly said, blinking rapidly. "He's *dead.*"

The woman stared at her. "How much did you inherit?"

Aly stared back. Did they hope there was a ransom? "I don't know exactly. Mom always looked after my money, she invested it for me, I suppose there's—"

She made an exasperated noise. "I'm not talking about his money."

"If you let me go, you can have *all* my inheritance. I just—"

"Shut up." The woman pushed away from the table, revealing a gagged man strapped to a chair behind her. She looked at him with a thoughtful expression. "Well. There is one way to find out if you're the one we're looking for."

Aly leaned to one side to view the man better. He was a few years older than her. A mess of dark hair fell over blue eyes set in an olive complexion. He was dressed in jeans, a flannel shirt and dark brown jacket. Had they met under any other circumstances, she might have thought him cute, but right now, the blood on his gag and the red mark on his cheek made her even more terrified.

The woman glanced at Aly. "Do you know him?"

Aly flicked her eyes up to the woman, then back down. Her brow creased as a bolt of recognition surged through her, akin to the flare she'd gotten from the girl at the funeral. Wasn't he the same one who tried to save her in the alley? "I—" She tilted her head in consideration.

Something flashed in the man's face, his eyes widening. A warning perhaps?

"—don't know. Maybe?" She addressed the man. "Did you go to Bellhollow High? I meet a lot of people cause I have a job in a diner. People come in and out of that all the time. My dad works at the hospital; we do all sorts of charity work—" Fear made her babble and there wasn't anything she could do to stop. "I might've seen him at one of those. He looks older than me, maybe he was a senior when I was a freshman? He looks kind of familiar but I really don't know—"

"Enough," the woman said, her hand cutting the air like she could slice up Aly's words.

"Please," Aly pleaded, leaning forward in her chair. "I don't know who you are, I don't know why I'm here. I just want to go home."

Ignoring Aly, the woman walked around the table to the man. Grasping his hair, she yanked his head back. "You should be just about ripe."

The man grunted.

Glad the attention was off her, Aly pressed her lips together and tried to compose herself. They had to see she wasn't who they thought she was. Perhaps if she waited, an opportunity would arise.

The woman untied the gag on his mouth and stepped away. "Name."

The man worked his jaw, then licked his lips. "Dick Grayson."

Aly blinked and sat up straight. She chewed on her lip and struggled not to laugh hysterically at the absurdity of the answer.

The woman didn't seem to know who that was.

"Good. That's a start. What's—"

One of the men behind her coughed. "Belinda, ma'am, Dick Grayson is a comic character."

Belinda scowled at the man who had spoken, who shrunk away with a muttered apology. Looking back at the bound man, she said, "I can see you're going to be one of *those*." She clicked her tongue. "Very well, I'll be specific. *Your* name."

The man grimaced. "Will Ward."

"Good. What's her name?"

"Alyson Rose Gale," he recited, then smirked. "But that's not a true test since I heard you before."

Belinda was stoic. Keeping her eyes on Will, she pointed to Aly with her thumb. "How do you know her?"

Will glanced at Aly, then rolled his eyes at Belinda. "Don't. Heard her screaming because of your thugs. Didn't expect this at all." He grumbled. "Serves me right for trying to play hero."

"You can't expect me to believe that."

Will shrugged. "How much faith do you really have in that drug? I think you gave me a placebo."

Belinda seemed unimpressed. "What faction do you belong to?"

"I don't belong to any of them."

"You're a mimic, you must belong to—"

"Shifter," Will corrected. "Mimic implies something else. Shifter is more accurate. Or changeling. Take your pick." He indicated Belinda with his chin. "And you're not, which makes me wonder—"

She gave him a stormy look. "I'll ask the questions, abomination."

Will snorted. "A Purist." He shook his head. "Brilliant."

Aly found it hard to breathe. Folklore about changelings said they were fae folk who replaced children in the crib with children of their own, but it seemed farfetched. There was a cartoon character called Beast Boy and he could morph his body into any animal. Perhaps that was what this man could do? Become an animal? Mystique from *X-Men*, she could change her form, she could mimic anyone's voice and appearance. A shapeshifter.

Aly stared at Will. Stories right out of fairy tales, but stories had to start somewhere. Mimic, changeling, shapeshifter, they all had something in common, the ability to copy or imitate, or change form. What if there was truth to the tales?

Fletcher hadn't fitted his face. Aly didn't remember why she'd said that, but he hadn't. Not at the beginning. She couldn't explain it. It seemed absurd. If Fletcher had warned her about the skin pricks, the pinpricks that occurred around these shifters, why hadn't Will given her any? And why had the one she'd gotten from Fletcher been sporadic? Had he been one? Why did one of the men behind her give such a strong and constant prickle?

Belinda hummed. "Do you know Rex Braddock?"

"Ye—" Will clamped his mouth shut and then swore viciously.

Belinda laughed in triumph.

Will shook his head from side to side in a disgruntled manner, then wriggled in his seat as much as he could. "C'mon. Everyone knows of Rex. He's one of the three."

She smirked. "I didn't ask if you knew 'of' him, I asked if you 'knew' him. That's the beauty of this particular serum, you can circumvent it all you like by being literal, but it'll get you in the end."

Will rolled his eyes. "So you say. I still say it's bogus."

"Do you know where Rex is?"

"No."

"Do you know his last location?"

Will sighed, sounding bored. "No."

"When was the last time you saw him?"

"Twelve years ago." Will tossed his hair away from his eyes and smirked at her. "I'm out of the loop."

"Do you know how to contact him?"

"No. Is this the twenty questions part?"

Aly watched the questions and answers bounce between them, more confused than ever. Belinda circled Will like a cat toying with prey. Round and round, her boots clipped on the floor with each step while Will stared straight ahead, occasionally glancing at Aly.

"Can you contact him?" Belinda asked.

Will appeared bored. "No."

Belinda seemed to be getting exasperated. "If I threatened to kill you, could you contact him?"

"No."

"If I threatened to kill *her*, could you contact him?"

Aly felt all the blood drain away from her face and her mouth went dry. Kill her? What?

Will met Aly's gaze. "No."

"Is she Rex's daughter?"

"How should I know?"

"Why were you in that alleyway?"

"Because she screamed." He snorted. "I already answered that. Did you think it would change?"

"Why were you in that town?"

"Passing through." Will smirked again. "You don't trust your serum, do you?"

"Where is Rex?"

"No idea. I can do this all day."

"Have you ever heard of the Faceless?"

Will's humor vanished in a heartbeat. "I think we're done."

Belinda laughed. Gripping his shoulder, she pulled Will so he was side on to Aly and loomed over him. "Did I strike a nerve?"

With a dark expression, Will looked up at Belinda. "You said there were two protectors, mistaking me for one."

"We weren't certain, he had such a weak reading," Belinda taunted. "Barely a blip. Friend of yours?"

"A blip? And you think Rex would send a *blip* to

protect someone?"

"Protect. Watch. Same thing."

"What happened?"

Belinda straightened, crossing her arms over her chest. "Sent him over a bridge."

Will's mouth thinned. "You were hoping to draw out Rex and when it didn't work— you know you've killed an innocent—"

Aly broke the wooden chair over Belinda's head. It came apart in her hands, the cuff slipping free. She panted, rage swelling through her like she'd never felt before. This woman *killed* her best friend. As she stared at Belinda's groaning form on the floor, tingles fired up her arms and down her spine. She whipped around to face the men advancing on her.

Will surged from his seat as though he hadn't been bound at all and threw himself on the two guards before they could get to Aly. Aly stared at them for a moment as they scuffled on the ground and the rage slipped to fear.

She bolted.

Through the door and out into the corridor, she picked a direction at random. Her mind didn't register her name being called. All she could feel was the need to flee. She didn't bother trying the doors scattered along the hallway, she sprinted straight for the end where an exit sign hung near the ceiling pointing right. She didn't slow down to take the corner, instead, she slammed into the wall and bounced off to change her trajectory.

The end of the hallway was blocked by double metal doors. A chain looping between the metal bars held the doors together and blocked escape. She reached the doors, shoving them as hard as she could in the hope they'd open enough she could squeeze through the crack. Although they opened, Aly was dismayed to discover the gap was too small for her.

Panicked, she looked around, hoping for something to pry the door open with. Barring that, something to use as a weapon.

Opening the closest door, she found a janitor's closet similar to the one she'd woken in. This one was mostly empty, except for an old, bristle-less mop. Not having much choice, she grabbed the mop. Perhaps she could use it to hold the door open while she slipped through.

Will slid around the corner, his shoulder hitting the wall. "Aly! Wait!"

A shriek burst from her lips before she could stop it. She retreated until her back was against the fire doors. Even with the mop, she didn't think she could get the doors open enough to squeeze through, so she'd have to fight. Holding the mop out in front of her with both hands, she prepared for whatever came.

Will skid to a stop and held his hands out before him. "I'm not going to hurt you."

She shook the mop at him. "I don't know *you*," she told him. "I don't know *her*, I don't know what's going on, but I *do* know a death threat when I hear one. If you think for one second I'm going to stick around and let—"

Will kept his distance. "It's okay—"

"It's *not* okay."

"Aly," he said. The corner of his mouth crinkled up into a lopsided and somehow familiar smile. "Snickers."

CHAPTER 15

"I… I don't understand." Aly rubbed her wrist where the cuff had been, watching Will as he slid her handcuff and the key's he'd snatched from Belinda into his pocket.

"I know," Will said, turning to use a pocket knife to jimmy the lock on the door. "I can't explain right now; we're pressed for time."

She held her broken wrist to her chest. "… You knew Fletcher?"

Will glanced at her, then nodded.

She swallowed. "Is… is he alive?" Her whole world teetered on its axis. Will's answer would either make her tumble or keep her steady.

"Now is really not the time," Will mumbled. The lock clicked open and he slid the chain off. "They'll be after us once they figure out how to open the door."

She stalled him with a hand on his arm. "Please, Will. I *need* to know."

He froze, the chain falling from his fingers, clattering to the floor. He snapped his eyes to hers; they were so wide Aly could see white around the entire iris.

Aly snatched her hand away. "Sorry! I didn't mean to."

He shuddered and looked away. "That name sounds so

wrong when you say it."

Her head spun. "I don't understand—"

"Look," he said, pushing the door open, "answers will come, I promise. We just have to get somewhere safe first." He gave an apologetic smile as he stepped into what appeared to be a large, abandoned underground parking garage. Not much light as most of the overhanging lights were broken, but there were enough with power to emit a glow bright enough to see. Given the dilapidated state of the building, Aly was surprised they had power at all. There was a ramp at the far end heading upward and Will went toward it. "It is not my intention to scare you."

She followed him, trying to keep her distance and yet not stray too far away either. He was the first semi-safe thing in this place. She eyed him, then cleared her throat. "So... do you know where we are?"

"No idea," he said. "We need to find a car."

"Or a phone."

He glanced over his shoulder at her. "I can't permit you to call anyone. Not yet."

Aly about-faced. "Right. Thanks. Bye."

"Be reasonable," Will said.

"Reasonable?" she spat, turning to glare at him and still walked backward. "I think I'm entitled to be—" she backed into a concrete support pole, and then put it between her and Will. "—angry and unreasonable—"

Will watched her retreat without following her. "Say you actually manage to get home without them catching you again. What are you going to tell the police? What are you going to tell your parents?" He gestured back the way they'd come. "These guys think you're Rex's daughter. Do you really think they won't try again?"

She hesitated. He'd gotten her to trust him with a safe word, but that didn't mean *he* was safe. He made her feel weird and she didn't know why. The letter had been moved from her pocket to her cast. They could have read it while she'd been out. There'd been four of them when they'd taken her, plus Will. She'd only seen three, Belinda and the two guards. Where had the fourth man been? This could all be some elaborate ruse. "I don't even know who Rex is!"

Will turned his head, staring at the way they'd come. Aly's arms tingled and the sensation seemed to be coming from Will *and* the direction Will was looking. "Hate to rush you," Will said in an absent tone, his attention elsewhere, "but they're coming. Are you with me or not?"

She pressed her fingers against her skull. "God. Why is this happening to me?"

Will thrust his hands into the pockets of his jeans. "Don't know, but it is. Not much we can do to change that now. It really only matters what you do next."

She looked up at Will and his image blurred. Blinking to clear her sight, she said, "You know what? No. No. I'm not going with you. This whole situation *stinks* of setup."

Will sighed. "Aly—"

"No," she told him, firmly. Shaking a finger at him, she backed away. "It's wrong." Her gesturing widened until she indicated the area around her. "This whole thing is wrong." She rested her hand on her cast. "There's no proof at all you know Fletcher and you make me feel weird and I'm not going with you—"

Will's eyes flicked back the way they came and then to her. "His last name is Norman. He had an Uncle Lee. His best friend's names are Aly, Grace and Del. His favorite pastime is going to the arcade with you and your brother, Tim. He works at the hospital. He was going to take you to prom. You haven't told your mother about the Otis acceptance letter because she wants to buy an apartment for you to use and you want to give dorm living a go before transferring to CalArts."

Aly's hands crept up to her mouth as Will spoke. One thing that stuck in her mind, beyond the fact Will used present tense, was he knew about her plans for Otis. She'd sworn Fletcher to secrecy and she hadn't told Grace or

Del.

Will shook his head. "If we don't get out of here right now, we're both dead."

Confusion descended over her and her stomach clenched as she struggled to make sense of what her heart told her. The ache of familiarity returned full force.

Will thrust out his hand to offer it to her. "Aly!"

A crash and voices behind her spurred her onward. Fear rising again, she darted out from behind the pole to Will, who took her hand. They ran.

Will was faster than Aly and his longer legs outpaced hers. The vice-like grip on her hand forced her to match his speed, else he would drag her. He pulled her toward the ramp at the end of the parking garage and Aly hoped there'd be an easy way to escape. Running closer, she was appalled to discover a roller door blocking the ramp exit.

As they reached the bottom of the ramp, Aly glanced over her shoulder, horrified to see Belinda and her goons pour through the door at the other end of the parking lot. Will stopped halfway up, giving Aly a heave to slingshot her up the ramp to the top.

She stumbled, unprepared for the move and slowed.

"Go!" he called, crouching down and pulling a gun out from the back of his belt.

A surge of dread passed through her. "But—"

Will fired off three shots.

Terrified, she bolted. Hoping the roller door wasn't locked, she scrambled for the handle and yanked. The door groaned but didn't budge.

Will fired a few more shots toward their pursuers.

"It won't open!"

"Take cover!" Will said, gesturing the corner near the roller door where she'd be protected. Aly fled to it to hide. Upon reaching the door, he reached down and yanked. The door groaned again, much louder this time. With a metallic ping, it launched upward and clattered into its holder.

An empty parking lot but at least they were outside. Aly stepped over the broken lock on the ground while her eyes adjusted to the sudden light. Early morning judging by the cool temperature of the air. So she'd been missing most of the night. Her parents must be frantic by now.

Nothing but open space, nowhere to hide. If they ran across the lot and into the farmland beyond, they'd be easily seen and Belinda and her men had guns. There seemed to be some sort of main road in the distance since she could see the flash of sunlight off a windscreen. A few scattered, dead trees were clumped in small bricked gardens, and there were several broken lamp posts, but nothing that could be used as cover. This place had been long abandoned.

Aly's breath was hard to catch and panic made a permanent home in her chest. At a loss of what to do now, she looked at Will. Should they run? Should they try and make the road?

Will glanced around, turned, and took several steps backward to study the building above them. In a sweeping movement, he stuffed the gun in the belt of his jeans, grabbed Aly, threw her over his shoulder, and leaped.

Aly watched the ground fall away, too startled to cry out. She clawed the air, unbalanced, and caught his jacket with both hands. Will's arm encircled her thighs to hold her steady and he hit the wall with a small grunt. She caught a flash of his foot slipping against the wall before she was hoisted through a broken second-floor window. Her feet hit the ground and she staggered backward, while Will scrambled into the room after her.

Will crouched under the window sill with his gun drawn and placed a finger to his mouth to request silence, then gestured she should make herself smaller. Obeying, Aly huddled beside him just as Belinda and her men burst into the parking lot below.

"Where'd they go?" Belinda yelled. "Fan out. Find them!"

Will relaxed as the three men each took different directions, none of them looking up. He sat with his back to the wall and breathed out slowly. "We'll be okay for a while," he whispered. "Catch your breath." He checked his gun. "Two left," he murmured and rested it on the floor beside him.

Aly drew her knees up to her chest and pressed her back against the rundown wall. Judging by the stands on the wall they were in an old shoe store. There were a few stacks of boxes in the corner and a few scattered ones that had been knocked over. A roller security door separated the room from what appeared to be an old mall.

There weren't any abandoned malls close to Bellhollow. The closest Aly knew about was a distance away; someone had built one that was supposed to become a shopping hub for the towns around it, but the economy hadn't been able to support such a large mall. If this was the same mall, she was at least three hours from home. Judging by the landscape, they might be even farther.

With the security roller down, how would they get out of here? Aly didn't relish the idea of going back out the window. She fixed her eyes on her dirty sock and remaining shoe and tried very hard not to think about the man beside her.

"Are you okay?"

She curled in on herself and struggled not to cry. "No."

"I'll get you out of here. We just have to—"

"I thought you were dead."

His breath hitched, his outstretched hand dropped to his side.

She hugged her knees tighter. "I don't know *how* I know. I don't even know how it's even possible. Its like— and I can't—it's impossible. People… people don't *change* like that. We can't—it's not scientifically possible… I've gone crazy, this is all a dream. The letter, the letter said— Maybe—I know in my heart this isn't—I just—" She squeezed her eyes shut and buried her face in her knees.

"God."

"Aly, I… I—"

"It's impossible," she continued. "What is it they call it? Imprinting? Projecting? I don't know. Hallucinations? We want so much for someone not to be gone we see them everywhere. God, Mom was right. I need therapy."

"Aly—"

"I keep seeing him in you," she said, the lump in her throat making it difficult to speak but it didn't stop her. "The way you speak, the things you say, the expression on your face. You're so familiar and yet wrong. It's wrong. This is wrong—people don't… No one else knew about Otis and CalArts; he promised he'd never tell and yet *you* know. She said 'mimic' and 'shifter' and all I could think was… Mystique." A sob broke from her throat. "It's wishful thinking, but…" A wave of remorse swept over her and her throat ached with the need to cry. She tingled and rubbed at the goose bumps on her arms. Now was not the time to succumb to fear; they had to escape from Belinda. "I'm sorry, really I am," she blurted, trying to control herself. "I'm frightened and—"

"I told you to trust your gut," he said. "That you had good instincts. And you do."

His voice. Fletcher's *voice.*

Aly snapped her head up.

Will had vanished. In his place, wearing his clothes and in almost the same position Will had sat, was Fletcher. Floppy-haired, dark-eyed, crooked smile, lanky Fletcher.

Aly's heart threatened to burst from her chest. She'd hoped, she'd wished, she'd dreamed but never once believed it was possible. She gaped open-mouthed at him, unable to do anything else but stare.

"Aly," he murmured and offered her a sheepish smile, "I didn't have a choice. It happened so fast and… by the time I'd made it out of the river, the police were there. If I'd been alive, without a scratch, especially after the state of my bike and the body they found, they would have asked too many questions and…" he swallowed and looked away. "Things would have come to light with that much scrutiny. I knew I was going to have to leave eventually; it seemed like as good a time as any."

Aly couldn't find her breath. It caught in her throat as her windpipe closed up. Tears crept down her cheeks.

"Aly?" he asked. He shuffled so he knelt beside her, both hands gripping her upper arms and gave her a little shake. "No, Aly, breathe."

She squeaked, her limp knees flopping to the floor. "Fletcher?" She flexed her fingers. If she touched him, would he disappear?

Fletcher's lopsided smile bloomed as he took her good wrist, directing her hand to his face. His cheek felt warm to the touch and his jawline rough with emerging stubble. "It's me. It's really me."

She lunged for him and Fletcher was unprepared for the action but still tried to catch her. They tangled, a mess of arms and legs and somewhere in the middle Fletcher was clouted with her cast as he lost his balance. They ended up sprawled on the floor. Aly buried her face into his shirt to hide the tears and held on. His arms wrapped around, holding them together.

He was alive. He was alive and he was here and the past weeks seemed like a giant nightmare she'd been released from. She was angry and elated; so many different emotions it was hard to pinpoint exactly how she felt about this whole situation.

Settling on anger, she whacked his chest once. "You let me think you were dead." She rested her cheek on his chest, listening to his heart to make certain.

"There's so much to explain and I don't know that we have time for everything."

His heart's rhythmic thumping, along with the way his voice echoed in his chest soothed her. Taking a deep breath, she let it out slowly and sniffled. "I *knew* something was wrong."

"I need you to be strong for a little while longer, okay?"

"Okay." Turning her head so her chin was on his chest and she could see him, she asked, "What are you?"

He let out a puff of breath. "There's a very long, involved answer to that. Mystique... is a pretty apt explanation, actually. We can start from there."

Lifting her chin, she shoved her hand in the gap between it and his chest so she could prop her head up. "Are you blue?"

He rumbled a laugh. "No. Can we sit up?"

"No. I am going to lie here for a while and be happy you're alive."

He grinned at her and gave her a squeeze.

"Can you change your clothes too? Like Mystique?"

"No." He smirked. "I don't walk around mostly naked either."

She frowned. "I mean... it is you, right? If... people exist in this world who change shape... couldn't they—"

"Copy my form?" He shrugged. "Yeah, they could."

"Then—"

"Think of it..." His brow furrowed, then he smiled. "Like identical twins, I guess. You can tell them apart, right?"

"Sometimes. Depends on how well I know them."

"Exactly." He stroked his fingers down her spine and rested his other hand on the small of her back. "Unless you know they have an identical twin, you won't be looking for differences to tell which twin they are. And with twins sometimes your brain can trick you into believing they're either one or the other."

"Yeah."

"Same with shifting. Unless they've spent a lot of time studying my face or my body, they'll produce a form of what they think I look like. And, as long as the image is close enough, the people who know me will be tricked into thinking it's me."

She rested her cheek against him to listen to his

heartbeat again. "Makes sense, I guess."

"I suck at acting. I'm not good at hiding who I am. I'm just very good at hiding what I look like. I think you could recognize me no matter what form I took."

She blinked lifted her head again. "I could?"

"You did at the funeral."

"That was *you*?" Staring at him with wide eyes, her voice rose in disbelief. "You can change sex?"

"I can change everything. Skin tone, voice, body mass. Everything."

She let out a whistle. "Wow."

He chuckled. "It's just a body."

She frowned. "Wait. So. If you can change shape, why don't you just be a girl all the time?"

"Girls have it tough," Fletcher explained while his hands roamed her back. "Hormones, body image, all of that. I was built to hide in plain sight, not to be noticed. Girls get noticed when traveling alone. I always pick a form that will hide the best in the area I'm in. Normally, that's a white male, but I mix it up sometimes."

She flushed. "Sorry. It's... just weird."

"I identify male, just because I can change my sex, doesn't mean I want to."

She smiled and blinked back a sudden influx of tears. "I missed you."

The hand on her back lifted so he could brush the hair that had fallen from her messy ponytail back over her ear. "I missed you too."

"I can't believe you snuck into your own funeral."

He snorted. "Didn't intend to."

A random thought occurred and since she was having trouble processing, she blurted, "Who did we bury?"

Fletcher hummed. "A homeless man in the wrong place at the wrong time. They found him in the river and just... assumed. There wasn't much left and since it was my bike..."

"How did you survive the bridge? There was... they

said there was so much blood. And—" she choked.

"Well, whoever gunned me down used a missile of some sort—"

She grimaced, deciding against hearing. "No… don't tell me. Probably not the time."

"Not really," he admitted.

She frowned as another thought occurred to her. Placing her good hand on the floor beside him, she pushed herself up. "Hang on. You have no intention of returning to Bellhollow, do you?"

Fletcher cringed and that gave him away.

Her eyes widened. "If these guys hadn't kidnapped me, I'd never even know you were still alive."

He propped himself up on his elbows as much as he could without bumping into her. "Aly—"

Crawling backward, she moved away from him. "You would've let me spend the rest of my life thinking you were dead!"

"Aly, please. There's a lot you don't know."

Getting to her feet, she continued to back away. "You're going to get me out of here and then *leave*."

He heaved up from the floor. "No. I'm—"

"Oh really," she scoffed. "So what was the plan?"

"I don't have one!" He cringed and shushed her with his hands while looking around. "We're still in danger. Can we save this till later? You can yell at me all you want later."

She glanced toward the open area of the mall. He was right, as loathe as she was to admit it. The danger they were in was more important than her feelings. It would have been nice not to be reminded. "Yeah. Okay."

He relaxed, his hands dropping to his sides. "Thank you."

She shook a finger at him. "I'm still angry at you."

He smiled. "Yup. I owe you a Snickers."

She didn't fall for that one. Itching the edge of her cast, she looked at him. "What now?"

"Well..." He rubbed the back of his neck with a hand. "I have to change back."

She tilted her head. "Why? They already know you can change shape."

He cleared his throat. "Most shifters can't shift as fast as I can."

"Huh? Why?" She held up her hands. "Wait. Let me guess. Long, detailed explanation that we don't have time for."

"Essentially."

She sighed. "Right." She grasped her arm above her elbow with her good hand. "You'll change back after this is all over, right?"

He studied her. "If you want."

"Yes."

"Okay." He stared at her for a moment and she looked back, trying to memorize his features. A part of her was aware how silly it was to think she might never see this face again since until ten minutes ago she'd believed she'd *never* see it again. It seemed her scrutiny made Fletcher uncomfortable. He cleared his throat. "Did you... want to watch?"

Ill at ease, she shuffled and looked away, not sure she did right now. "I'll just... peek through these doors, see if I can see anyone."

"All right," Fletcher said as her skin tingled. Rubbing her arms, she left him to his shift and walked over to the security gate to peer through, careful not to touch it in case it made a noise. A lot of things were in shadow since the sunlight that streamed through skylights was insufficient to light the area. The ceiling panels were cracked or completely missing. Light frames hung at odd intervals, stripped of parts. Trees were dead in their pots. Fallen plaster scattered on the floor along with broken glass. The store across from them used to be a clothing store; three naked, headless mannequins still posed in the window.

"Do I call you Will or Fletcher?"

"Will. In case they overhear." There wasn't anything of Fletcher in his voice and unbidden tears stung her eyes.

He laced his olive toned fingers through hers, and although she clutched his hand, she found she couldn't look at him.

"Let's go."

CHAPTER 16

Aly picked her way across the broken glass covered floor. Having only one shoe made it difficult, but the glass pieces were large enough she could navigate them. She rubbed her hand along her arm as she reached Will's side and pressed her back to the wall. They were careful to speak softly to each other, as sound in this place seemed prone to echoing. "So, what about the tingles?"

The tingles had been intermittent as they wandered through the rundown mall, always in the background but occasionally a stronger prickle and she wondered about that. She couldn't glean any information, nor direction or number of shifters, or even how close they were. She couldn't even tell if it was Will she felt or another shifter. She did know that the weird, uncomfortable feeling took hold a few times, like she'd held her breath too long underwater, but she didn't know what it meant.

Will glanced at her, then peeked around the corner. Seeing it was clear, he gestured for her to follow. "All I have is a theory."

"Okay." She stepped up on the edge of one of the raised gardens, balancing along it as she walked. "Spill."

"Shifter's can... sense, I guess is the word, if another

shifter is out of his natural form. It's more a feeling. Some of us can even tell a shifter friend despite whatever form they take. It has varying degrees of strength; some scents are strong, some weak. It depends on how recently they shifted and how good they are at it."

Reaching the end of the garden, she jumped off. "Okay."

He smiled at her antics. "My guess is you have a shifter ancestor. You'll get the feeling of when someone's out of their natural form or... in my case, accessing the shift, but that's about it."

"So... why aren't you making me tingle now? This isn't your natural form."

"Neither is Fletcher," Will said. "I think you get those when I shift but for others, it's an alert they *are* shifted."

Aly blinked in surprise. "Fletcher isn't your natural form?"

"No." His smile was sheepish.

She couldn't explain why she was disappointed. There was so much to learn about him. "Why are your tingles so different?"

Will pressed his lips in a line.

"Long and involved answer?" Aly asked.

"Yep."

"Let me guess, you're a secret government experiment," Aly said, then laughed at her own joke.

He froze mid-step, turning his head to stare at her.

Aly's jaw dropped. "No way! I was only joking! I mean, it's always that in the movies, I never... I didn't think... wow..." Her laughter had a hysterical edge. "That's so cliché!"

"I guess."

The smile dropped off her face since he sounded insulted by her humor. "I didn't mean to laugh."

"Hmm."

She reached out to pluck the sleeve of his shirt with her finger and thumb. "Fl... Will, I am sorry."

"Yeah."

"Do you want to talk about it?"

"No," he snapped, then sighed and softened his tone. "Not yet. Let's get out of here first."

They traveled in silence, picking their way carefully through the mall. Will seemed to have a destination in mind. At times he took them on small detours through stores to come out on the other side of rubble or security barriers or broken glass.

"How old are you?" Aly asked eventually, tired of the silence.

"Hmm?" He glanced her way. "Why?"

She shrugged. "Just asking. Couple of things you said…" She touched her cast.

His eyes followed her movement. "My letter. About the war."

"Yeah. I guess… makes me think that eighteen's not your real age."

Will took a deep breath and let it out slowly. "It's as good an age as any."

"That's not an answer."

"Because I don't know."

"Oh."

"I have… um…" He paused tapping the tips of all his fingers to his thumb as he counted. "Sixteen years of memory." He shrugged. "Roughly."

That didn't make much sense. "Memory?"

He paused at the edge of another section of broken glass, turning to present his back to her. "It's… difficult to explain."

Accepting his unspoken invitation, Aly climbed up. "So, I'm older than you?"

He hooked his hands under her knees and she held his shoulders. "That's a matter of perspective. I never had a childhood until I met you… I… um… I would've liked to have told you."

"It's not exactly an everyday conversation," she said

tartly. "'Oh, by the way, I happen to be able to shift my form' and Del would answer, 'What else can you shift?' and do his suggestive eyebrow dance."

He laughed as his boots crunched against the glass. "No. Although I don't intend telling them."

She couldn't stop the remark, "You don't *intend* coming back to Bellhollow?"

"Oh, c'mon—" he started to complain.

She sighed and slid off his back. They were past most of the glass; she could pick her way across the rest. "Can I ask your real name then?"

He frowned at her like he'd been prepared for an argument. "Fletcher."

She gave him a confused look. "But you just said—"

"Fletcher is the name that means the most to me," he said, smiling at her. "Because the people who call me that mean the most. But, if you're asking what name I was given, it's—" He paused, then in one swift movement he grabbed Aly's arm and pulled her down. "Shh."

Fear returned full force, along with her noticing an increase in the intensity of her prickles. Talking to him, she'd almost forgotten they were in danger. She went quiet and still, listening and searching with her eyes to hear or see what Will did. She couldn't find anything out of the ordinary. They'd been walking near an open section of the walkway where a set of broken escalators led down to the first floor, but Aly couldn't tell if the danger was on this floor or another.

Will beckoned her with a finger and then crawled along the floor until he reached the edge of the walkway and looked down over the first floor of the mall. She crept along the floor and stretched out beside him.

Copying Will's position by putting an ear to the floor, she could barely make out some figures on the floor below them. She couldn't see them well, the angle of the floors made it difficult but there were too many legs for Belinda's group. They seemed to be milling around, perhaps waiting for instructions. Leaning in close to Will, she whispered, "They're… shifters, right? I think… I can feel that."

"Aly," Will whispered in a strangled tone. "Before… were you lying about your father being dead?"

She blinked. "No. You know that."

"We're in serious trouble."

"Why?"

"Those are Welcher's men."

She looked back at the group. "And who's Welcher?"

"Hmm…" He narrowed his eyes at the group. "Shifter society, it's broken up into a lot of factions. People with different beliefs about why we're here, what we're supposed to do, whether we're the greater evolutionary being. X-Men stuff."

"Okay."

He drummed his fingers on the floor. "There are three larger ones. Darcy's faction believes shifters are the next stage of evolution and should be treated as such. She believes our abilities were given to us by higher beings to lead this world into the next age. Welcher is basically old blood, stay with our own kind, do not interfere with humans, and uphold old traditions. Rex… I guess in a roundabout way he fights for everyone else, shifters and non alike. At least, that's how it used to be, I've been away for a while."

Since Aly couldn't see the group, she watched Will instead and wondered what he saw that she didn't. "And Belinda's faction?"

"Belinda's group isn't a part of shifter society; she's a Purist, as in pure human. Get rid of all the 'mutants'."

Her dislike of Belinda rose even more. "Okay."

"Both Darcy and Welcher's factions shun any shifter offspring that aren't born with the ability. It was happening more and more when I left."

"What about… that creepy name… the Faceless?" Belinda had mentioned them before and Will had clammed up. Aly didn't know what that meant.

Will stared straight ahead. "Shifter soldiers. Highly trained in combat. They also lack morals and judgment, following orders to the letter. They say you can't reason with a Faceless."

Startled, Aly gaped at him. He didn't seem like he wanted to add anymore so she turned her attention to the group. They were talking; she could hear the hushed murmurs of their voices, too soft to make sense of their words. "Should we get closer?"

"No."

"Should we leave?"

Will scrubbed a hand through his hair and made a frustrated sound. "I was not expecting this."

"What's wrong?"

"Lots of things… I kind of want to know why they're here. If Belinda's working with Welcher's group, then Rex is in serious trouble."

"And if they're not?"

"Then why are they here? And…" His head jerked up. "Oh. Wow."

Aly blinked rapidly. "What?"

Will touched his hand to his ear and shook his head. "Aly, I need to shift for a sec. Just some augments."

She nodded, mesmerized, as more intense tingles spread across her skin. Will's appearance didn't change. "What are augments?' she whispered.

"Slight changes in the way my body works. Like enhanced eyesight and hearing. Even voice pitch. Just a sec." The sensation dimmed and Will's lips kept moving. With two fingers, he pointed left, then up. When he nodded, Aly got the impression he talked to someone a distance away, which confused her because she couldn't see anyone.

The tingles returned to her skin, then were gone just as fast. Giving Aly a manic grin, Will shuffled away from the edge. "C'mon. We need to move, and fast."

Bewildered, she followed him. He had a spring in his

step that hadn't been there before, but he also seemed to be more cautious as well. He checked every corner they came across, his gun sweeping down each corridor as well as above and below them when they reached any opening in the walkways.

Tension rose in Aly, arising from the change in Will and the knowledge they were hiding from more than Belinda and her team. So when they reached an escalator, Aly was astounded when he went up instead of going down. "What are you doing; where are we going?"

He bounced as he turned around halfway up the escalator. "Trust me."

She hesitated at the bottom. "I thought—" She clasped her elbow with one hand and looked over at the other escalator, the one that headed down to the next level. "I thought we were trying to get out of here, not get ourselves more trapped."

"We're meeting someone."

"Who?"

He glanced up the escalator then down at her, exasperated. With a sigh, he trotted down to her again to take her hand. He tugged her. "It'll be fine."

"I don't like this," she replied and only allowed him to pull her onto the first stair before she stopped again. "All this sneaking, all these people with guns. Proper guns, not just paintball ones. I want to get out of here, and out of here is *down*."

"I know this is difficult—" He whipped about, brought up his gun and moved sideways so he covered Aly before she'd even realized there was danger. The movement caused her to squeak with fear.

A woman said, "Thought you were dead."

Against her better judgment, Aly peeked around Will.

An Asian woman descended the opposite escalator stairs, pointing a gun at them. She wore an ill-fitting camouflage uniform with the sleeves rolled up and hanging open at the chest, revealing a black tank top beneath. A braid of raven hair dangled over her shoulder.

Will kept his gun trained on her, moving so he was always between Aly and the gun. "Nice to see you too."

Hazel eyes fixed on Will, she said, "Perpetually stuck as a teenager, I see."

Aly stretched out her hand and gripped the back of Will's shirt. He backed into her, forcing her into the railing of the escalator.

Will replied, "Growing old gracefully, are we? Nice look. Very Lucy Liu."

"You're one to talk. Who'd you model that form from?" The woman waved a hand to dismiss the question, then clasped it around the gun again. "I didn't think I'd see you again. You just dropped off the face of the world."

"That tends to happen when you're lied to on a daily basis."

The woman frowned. "He never lied to us."

"Keep telling yourself that."

She reached the bottom of the stairs and halted. "What are you doing here?"

"What are you?" Will countered. "I've seen Purists and Welchers. Don't tell me you're mixed up too."

She frowned. "Are you?"

Will nudged Aly off the bottom step so they could back away from the woman. "I got dragged in."

"How?"

"You first."

She sighed. "Increased chatter on the network. One of my infiltrators said something was going down so I thought I'd check it out."

"Infiltrator?" Will asked. "The shifter with the Purists?"

The woman's lips thinned as she pressed them together. "No. He's not one of mine." The woman shook her head at him, then sighed. "There's four different factions floating around here. So, you can imagine my surprise to find you."

"You're not here under Rex's orders?"

"Not officially," the woman said. "Although, I have the feeling that'll change when I report in."

Aly peeked out from behind Will. The woman didn't appear threatening, even though she still held a gun on them. She was taller than Aly and had an air of authority. The conversation between Will and the woman was strange; cordial and familiar. They had history.

Seeing Aly's peek, the woman asked, "Who's the mouse?"

"Play nice," Will responded. "I came to warn you, that's it. You need to leave."

The woman shook her head. "You don't get to show up unannounced and command—"

"The Purists have a new serum. It's... difficult... to nullify and doesn't produce drowsiness."

The woman's brow furrowed. "Even for—"

"Several answers were borderline."

She gave him a skeptical look. "Are you sure you're just not going soft?"

He raised an eyebrow. "They want Rex."

The woman's face was impassive. "And you know this because?"

"They're after his daughter."

The woman's eyes narrowed. "Rex doesn't have a daughter."

"Apparently, the Purists think he does."

The woman looked at Aly again. "And that's who they think she is?"

Will lowered his weapon, startling Aly and she drew closer to him. "It appears they only have a name. Aly's a circumstantial match at best, but they took her because of my presence."

Abruptly the woman clicked on the safety and holstered her weapon. "I need to call this in."

"Leave my name out."

She pulled out a phone. "He's going to want to know. Stay put."

Will sighed.

Aly tugged on Will's shirt to get his attention. "Who's she?" she asked, nodding to the woman.

Will's smile was one she hadn't seen before. "That's—"

"Elaine," the woman said over her shoulder.

Will blinked in surprise. "Elaine? Really?"

"I like it."

Will grinned and turned back to Aly. "Elaine's my younger sister."

"Older," the woman said primly.

"Don't think so," Will responded in a teasing tone. "My number is larger than yours."

"Indicating I was first. Now shush."

Aly felt a familiar surge of protective anger. Fletcher's family, who had ignored him the entire time she'd known him, who hadn't supported him when... The anger derailed. Uncle Lee. He'd probably been Fletcher too, now she thought about it. It would explain why she always felt odd around him.

Her head hurt. Everything she'd thought she'd known about him had unraveled in such a short time. He'd been lying about everything. Their friendship had been built upon the lies he'd told her, what if it was a lie too?

Will seemed to notice her internal struggle and placed a hand on her shoulder. "Hey, what's wrong?"

"Nothing."

"Don't lie," he said, his voice soft. "In a situation like this, I would be surprised if nothing was wrong. You can tell me anything."

"Can I?" she questioned, frowning at him. "How much have you lied to me? Has *anything* you've *ever* said been the truth?"

Will's mouth dropped open. "What?"

"Your sister?" She glanced over at the woman who was astutely ignoring them. "The fact you're a shapeshifter? Your name?"

"Joseph, put me through to Rex."

Will rubbed his palms along her upper arms. "I know this is stressful—"

"You really don't know how I'm feeling."

"I'll get you out of here, I promise."

Aly hugged herself and stepped away from him. "You don't know that. You can't actually promise anything right now."

Will ran a hand through his hair in a gesture that was so like Fletcher's and yet so wrong.

"It's Elaine. I'm reporting in because…" Elaine looked taken aback. "Yes? … I'm already there." She glanced over at Aly and Will. "There was increased chatter, so I thought I'd…" Elaine straightened. "A girl?"

Will tensed and turned to watch Elaine.

Elaine raised her eyebrows at Will. "Yes… Her name wouldn't happen to be Aly, would it?"

"Don't," Will warned.

Elaine swept her sight over Aly. "Brown hair. Blue eyes. Looks about eighteen." She paused. "Mouse, what's your surname?"

Aly glanced at Will, who shook his head.

With a frown, Elaine asked, "Aly's short for?"

Will shook his head again.

Elaine sighed. "There's an Aly standing right in front of me. Along with Noah."

Will swore, throwing up his hands. He stalked away from Elaine, muttering under his breath. Aly skittered after him, stopping to stare when he about-faced and walked back.

Elaine tucked her phone away. "Rex wants to see her."

"We're not going with you."

Elaine brushed her braid over her shoulder. "Apparently, there's been a spate of kidnappings up and down the coast. All of them a variant of Aly. Alison, Alyssa, Alice, Alina. We're sending out people to recover them all."

Will rubbed his face. "So, he does have a daughter."

Elaine shrugged. "All I know is he wants to see her. And you."

"No."

"You can't keep running," Elaine chided.

He scowled.

"I can force you."

"You can try," Will replied.

A prickle ran up Aly's spine at the same moment Elaine and Will looked down the escalator.

"We should go," Elaine said, redrawing her gun.

"Yup," Will replied. He turned his back on Aly and bent slightly, holding his hands like stirrups. "We have to run."

Glancing down at her one shoe, Aly asked, "Are you sure?"

"Faster if we don't have to worry about broken glass."

"Right," Aly said as she clambered onto Will's back. He rested his hands under her bottom and she gripped his sides with her knees, her arms around his neck.

"This probably will scare you," Will muttered. "Try not to scream."

"Huh?"

He surged forward, bounding up to the top of the escalator with only one step in the middle and Aly almost lost her grip on him. She yelped, then stifled it as much as she could, clinging to him. He sprinted, darting through the mall faster than she imagined anyone could run while carrying someone. Elaine ran ahead of him, leading the way, her pace just as fast. The pair of them made it look easy. Their steps were sure and confident, and their feet made scarcely any noise as they ran.

Neither of them were out of breath as they pulled up where the walkway opened out onto a balcony over an old food court. Goose bumps sprung up on Aly's arms and she shuddered. Will shot Elaine a glance, "Where now?"

"Car's outside about a mile away."

"Brilliant," Will muttered.

"I did *not* expect to need to make a dash for freedom," Elaine replied tartly. She pointed down to the first floor. "We need to exit through there. I can't see anything. You?"

Will peeked over his shoulder and Aly nodded in acknowledgment. "Probably going to be doing a lot of it intermittently," he warned.

"Do what you need. I'll cope."

Elaine gave them a questioning look.

The tingles engulfed Aly as Will said, "She can sense when we shift."

Elaine's eyebrows shot up and her mouth dropped open. "Really?"

"Yes."

"It's like being dunked in ice water," Aly muttered.

"We barely have a scent," Elaine said.

"Yup," Will said with pride. "She can also tell a normal shifter out of their natural form."

Elaine blinked rapidly. "Holy… we'd better not let the Purists get hold of her then."

"That's the idea." Will turned and Aly leaned around to see his eyes on the floor. He looked the way they came, then, with returning tingles, back to the exit. "Nothing close. We should be right to sneak out."

Elaine holstered her gun again, winked at Will, and leaped over the hand rail.

Aly gasped in shock, jolting forward as though she could somehow save the woman.

"She'll be okay," Will said, uncaring. "She's grabbed onto the railing." Removing a hand from her bottom, he coaxed her legs straight. "Hook your ankles around me, put your arms under and around my shoulders, and hold on real tight."

"What?" she squeaked, as she crossed her ankles in front of him and changed her grip on his shoulders. Surely he didn't plan to jump over the edge too.

"I've done this before; trust me. All you have to do is

hold on." Keeping one hand on her, he placed his other one on the railing.

"I don't—"

He threw them up and over the railing. With a startled cry, she gripped him as tightly as she could, certain they were about to die. Gravity tried to pull them apart and, as they fell, Will twisted and caught onto the railing below them with one hand. Their bodies jolted and her face squashed into his shoulder as he halted their fall. Both his feet planted on the stonework edge and he hung there.

"Oh, God."

"You're okay," he soothed. He glanced below them, then monkeyed along the railing until he had a better landing spot. "Here we go."

Even though she was ready for the fall, it was no less terrifying.

Elaine waited for them, a smug smile on her face. "You did get slow."

Will rolled his eyes and returned his hand to aid in supporting Aly on his back. "Let's go."

Aly wasn't good at horse riding. She'd done a few trail rides but never had a horse any faster than a walk. She imagined this might be what a gallop was like, except the horse didn't hold onto you as it ran. She jolted and bumped against him and felt her stomach doing massive flops.

"Don't tell me you sparkle," she muttered.

He laughed. "I would be considerably slower. And I'm not planning on climbing trees."

"No, you just jump off balconies."

"Yup."

"Just be glad I don't get motion sickness."

He grimaced. "Thanks for that image."

"My pleasure."

Turning her head, Aly looked behind at the mall as it grew farther away. She felt like they were both running away from and running toward danger.

Elaine slowed, then stopped to turn and look behind them. "Seems like we're clear."

Will slowed to a walk. "Doubt it," he said. "The Purists didn't strike me as ones to give up so quick."

"I'm just glad we made it out of there," Aly murmured. She relaxed her death grip on Will, expecting to be let down to walk, but he kept her on his back.

"So," Elaine said, falling into step beside Will. "Where've you been for the last... what do I call you now? Did you pick a name?"

"Not really. Not in this form. But call me Will."

Aly felt her heart twist from his response. He couldn't even tell his sister his name was Fletcher, despite saying to her earlier it was the name that meant the most to him.

"Serviceable," Elaine said with a nod. "So, where have you been?"

Will glanced over his shoulder at Aly, wariness written all over his face. "I've been... around."

Tears pricked Aly's eyes, but she refused to acknowledge them. The way he spoke, the sheer blankness in his voice, it sounded like all the time he spent in Bellhollow meant nothing.

Elaine looked at Aly with a curious expression. "Who is this mouse of yours?"

"The 'mouse' has a name," Aly snapped, turning the hurt into anger. "I'd really like to go home now."

Elaine shook her head. "Can't. Rex wants to see you."

"What makes him think I want to see him?"

Elaine shrugged. "Squeak at him then. I'm following orders."

"Stop it," Will snapped at Elaine. "She was kidnapped off the street and she's only just found out what I am; it's a hard thing to process. Lay off."

Aly tingled. Will's lips moved, whatever he said was lost to Aly but Elaine halted in her tracks.

Aly rubbed her arm as the feeling faded. "I can tell when you shift," she muttered. "Warning next time."

"Right," Will mumbled as he walked.

"You're shitting me," Elaine said, jogging to catch up.

"No," Will said. Aly wondered what had passed between them.

"*Wow*. I never thought… I never thought *you'd*… wow."

Will seemed unimpressed. "Hmm."

Elaine was flabbergasted. "And shift sense too."

"Hmm."

Elaine's gaze flicked between Aly and Will. "She must be strong if she can sense our shifts."

Will shrugged. "Or prolonged exposure. Not too sure."

Elaine cast Will a calculating look. "Prolonged… how long?"

Will sighed. "Nine years."

"Nine years!" Elaine hit Will on the arm. "You lasted nine years in one fucking place and didn't care enough to call and say you were okay? Jesus Christ, Noah! Do you have any idea how worried I've been about you?"

Aly turned her attention to Will at the slip of a different name. It wasn't the first time Elaine had used that name. Was it his real name?

Elaine ranted, "Every clone that comes from that place with your face, and the real you can't be bothered checking in."

Aly's mouth dropped open. *Clones*?

Will sighed. "They're still coming?"

Elaine regained control of her emotions like she'd snapped her fingers. "Like clockwork, every year. I think Darcy's allowing them to escape now."

"Sending them out to die, you mean."

She smiled. "Four years ago, both Seth and Solomon lived."

Will's eyes shot to Elaine. "Really?"

"Yeah. They weren't the same as our Seth and Solomon… but still." She sighed. "It was nice. Seeing them."

Full of melancholy, his sigh echoed hers.

"I wish you'd been there. If I'd known how to contact you, I would've sent for you."

Will ignored that. "Who lived this time?"

"Solomon died from shift dysplasia. Adam has several gunshot wounds; he doesn't look like he'll make it. Jonah was hit; doing okay. Seth's dead, Boaz's dead, Ruth's MIA."

Will grunted. "Sounds like our escape."

"Yeah. It's surprising how frequently that setup occurs. I often wonder if this is an experiment by Darcy on destiny."

"I wouldn't put it past her. Are they still…?"

She heaved in a breath and let it out slowly. "Seems to be hardcoded now. The breakdown occurs within a few weeks of their arrival."

"And I bet they still don't know what's going to happen," Will said, sounding bitter.

"After you left, we did tell the first few. It was… bad for them. One of mine committed suicide within the first week. Yours two weeks later. Now… we make them as comfortable and happy as we can with what time they have left." She sighed. "It's funny, though. Comparing experiences. Subsequent clones don't have the depth of access we have. Some of them can't even access it."

Will grunted. "Sounds like a decoy."

Elaine paused. "Possibly."

"Rex really should've let us destroy the facility."

Elaine nodded. "I did. Eight years ago. Two years later, they sprung up somewhere else."

"Fuck."

"Yup. Did you hear…?"

"About Adam?" He sighed. "Yeah, I saw the obituary. What happened?"

Aly tilted her head as she listened.

Elaine kicked a stone. "Mining accident. It was quick."

"How's Naomi?" He squirmed and adjusted Aly on his

back.

"Taking it hard. They were in the process of adopting."

Another heavy sigh. "Jonah?"

"Vanished, same as you. I get postcards every six weeks."

"Hmm."

Aly had been alternating between staring at them both, her mouth dry and hanging open. Now, since it seemed like the conversation had stopped, she squeaked, "Clones?"

Will looked over his shoulder. "Like I said, there's a lot to discuss."

Elaine said, "We have time."

Will removed one of his hands from beneath her and scrubbed it through his hair, then over his face. "All right, I suppose… first off, the name they gave me was Noah and there's a lot of Noahs exactly like me. Let me tell you about the Faceless."

CHAPTER 17

Head resting against the window of Elaine's car, Aly stared out into the world and watched as farmland passed by. Trapped in an unforgiving moment, her mind churned and her heart felt burdened.

She couldn't process what Noah-Will-Fletcher had been through. There wasn't a place for her to start. It was so far outside the realm of what she'd expected—what had seemed *possible*—her mind refused to comprehend it.

Fully grown in a vat. Experimented on. Almost dying. Discovering augmentation. It didn't seem real.

Will and Elaine, realizing Aly needed time, dropped into silence.

Will stared out his window, his hand over his mouth as he rested his elbow on the door. Aly alternated between glancing at him and staring out the window. She knew that stance; he was upset but she didn't know how to help him. Could barely help herself.

Aly wanted to ask questions. Will invited her to ask, but she impersonated a goldfish, opening and closing her mouth, unable to form the words until Elaine mumbled something about shock. There had been desperation in Will's eyes. He wanted her to understand. Ready and eager to answer and help her come to grips with his life. He was so different.

She felt shattered. It made her wonder how Will felt about all of it. He'd bared his soul and she'd shut down. She wasn't sure how to react but she knew keeping silent was the wrong way to go about it. That led her to think about what she would have done if *Fletcher* had come to her and told her this story. If it had been his earnest expressions and his voice she'd been listening to. Her mind had partitioned the two. Will and Fletcher; Will the enigma with a familiarity that made no sense, and Fletcher with their shared past and in-jokes. Separate somehow, but still the same when it mattered because they were the same person.

And since they *were* the same and she could understand that, she knew what she should be doing right now. Talk to Fletcher. Tell him how she felt. Ask about his feelings. She'd be his friend.

She wasn't doing that right now.

Clicking off her seatbelt, she slid across. The leather seat squeaked against her thighs, causing Will to turn his head. Not looking at him, she redid the middle belt. Breathing out, she took his wrist and looped it over her shoulder, half turning so her back was against his chest and relaxed into him.

After a stiff moment, Will maneuvered so they melted into a more comfortable position. He rubbed her upper arm and then gave her a squeeze.

"I don't know what to do with this," she mumbled.

"I know. I don't know how to make it easier."

"Snickers would've been a good start."

He rumbled a laugh. "Yeah. Stupid me for forgetting that."

Aly closed her eyes.

His thumb brushed against her arm. "Are you okay?"

"Not even remotely."

Will pressed his nose against the top of her head.

"Oh."

She stretched out her legs on the seat beside her. "I'm tired, hungry and I need a bathroom. Sort that out and we're on the way to being okay."

"There's a gas station in ten miles," Elaine said. "We'll stop."

"Thank you," Aly said. "Can I call my mom?"

Will squirmed. "Please don't."

"She'll be panicked." Aly tilted her head back to see him. "Grace and Del too. And Tim! Think of what this must be doing to Tim. We've all been through a lot these past few weeks—"

"I understand, but I don't know what we'd tell her yet. Just give me a few more hours. We'll think up a cover story, practice it a bit and then you can call them."

Aly sighed.

"Who are Del and Grace?" Elaine asked. She drove one handed, the other hand pillowing her head as she leaned her elbow on the door frame. "And Tim?"

"Tim is Aly's brother," Will explained. "Del and Grace are our other friends in Bellhollow."

Aly toyed with Will's fingers. "Why'd you decide to stay in Bellhollow?"

"Um…"

"I'm interested in that one too," Elaine said.

Will sighed. "I was tired. Lonely too, I guess. I'd been traveling, the bus stopped over in Bellhollow for lunch and… well… there was a girl sitting in a tree reading and…" He shrugged. "I don't know… I felt like saying hi. The rest is history."

Elaine hmm-ed.

Will raised an eyebrow. "What?"

"You're not usually impulsive."

"Best decision I ever made."

Elaine appeared skeptical. "And his age didn't alarm you, Aly?"

Will tensed. "Age shift. I was the same age as her, all

the way through."

Elaine's hand gripped the steering wheel. "I guess you *can* do things I can't. Why eight?"

"No one looks at an eight-year-old traveling, because, *of course*, there has to be a parent nearby. As long as you look like you know what you're doing, people ignore you. Aly saw me and was nice."

"I ate your Snickers," Aly said. "Explain how that's 'nice'?"

Will laughed, "And then invited me over for snacks and I met your mom and... it'd been a long time since someone was nice to me for no reason at all." Looking back at Elaine, he said, "A night turned into a week, then her mom asked why I wasn't in school and... well. You can guess from there."

Aly touched her cast. It wasn't exactly like what he'd said in his letter, but she assumed it was because there were things he didn't want to tell his sister. Or didn't want to tell her. "You said the Faceless were mindless killers."

"Yeah," Elaine said. "We grew faces." She paused. "Did that sound as weird to you as it did to me?"

"Yup," Will said with a rumble of laughter. "True, though. Our facial features were not defined at all. It was a way to brand us."

"Darcy fed us a story about alien DNA," Elaine said. "And we were mixed human and alien to get a better understanding of their abilities. It wasn't until we saw people up close we realized our faces and skin were different."

"First time was a shock," Will continued. "When we started to discover our shifting ability, we changed. We started thinking for ourselves, rather than following orders."

"Can I see?" Aly asked.

Will jolted. "Um..."

"I wouldn't advise it," Elaine said.

Will's twitching jostled Aly. "It's... it can be a shock."

"Why?" Aly asked.

"Think... hmm... think Voldemort," Will said, scratching his face.

"More snake-like," Elaine added. "Scales and all."

"Scales?" Aly blurted, astounded. She tilted her head to look up at Will. "Really?"

Will nodded. "We call them scales anyway. They look very similar, but they can grow hair and they don't overlap." He shrugged. "Scales seemed like the best name for them."

"Some of the conspiracy theories about reptilian people weren't far off," Elaine said with a light laugh.

"You're not human?"

"We are," Will assured her. "Genetics is a funny thing. Change a chromosomal string and you get a host of side effects." He lifted his arm, reaching around her so he could tug up his sleeve. "Genetic codes that can be either good or bad for the carrier. Take color blindness, for example. Sure, it's hard to tell a red light from a green light, but it kicks ass for detecting motion." He left his arm in front of her and wiggled his fingers. "Skin color. More melanin, darker skin, more resistance to sunlight, more chance of disfiguring patches from something as simple as a rash."

Tingles rippled and Aly watched, fascinated, as Will's arm changed color. It was like water droplets hit his skin, circles of changes that crept outward.

"As for our skin... somewhere hidden in the human genome is this."

She could see why he called them scales. Miniature diamonds no larger than a mole patterned his forearm as it turned ash gray. There were slight variances in color from scale to scale.

"We suspect it might be connected to evolving from the ocean," Elaine said. "Or a version of ichthyosis. We'll probably never really know."

"And... all shifters have skin like this?" she asked.

Stretching out her hand she reached for his arm then hesitated.

"It's unique to the Faceless," Will murmured and brought his arm closer in invitation.

She ran the tips of her fingers against the patch of scales. They felt warm to the touch, which was a surprise since she expected them to feel cold. Firmer than skin, but with a silky quality. "They're pretty."

Will lost some of the tension in his body and he rumbled a laugh. "Pretty is not a word I would have used to describe them."

"Do you have a forked tongue too?" she asked, teasing.

He laughed again. "Only if you want me too." Another tingle and the scales disappeared from his arm. "But no, not naturally."

Smiling, she withdrew her hand. He caught her fingers and laced his between hers.

Elaine turned her head, grinning at them for a moment. "Look at you, being all snuggly. It's nice to see you like that."

"Hmm?" Will lifted his head. "What's that?"

"Hugging that guy used to be a pain, he'd go all stiff," Elaine told Aly, her tone bright and cheery. "It's good to see he found someone he can relax around."

Will tensed. "That's just the way we are. Aly's very tactile."

"It's a rare person who will allow us to be affectionate and never expect it to progress. I'm happy for you both. I never thought you'd find someone to love."

Aly snuggled closer. "Of course he loves me, we're best friends."

"Uh-huh," Elaine teased. "That's why he thinks of you as his Seth."

Will's sudden jerk knocked Aly off his chest. "Elijah!"

Elaine blinked. "What?"

Will squirmed. "Drop it."

"Your Seth?" Aly said. She turned to face him, startled

to discover him pale and avoiding her gaze. "She's…" She struggled with their names. Strange and biblical, their gender often didn't match the name. So much information to sort through. "She's your sister, right?" She smiled. It was a nice way for him to think about her, even if she didn't think of him as a brother. "That's sweet."

He still didn't meet her eyes. "Yeah, um—"

"That's not what being his 'Seth' means."

Will groaned in exasperation.

"He didn't tell you?" Elaine asked.

"Tell me what?"

A flash of tingles as Will spoke without sound and Aly frowned.

Elaine jerked her head around and the car swerved. "You told her you were gay?"

Will covered his face with his hands and rubbed, muffling the "Jesus."

"Noah!"

"She was thirteen!" Will protested. "What was I supposed to say?"

"The truth," Elaine snapped.

"What truth?" Aly looked at Will for an answer, but he didn't respond so, Aly turned to the woman. "Elaine?"

With an over the shoulder scowl at Will, Elaine said, "Tell her."

Will kept his eyes on the horizon. "I'm not gay."

Astounded, Aly looked at Will. "You're not?"

"I'm asexual."

Aly didn't think he was referring to the ability to reproduce with himself. In this sense, asexuality was a lack of sexual attraction or an absence of sexual desire. "Really? But…"

Will scowled at Elaine. "Thanks a lot."

"She deserves to know."

Aly sought an explanation. "Why did you lie?"

He shrugged.

"Seems like a silly thing to lie about considering—"

Will snapped his head toward her, his mouth twisted and his face settled into deep frown. "A silly thing?"

"You've lied about so many other things, it seems like something small in comparison."

Twisting his torso, he faced her completely. "My sexuality is *not* a silly or small thing."

Aly shrank back, intimidated. "I didn't say it was. I accepted it when you said you were gay. Do you really think I wouldn't have—"

"It got you off my back."

Aly blinked. "What?"

"What's it matter?" he spat. "You're going back to Bellhollow and I'm getting out of your life."

She recoiled, feeling his words like a physical blow.

"Stupid, Noah," Elaine muttered. "Really stupid."

Will puffed out a breath and closed his eyes. "Aly—"

"No, you're absolutely right," Aly said. She unclicked her seat belt and moved to the window seat. "You don't owe me anything."

"Don't be like that."

Clipping up her seat belt, she ignored him, returning to the boring view of watching the scenery flash past her.

"You're still running," Elaine commented.

"Stay out of it," Will told her.

"I don't know why you told me about shifting," Aly commented off-handedly. "You could've just called me delusional and that would've been the end of it. Did you need to be validated or something?"

Will opened his mouth, then closed it again.

Aly pressed on. "You're so set on not coming back, what's the harm of allowing me to think you were dead?"

Elaine turned her head sharply, then decided against interrupting.

"Would you have preferred I stayed dead?" Will asked.

"Yes, I think I might have," Aly said, resting her head against the window. "I knew where I stood with Fletcher. I loved him, he loved me, there were no lies or half-truths

223

between us." She waved her hand in the air. "All this has tainted his memory."

Will's voice was strangled, "You can't mean that."

Curling up, Aly didn't reply.

The gas station was nestled in among large pastures and was nothing more than a building on the side of the road with several RVs for staff. It had two measly browsers and a dusty, rundown look that told Aly their customers were few and far between.

Elaine warned her not to let herself be seen. She'd pointed out the security cameras before Aly was allowed to get out of the car. Aly made sure to keep her face away from them. The uniform she wore was a dead giveaway if her story was on the news, so Elaine said she would check the little store to see if they had anything else she could wear. Aly doubted there would be anything. Half-tempted to disobey, Aly followed their instructions with a small sense of frustration.

The bathroom was tiny and stank of stale urine, but Aly was glad for the privacy. After using the facilities, she washed her face, undid her ponytail, and combed her fingers through her mess of brown hair so she could braid it.

Elaine rapped on the door. "They didn't have any clothes," she called through the door.

"I didn't think they would."

"Aly?"

"Yeah?"

"Can I ask about Fletcher?"

She sighed. "Fletcher was my best friend. He died a few weeks ago."

"I see. I'm sorry Noah did this. He's... he can be... Ours is a difficult life. He must've felt he had to."

Watching herself in the mirror, Aly willed the tears away. "You don't need to explain."

"From what I've seen, I don't think he would have willingly—"

"Elaine, please."

A pause. "Sorry. I'll be by the car."

Aly stalled in the bathroom, rewashing her face and deciding her braid was too messy and required redoing. She straightened her dress and unlocked the door.

Will waited. He leaned against the wall beside the toilet door holding several sandwiches wrapped up in plastic and a bottle of water tucked under his arm. "Hi."

Pausing in the doorway, she frowned. "Hi." Stepping past, she headed to the car.

He followed her. "Can we talk?"

"Seems like we've been doing nothing but talk," Aly muttered.

"I'm sorry."

She rounded on him. "See, that's how I know you're not him. Fletcher *never* says sorry."

His smile was contrite. "They were out of Snickers."

"Oh, great." She threw up her hands and stalked away. "World's ending and they're out of Snickers."

"I was scared."

Things began to click in her head. Seth and Solomon. There had been a budding love between them that was never fully realized. Siblings, but not in the true sense and if Aly was Will's Seth, then... her eyes widened and she turned back to him. "No. No. You don't get to do this. Not now. Not after everything."

He pressed on anyway. "You were getting too close. I've never had anyone in my life like you, Aly, and I didn't want to lose that because I couldn't be what you needed."

She curled her hands so her fingernails dug into her palms. "And what did you think I needed?"

"You wanted to explore a more... intimate relationship and I... I can't... I couldn't give you that."

She raised her eyebrows and waited.

Will had never looked more nervous. "I..." He swallowed. "I want to be with you. I need to be a part of your life. I want... to see you smile and be the first face you see in the morning and hold you in the dark. I want to make breakfast in the morning and stay up late playing games; I want to be part of your triumphs and your failures. I want to see the sunrise and steal all your Snickers. I want our lives to intermingle so much we can't tell where one begins and one ends."

It cost her, but she refused to be swayed. "We *had* that."

"Yeah, but you still—I never expected to remain in Bellhollow as long as I did. I thought I'd never see... you had boyfriends—I wanted... exclusiveness." The words tumbled out in a rush. "None of them really understood what we had and you always chose me and maybe one day you wouldn't and—and all the time I worried about what'd happen when I had to leave and—"

"You... really?" She tilted her head in astonishment. "You'd never be with me, but you didn't want anyone else to be? You realize how juvenile—"

"You're my favorite person, Aly," he said, looking like he was on the verge of confessing something. "More than that, I'm—"

"Don't," she snapped and waved her hands at him. "Please. Just don't. That's not fair, you don't get to do this."

He jerked his hand through his hair. "I regret not kissing you back."

Clamping her mouth shut, Aly thought maybe once everything had settled down she could fully appreciate that remark. Right now, she felt numb. "But?"

"But..." Staring at his free hand, he opened and closed it several times before he answered. "I don't want... I don't feel desire. Sex is... not interesting and I'd rather not."

She raised her eyebrows.

He swallowed. "Sexuality is hard, especially when you're thirteen. It changes as you grow and at the time... well, I wasn't attracted to you, I didn't see you as more than a friend at that time so… I thought… You assumed I was gay, I went with it. I knew eventually it could be an issue."

She huffed at him.

"Being in love with someone is different than being in lust and there are other ways to be intimate—"

"You jerk."

He looked taken aback. "What?"

"What makes you think I still want to be with you?" she asked. "What if I'm over it? What if all I want—" Her hand cut the air like it could cut her words in two. "All I *wanted* from you is friendship?"

Will looked sick at the prospect. "But—"

"I was thirteen! I was stupid and impulsive and I confused platonic with romantic. You're standing there, telling me you don't want our relationship to change, that you don't like sex, yet you regret—You said you don't want me to see other people; you can't still expect—I'm not exactly the most sexual person myself," she snapped.

He raised an eyebrow. "You have a file on your computer entitled '*Bee Gone*' that says otherwise."

"Anatomy practice!" she snapped, her cheeks flushing. "You're making me sound like some sort of hormonal driven bitch! Did you think I'd force myself on you? Thanks a lot!"

"No, I—"

She shook her head. "I don't want to hear it. We could have grown up with this. I could've had time to process. We could've worked something out! Instead, I was left to measure up every single boy who tried to date me against you. And now I find *everything* we had was a lie!"

Taking a step toward her, he implored, "Aly, please—"

"I took a chance and you threw it back in my face!" Aly spoke around the growing lump in her throat. "You never gave me a chance with *any* of this. How can you possibly—"

"I'm giving you one now."

"Bit late," Aly pointed out. "Fletcher's dead."

"I'm still here."

She swallowed and her throat closed up. "Are you really? Because it doesn't feel like it."

Pain etched lines on his face. "These last few weeks have been... hideous... watching you go through... and I couldn't... I couldn't..."

It devastated her to know he'd been around, watching her grieve and not done a thing to help. "That's *so* creepy. And stalkerish. Jesus, you came to your own funeral. Do you know how messed up that is?"

He defended himself. "I had to make sure... Adam just died but Fletcher was *murdered*, I wanted to find out why! I had—"

"The *only* reason you're here now is because those people kidnapped me. Did you know they were going to?"

"I wasn't stalking you, I was stalking *them*!" He paused. "Okay, that sounds bad, but I had to know! If I'd known they were after you, I would have stopped them before they got close."

"Then... I wouldn't ever have known, would I?" Aly bit her lip to keep from crying. It didn't work. "You didn't intend to come back!"

"Aly—"

"What do you want from me?" she asked. She shoved the tears off her face with her fingers and hugged herself. "Do you want me to say everything's okay? I forgive you? Fine. Everything's okay. I forgive you." She marched over to shove his chest. "Happy?"

Will hung his head. "No."

"Me neither." She sighed again. Her chin dropped toward her chest and she cupped her forehead in her palm.

Shoulders hunched, he had the look of a dying man as he held out the sandwiches and bottle of water to her. "Here."

She took them only because it seemed he'd drop them otherwise. "Thanks."

Thrusting his hands into his pockets, he nudged his shoe against the ground. "We should get back in the car."

Helpless and torn between wanting to make him feel better and needing comfort herself, she bent forward until the top of her head butted against his chest. She transferred the sandwich and the drink to one hand, using the broken one to grip his jacket.

He made a soft noise. "Aly—" The way he moved his body suggested he wanted to hug her.

"Don't."

His hands flopped to his sides. He puffed his chest to push against her head, cheating his way into returned contact.

"I need space. Time. You've... shoved all this information at me and I can't... I can't... just... I don't know how..." She couldn't find the words.

Will's answer came slow. "All right."

She squeezed her eyes shut then said, "I love... I loved Fletcher, okay? Even when he was a bumble-butt, he was my best friend and I loved him and I regret not telling him more. You're still here, but *he's* gone and I don't know what that means."

He lifted one hand and splayed his fingers on her back. "I never meant—"

"I know," she whispered. "Doesn't make this easier." With a sigh, she pushed away from him and stalked toward the car with Will trailing behind.

When they returned, they saw Elaine rummaging in the trunk. She pulled out a duffle bag and closed it before they reached her. "We have several hours travel. Rex wants us to go to our alpha site. He'll meet us there."

"Hours?" Aly asked in disbelief. "But—"

"I'm under orders," Elaine interrupted. "I will force you into the car if I have to."

Will sighed. "Elaine—"

"I don't have any answers," she responded. "Rex *does*. If you want them, I suggest you wait."

Aly shook her head and backed away. "No. This has gone on long enough. I need to call my mom. I need to—" Prickles spread across her entire body and her breath snatched in her chest from their intensity. She shivered so hard her teeth clattered together, prompting Will to shoot her a concerned look.

"Elaine," he snapped. He stepped in front of Aly as a tingle intensified the prickle. With clenched fists, he growled. "Stop it."

Elaine met him with a scowl, copying his position. "I've been training. Have you?"

"Never stopped," Will spat and something in his voice changed. It seemed deeper, somehow, with an accent Aly couldn't identify. "I can do things now you will *never* circumvent. If you wish for me to share, cease hostilities."

One final ripple down her spine and the prickles returned to a tingle and Aly gasped with relief.

Will held his position a moment longer, then, as he shook his hands out of their clenched fists, Aly's tingle vanished. "You okay?" he asked Aly.

Rubbing her arms, she voiced her thoughts. "It's... different when you do the augmentation thingy. Stronger, I think. I can't really... I don't know."

"Interesting," Elaine said, regarding Aly.

"Give her some warning," Will replied and pointed his finger at Elaine. "Threaten her and you threaten me. Make sure Rex knows that."

Elaine looked displeased. "Her safety is paramount. Rex made that perfectly clear."

"Safety is a state of mind," Will responded. "You force her to do anything and she protests, I will stop it."

"Right here, you know," Aly muttered, disliking the way they talked about her as though she wasn't there. Will looked at her with an inquiring expression. She threw her shoulders back. "If I said, 'I want to go home', what would you do?"

Will's hands went to his pockets as his shoulders

hunched. "See that you got home."

Aly heard his unspoken words. She'd likely never see him again. Never learn more about what he was and his life. He'd fade into memory. Whatever occurred between them, she didn't want that. When she thought he was dead, all she wished for was more time. Now she had it. Looking to Elaine, Aly said, "Give me one reason why I should see this Rex guy."

Her lips thinning as she pressed them together, Elaine shook her head. "I have no compelling reasons. All I know is he wants to see you."

"And after?"

Elaine shrugged. "No idea. It depends on why Rex wants to see you. Pretty sure it's connected to those Purists. You have no guarantees they won't come after you again, especially since they're taking other girls with your name."

Aly chewed on her bottom lip. Although Elaine's words troubled her, the need to have the appearance of having a choice in the whole situation overrode common sense. "I want to call my mom. Then I'll see Rex."

Will nodded. "Okay."

Elaine shook her head. "I'm not allowed to—"

"We're not kidnapping her," Will snapped. "And until you cross that line, she has a right to do so."

Elaine ground her teeth. "What are you going to tell her?"

Aly said, "That I'm safe and not to worry."

"And the police?"

Aly shuffled, unsure.

"You have to have a plan," Elaine continued with an air of smugness. "This isn't the kind of thing where you can just say you're safe and everything'll be fine. There are *other* girls taken, girls we haven't liberated yet. What if your phone call to your mom means the media gets wind of an escape, the Purists assume *you* must be his daughter and kill the other girls—do you want that on your conscience?"

Aly covered her mouth with her hands. "No."

Will glared. "That was unnecessary."

Elaine didn't appear fazed and shrugged. "It's up to you."

Will rubbed the back of his neck, looked at Aly and waited. Aly fidgeted, kicking the dirt with her toe before she walked to the back door of the car.

To give Aly some space, Will sat in the front. Elaine's duffle bag sat on the floor behind him, allowing Aly to stretch out along the back seat. Elaine switched on a CD of classical music; Will grimaced and complained about her taste. Both of them ignored Aly's tears.

Staying quiet, Aly wiped her face and ate her sandwiches, glad to have something to fill her grumbling belly. When that was done, she stared out into the world until, exhausted, she closed her eyes.

What seemed like moments later, Aly jerked forward in the seat with a cry, jolting awake as Elaine locked up the brakes. The car slid on the road, the tires screeching as the car spun sideways. Aly caught a flash of a barricade of cars and then green as the car turned.

"Get down!"

Metallic pings splattered against the passenger side door. The front and back windows shattered, spraying glass. The windshield cracked. A tire exploded, punctured by a bullet. The wheel hit the edge of the road at the wrong angle and the next thing Aly knew, the car was airborne.

CHAPTER 18

Visible through the broken windshield was a lot of green. Some sort of dense forest. Ferns, trees, shrubs, wildflowers, moss and bracken-covered ground.

Aly fought for consciousness. She was upside down. Something ran up her face. Her limp arms were pooled against the roof of the car. Something warm dripped onto her palm.

With eyes that wouldn't remain open at the same time, Aly tried to see. Will's mop of hair hung on its end. He didn't move. Aly blinked one eye, then the other. She felt foggy. A pressure against her chest, the seatbelt. Breathing hurt, but not as much as not breathing.

She could smell… what was it? … blood… fear… burned rubber and the fiery stench of leaking fuel. Coughing, she trailed her fingers along the pressure on her chest until they reached the buckle. It didn't want to release and she couldn't remember how to work it.

The buckle release was unexpected and she landed in a heap on the battered roof of the car. Ankles up near her head, it took her a moment to orientate herself. Fingers found the door latch and it creaked, stalling part-way open, so she crawled through the broken window instead.

Nowhere in her mind did she register a lack of pain.

Crawling from the wreckage, she felt grass beneath her. Her chin stung and she wiped her mouth with the back of her hand, leaving a smear of blood. Her eyes slid across the trees, unfocused. Prickles fired along her arms in warning.

From the row of cars spread across the road, people approached.

Will! Will was in the front seat. She staggered around the car to his door. Stuck, it creaked heavily and didn't move. Dropping to her knees, she peered through the broken window.

His eyes were closed. Blood splattered against the deflating airbag. He was held in place by the seatbelt. Reaching out a hand that wouldn't stop shaking, she searched for a pulse.

"You, get the girl."

Aly woke up fully. Her eyes snapped to the approaching man as the danger she was in became forefront in her mind.

Elaine. She appeared awake, if groggy, but Aly wasn't sure she could reach her. Instead, she scrambled for Will, unclipping the belt. He collapsed on top of her and she grunted. Looping her hands under his arms she tugged, inching him out of the car through the window. He tangled in the door and she heaved. "C'mon!"

Something tore. Will popped free of the car and they crumbled in a heap perpendicular to it. The man was coming and the rest waited at distance. They were going to hurt Will and she couldn't allow that. She couldn't carry him and they'd catch her if she dragged him, but she wouldn't leave him to be killed. What was left?

She shot a wild glance at Elaine, who now struggled with her seatbelt. Then her attention fell on the gun tucked into Will's jeans.

She lunged for it. Will was heavy and awkward and her legs were trapped by his weight. The car door offered little cover but the distorted front wheel hid her actions from the approaching man. Aly knew she didn't have long. As the man came level to the upside-down hood of the car, she found the safety, then, with shaking hands, her finger hovered over the trigger and the muzzle pointed at the man.

"Stay back!"

The man dove out of sight. "Drop your weapon!"

"Stay away!" Aly screeched. Her broken hand gripped the front of Will's shirt, the other shakily holding the gun as she wriggled her way out from beneath him.

"Drop the weapon!" the man called again.

If she angled herself right, Aly could see his foot and judged he cowered near the hood. For a brief moment, she wondered if she could shoot him through the windows of the car. The thought appalled her. Feet freed and Will's head cushioned on her lap, she had no idea what to do now. She had a weapon, little coverage, an unconscious man, a broken wrist and no chance of hiding. "Who are you? What do you want?"

"We're trying to help—"

She couldn't believe his gall. "You're lying! You gunned us down!"

"You need to calm down—"

She laughed, a bitter, harsh sound. "Look, I don't know who you are or what you want, but you've got the wrong girl."

"Trust me, we can—"

"Please," her voice cracked. Strength drained from her and her arm drifted down until it rested on Will's chest. Sobs bubbled up from her belly. "I just want to go home." She bent in half, encircling Will's head. "Please. I can't do this. I want to go home."

Something niggled at her and it wasn't the pinpricks firing up her arms. Pain wormed around the edges of her awareness, squirming its way in through the cracks of faltering adrenaline. She pressed her head against Will's, tears dripping onto his cheeks.

Will's eyes snapped open. He blinked at Aly, his eyes searching hers. He reached up to cup her cheek and his thumb brushed away the tears. She tried to smile for him, but it crossed her features as more of a grimace. His lips parted, forming her name and she nuzzled his hand.

A shadow loomed. "Easy. There's a good girl."

Will's gaze flicked away and the moment shattered as he took the gun from her and fired. The man cried out and hit the ground.

Ears ringing, Aly fell away from Will in shock. He rolled off her lap, onto his knees and flowed upward to fire over the car. Her hands covered her mouth in horror, then her face so she couldn't see.

"Take cover!" Will gripped the front of her dress, dragging her so she was shielded by the slanted hood. "Elaine!" He fired his gun again and ducked down behind the car.

"They're retreating."

Aly lifted her knees and buried her head in them. Her hands covered her ears, fingers in her hair clawed against her skull. Didn't want to see, didn't want to know, and couldn't feel.

"Ammo?"

"Grab the duffle bag."

He'd killed before. He'd been forced to kill at the Institute, obeyed orders because he didn't know any different.

Will's foot nudged her. "Aly, grab the duffle bag."

He knew different now.

Was the man dead?

Aly peeked open one eye but she couldn't see him. Another gunshot and she squeezed her eyes shut again with a whimper.

"Shit, we don't have time for this." His whole leg bumped against her, pushing her sideways. "Aly!"

Aly blinked and looked up at him. There was a dark

patch on the back of his jacket; blood that seemed to glisten. The blood on his face also shared the shimmer and she was lost to the shine.

"We need to go," he snapped at Aly. "Get the duffle bag!"

The back passenger door was kicked open and the duffle bag tossed out. "Got it," Elaine said, climbing out as well.

"You okay?" Will asked, squatting down to rummage through the bag for ammunition.

"Yup," Elaine said, dragging out a pair of pistols. She eyed Will's back as she loaded them. "You?"

"Patched," he rolled his shoulder. "Needs more work but I don't think I have the time to concentrate. Aly's in shock. Run or fight?"

Elaine stood, stretching both weapons out and firing of the top of the car. Six shots in all before she ducked down behind the upturned car for cover. "Run." She reached into the duffle and pulled out a grenade and a smoke bomb. "These'll give us a chance."

A grin spread across Will's face. "Blow the car?"

Elaine's grin was as manic as Will's. "Blow the car."

Aly whimpered.

Elaine threw the smoke grenade into the carriage of the car. Will fired over the top to keep people away. There was a hiss and smoke bloomed. "This'll confuse them," Elaine said, hunkered down by the door. "Go!"

Will grabbed Aly's wrist, pulling her up and over his shoulder in one swift moment. Then, concealed by the plume of smoke, he charged off into the surrounding forest with Elaine a few steps behind him.

Neither of them turned at the sound of the car exploding, but Aly could see the inferno occurring between the trees. She gripped Will's shirt so she could lift herself up to see. The men who had been accosting them were recoiling or shielding themselves from the heat of the blast.

Another black car screeched up to the barricade from behind and a man leaped out. Unruly hair and beard, his somehow familiar face was twisted with horror. Behind him, Aly thought she saw her mother exit the car.

She lost sight of the fire as the forest closed around them. Will and Elaine ran on.

The ground wasn't even; it rose and fell like the swell of the ocean and Elaine and Will followed its wave with ease. They bounded over logs and rocks, dodging trees as though the obstacles weren't there. Aly couldn't imagine sprinting through a forest; she'd likely fall and break something.

Aly's trip wasn't as smooth. Bounced and jostled, her head bobbed and her stomach flopped with every step. Even holding onto him didn't make the trip easier. Will's bony shoulder mixed with gravity wasn't kind.

"Remind you of old times?" Elaine laughed as she bounded over a fallen log.

There was humor in Will's voice when he answered, "Somewhat."

"Face it; you missed this."

"This? No." He laughed. "You, I missed."

Aly endured as long as she could. The rough travel was too much for her. "I'm gonna be sick."

Barely managing to stumble away after she was on the ground, Aly rid herself of the little she'd had to eat that day into a bush of ivy. Dizzy, sore and confused, she slumped at the base of a tree and wiped her mouth with the back of her hand.

"We can't stay here." Elaine planted her duffle bag on the ground and caught her breath. "You should fix yourself while you have a chance."

Hands on his hips as he panted, Will nodded. "Yeah."

Aly raised her head. "Fix yourself?" Lifting her hands, she saw blood stained palms and her eyes zeroed in on the blood on his shirt. "Are you hurt?" It didn't seem possible, after all the running, he could be hurt.

Will waved his hand at her. "It's nothing."

She would have liked to get up, but her legs felt like jelly. She tilted her head. "You're sparkling."

Elaine and Will exchanged worried glances.

"I mean, your blood is." She touched a finger to her head. "There." Her fingers plucked at her shirt. "There."

Will touched his head in the place where she indicated, looking at the blood on his fingers. "I'm what?"

"You've done that before," she murmured. Turning her eyes to Elaine, she said, "You don't sparkle." She laughed. "Guess you're not a vampire." The laughter died. "I think I saw... but that's not possible... I mean, it could be, right? She wasn't really there. With the whole 'any form' thing it could—"

Will stared at her. "Did you hit your head?"

Aly blinked and lost her train of thought. "Huh?"

Elaine snorted. Rummaging through her bag, she grabbed a sniper rifle. Shouldering her bag again, she headed back in the direction they'd come. "I'll cover us. We don't have long."

"Understood," Will replied. He rested his back on a tree close to Aly and slid down until he sat at the base. "Aly, I'm shifting for a moment, okay?"

"Uh-huh." She looked up into the foliage, her hands resting on her lap. "Why?"

He extended his long legs in front of him. "I'm able to heal myself, but it takes a bit of concentration."

She focused on his chest. "You're hurt?"

He dismissed it again. "It's nothing."

"You said that before."

He wouldn't look at her. "Nothing I can't fix. Rest a bit, but don't sleep."

"Not tired."

"Just loopy?"

She considered. She didn't feel right; her brain didn't seem to be able to filter her mouth like it usually did. Plus, she was hallucinating. Penelope hadn't been there. "A bit.

Sorry."

Will nodded. "Don't apologize. None of this is your fault."

"Who were those guys?" she asked, and then her arms layered tingles. "Oh. Right. Sorry." She studied her arms, watching as the wave of tingles tumbled over them. The feeling was interesting, like someone blowing on her skin. She wished she had more time to study them. Maybe if she knew how they worked, she wouldn't have to endure them. Her thinking felt thick and all she could do was stare at the patterns the tingles made as they swept over her skin. Oddly, they seemed similar to Will's diamond scales and Aly wasn't sure what that meant. Or if they were really there.

Will broke the silence. "Did they decide on a prom theme?"

Aly blinked, then pulled a face. "Grace said Victorian era."

"Ahh."

"Ruffles, corsets, pleated skirts. All that."

"Tamara'll be pleased."

Aly giggled. "Del's going to wear a top hat."

Will gave a pained laugh and pushed his hand onto his side. "What about you?"

"I'm not wearing a top hat."

"No, I mean a dress. Does the Victorian era have slinky dresses? You'd look nice in a—"

She tilted her head and frowned. "What makes you think I'm going?"

Will frowned. "Why wouldn't—"

Her legs didn't feel like jelly anymore. The world wasn't swimming, but she wasn't sure she should get up just yet. "My date died."

Will blanched and hung his head. "Oh. Right."

"Kinda puts a dampener on the event."

"Yeah." Will reached under his shirt, fiddling with something. He grimaced, grunted, then shoved something

240

in his pocket.

"What was that?" Aly asked.

He wrinkled his nose. "Bullet."

Aly jolted. "What?"

"I've had worse." He waved his hand at her, dismissing her worry.

"That's not the point!"

"I'm fine. You don't need to worry—"

"Fletcher!" she scolded. "You just ran all this way with a—"

He gave her a look. "Decided I am Fletcher, then?"

Aly clicked her teeth together and stared at him. She turned her face away while keeping her eyes focused on him. "Well… You're both idiots. You have that in common."

His smile was lopsided and so Fletcher that it made her heart hum in her chest. "I know."

She itched under her cast. "You said you would have left anyway."

The smile melted into sadness. "Yes. When you went to college… I was… just going to fade."

That surprised her. "Not die?"

"No. I wouldn't have done that if I had a choice." He sighed. "College changes things. I thought… you'd go away, make new friends, have other boyfriends…" His lips twisted bitterly. "Go on without me. I'd fade back to the 'best friend in high school' memory. Cherished, but not needed anymore."

It hurt he thought so little of his importance in her life and that she was the sort of person who would allow their friendship to deteriorate. "You really thought I could do that to you?"

He sighed. "I don't know, Als. I don't even know if I could've gone through with it. I… kept making excuses. I think… if they'd never come after me, I would've kept making them."

"Hmm."

"Forgive me?"

She held up her hands, fingers spread. "I remain Snicker-less."

He laughed, a gentle peal with a hint of relief.

She smiled, even though she didn't feel humor. Her tingles died and she assumed he was finished. "Are you okay?"

"Yup." He got to his feet and stretched, twisting his torso from side to side. "All better. You?"

She watched him. "I don't know."

He knelt in front of her. He checked both her eyes, then ran his fingers over her head. "Couple of bumps," he said. He touched her chin and she hissed but kept her face still. "You've cut your chin, deep, but it's congealed already." Lifting both her hands up, he held them in his palms. "Couple of other scrapes. Nothing too serious."

Tingles spread and vanished fast enough to make her shudder. "That's getting old, fast."

"I don't normally shift this often," he said with an apologetic smile and his eyes scanned her from head to toe. "No broken bones… oh, your wrist is healing nicely."

She frowned. "How…?"

"X-ray vision," he said with a wry smile.

She started. "You're messing with me!"

"Nope." He squeezed the fingers of her broken hand. "S'how I knew."

That made sense. "Oh."

He nodded at her head, concentrating on a spot above her ear. "Nasty bump. Explains why you're out of it. You must've hit the window. You may be concussed." Another tingle and Aly guessed he returned his sight to normal.

Aly bit her lip.

"What?"

She dropped her eyes. "That guy… you shot him."

"Oh." He gently placed her hands on her lap and withdrew. "Yes. I did."

Aly swallowed and met his gaze. "Did you kill him?"

"Does it matter?" he asked.

"I... I don't..."

"He took it in the shoulder. He should be fine."

"Oh."

After a long, searching moment, Will said, "I have killed before. Might be forced to again. I don't expect you to be okay with that but it is part of who I am. And it's not a part I can shift."

No excuses. None at all. He didn't deny it. Didn't make light of it. Didn't try and convince her of right or wrong. It only was. She could either accept it or not. But why did he look as though the last nail had been hammered into the coffin of their friendship?

Elaine cleared her throat as she walked toward them. "We have a problem."

Will stood, alert. "What?"

Sniper rifle placed on the ground, Elaine dumped her bag, yanked the zip down and thrust away the sides to reveal an assortment of weapons. "They have Faceless. And they're not ones I recognize."

"Not ones you recognize?" Will asked. "How is that possible?"

Elaine added a different sight to her weapon. "The instances are occurring with more frequency," she explained. "Darcy is branching out. These new batches, they can't shift, but they're already..." She sighed. "They're Solomon. Whatever Darcy has done, they're all like Solomon."

Will stared at Elaine, then turned and punched a tree and swore.

"What does that mean?" Aly asked, startled by Will's vehemence.

"There's a movie," Elaine said, watching Will. "Hulk. Have you seen it?"

Aly nodded, her eyes on Will as he thudded his forehead against the same tree. Fletcher always made excuses not to watch it or anything with that character in it; something she hadn't understood at the time.

"You know how he changes back from that?" she continued and left her sniper rifle on the ground beside her to pull out another gun. "Becomes Bruce Banner again?"

"Yeah."

"We can't," Will said, his voice cracking. "Shift dysplasia. We can't return. Shift too fast, too angry, too much and do it wrong and it's all over. Solomon... he did it out of anger and love and hate and... he got stuck and couldn't... It killed him. It killed a lot of hims."

"Darcy's been trying to get shifter clones into that form and stable," Elaine said. "They don't have a long life and they're a *bitch* to fight."

Will eyed her. "Fought them before?"

"Ran from them. If it were just you and me, we could try." Elaine tossed Will several pistols. "But not with her. Can't risk it." With a frown, she heaved off her jacket and tossed it at Aly. "Put that on. It's better than the blue."

Nodding, Aly shoved an arm into one of the sleeves.

"Can't risk them getting to Rex either," Will said, and checked the pistols were loaded and safety engaged.

"Camp can clear within twenty," Elaine said. "And I know where it is. If we're sneaky and fast, they'll have a hard time tracking us."

"How far?" Will shoved one of the guns into the belt of his jeans, offering the handle of the other to Aly. Aly took it, storing it in one of the pockets of Elaine's jacket, and finished buttoning up the front.

Elaine noted the exchange. "Can she shoot?"

"Yep," he responded, sounding proud. "Even sniped me once."

Elaine raised an eyebrow. "Oh?"

"Paintball," Will answered. "She's pretty good with traditional weapons too."

Elaine smiled and shook her head. "Made sure of that, huh?"

"Grace's dad's a cop," Will said with a light laugh. "Came in handy."

Aly gave Will a look. "I'm not shooting anyone."

He shrugged at her. "Precaution only."

Extracting a sawn-off shotgun and an ammunition belt, Elaine tossed them to Will. "Here."

Clipping the belt around his waist, Will bent to tie the holsters to his thigh. "You kept this?" he asked, looking at the shotgun. His hands caressed the stock like he was greeting an old friend.

"It's a good gun," Elaine replied. She zipped up the bag and grabbed the handle. "Let's go."

Storing the shotgun in one holster and the handgun in the other, Will turned his back to Aly and crouched.

Aly didn't like that idea. "I can—"

"You have one shoe," Will told her.

"It's a long run," Elaine added. "And you won't be able to keep up, not with us."

"I can manage—"

"Plus, you hit your head," Will said. "Now, stop complaining or I'll carry you over my shoulder again."

Aly pulled a face. "Ass."

He grinned. "Yup. Hurry up."

Clambering onto his back, she muttered, "I don't like this."

"I know," he said, putting his hands under her thighs to help support her as he stood up.

Aly looped her arms around Will's neck. "Do you need to shift?"

Glancing at Elaine, Will said, "No. I'm good."

"So. Um… giddyup?"

Will laughed.

CHAPTER 19

Within minutes, Aly decided being carried by a shifter charging through the woodlands was ten times worse than any rollercoaster she'd ever been on. Rollercoasters were thrilling and fun, this was not.

The pair didn't travel at constant speeds or directions. They changed everything at a whim, from slowing down to check their surroundings, to sprinting through the woods. She had no control over the situation and her seat grew uncomfortable the longer she stayed on. Her legs were cramped, her arms hurt, she was sick to her stomach and she felt dizzy. No talking beyond the occasional call of "Pothole!" from either Elaine or Will.

Even when they slowed to a walk so Elaine could check behind, Will didn't allow Aly to slide from his back. Although the brief interludes did help her stomach settle, once he started running again, the nausea was quick to return. Closing her eyes didn't help. Having her eyes open didn't help either, not when the woodlands passed at a rate much faster than she could run. She found fixing her sight on the nape of Will's neck was her best solution and even that wasn't much better.

She supposed she should be grateful they weren't

running close to trees or catching her clothes on stray branches or powering through groves of ivy. Their twisted route kept them clear of most obstacles.

Despite all Will's claims of being different, it appeared sweating was a normal body function. She realized how much when he altered his grip on her thigh, the spot vacated created a sudden chill and the new purchase felt clammy.

She endured for as long as she could, but when they reached a rock stream, Aly'd had enough. "I need to get down."

Elaine, having crossed the stream, paused, "That's probably not a good—"

"My legs are cramping, my butt is numb, I'm thirsty and Fletcher's sweating like a pig."

"I'm what?" Will panted and he paused, poised on a stone halfway across the stream.

"It's gross." She squirmed hard enough so his clammy hands slipped from her leg and one foot touched the ground.

"Aly—"

"We can keep moving; I just want to walk for a while." She pawed at him until he released her other leg. "How far away are we?"

"Hmm," Elaine said, studying their surroundings. "I'm hoping we'll come up on a nest soon, we can borrow their vehicle."

"Nest?" Aly asked, shaking her legs to get the blood flowing through them again.

"A lookout," Will supplied, keeping a hand on her to steady her.

"So, it's probably better we don't go charging in," Aly said.

"Yeah," Elaine agreed. "Probably." She looked the way they'd come, then upward at the trees. "We should have lost them by now. I'll scout."

"Okay," Will responded.

Elaine started to walk away and paused. "Um… Aly, I'll probably be shifting a bit."

Aly nodded and smiled. "Thanks for the heads up."

Elaine returned the nod, then jogged away.

Looking down at the trickling river, she crouched at the bank and ran her hand through the cool water. "Can I drink this?"

"Free flowing," Will responded and crouched down beside her. "Should be fine." He cupped his hand, dipped it in the water and lifted it to his mouth. "Tastes okay."

Aly cupped her hand and copied Will's action, wishing she could use both hands to drink her fill.

"You okay?" Will asked.

"Please stop asking me that," Aly said.

"Right."

After drinking, she washed her face and the back of her neck. "What's this Rex like?"

Will paused, then shook his hands free of water. "I'm not sure I'm the best person to ask."

She snorted. "You're the only person I can ask."

Will considered. "He's… do you think he might be your dad?"

Aly sighed. Hopping up onto a rock, she crossed the water. "I think… there's lots of things going on right now I have no clue about and I'm trying to make sense of things. Do you think he could be? If he's a shifter, he'd have aliases… maybe that's why that woman thought I was his daughter?"

"I don't know."

"Does he…" she frowned. "I suppose it would be pointless to ask if he looks like me."

Will scratched his chin. "I don't know how… Actually… Um…" He rubbed the back of his neck. "Well… let's put it this way. I can change everything, yeah? Right down to blood type, genetic composition and such."

Aly nodded, knowing what he meant in a roundabout way.

"Other shifters can't do as much as I can. It's more… a surface change. A skin shift, I guess, if you want to call it that."

"So… no eye change either?" Prickles flittered up her arm, not as strong as she expected and Aly assumed Elaine was shifting.

"Sometimes. Depends on the skill of the shifter."

"How would they do different faces then? Padding?"

"Something like that." Will shrugged. "It's complicated."

"Everything's complicated."

Will barked out a laugh. "Yeah." Losing the smile he said, "I think, if he was, you'd share characteristics with his natural form."

"And do I?"

Will tugged at his hair at the back of his head. "Aly… you have pictures of him, right?"

"A few fuzzy old ones." It was her turn to shrug. "You know Mom."

"She doesn't like to mention him."

"No." She flashed him a smile. "And you're avoiding the question."

Will sighed. "I am."

"Well?"

"Well… Um…"

She stared. "Fletcher."

He closed his eyes and looked thoughtful. Aly got the impression he cataloged in his mind. "Yeah. There… could be some resemblance." Opening them up again he said, "Doesn't mean a thing."

"Yeah. Right." She turned away. "Doesn't explain the 'Madeline Spenser' part either."

"No."

Aly sighed. "Which way?"

Will stood and dusted off his hands. "Shifting; sec."

Aly turned her gaze away as the tingles ran down her arms. After a moment, Will said, "Straight ahead. Elaine will join us in a minute."

Aly nodded and began to walk. "So… tell me what happened after you escaped."

Will sighed. "No."

Surprised, Aly glanced over her shoulder. "Why not?"

He followed sedately. "It's not important."

That confused her. He'd been so open about everything else. "It's a part of you."

"Not a very good part," Will said. "I worked for Rex for a while, got disgruntled and left. That's about it."

"Doing what?"

He made a frustrated noise then said, "Aly, I need my secrets. I can't— I *won't* tell you everything. I've told you all I'm willing to let you know."

She blinked several times in rapid succession, then turned away.

Will sighed and jogged forward to walk beside her. "Look—"

"I get it," she responded and tried to subtly step away, putting a tree between them. "You don't have to tell me anything."

"And now you're back to pouting," he said with a groan. "I can't win."

"So what if I am?" she snapped and brushed past a shrub, startling a bird hiding in its nest. "I'm just trying to understand and if you're not willing to—"

"Don't be petty."

With a scowl, she said, "You know what? Don't talk to me."

Will rolled his eyes. "Aly—"

"Nope."

"C'mon—"

"It's strange," she told him as she walked through the woodlands. "All I've wanted to do for ages was to get out of Bellhollow and on my own. Go traveling. Do things on my own terms. Now, all I want to do is *go home*. So shut up and get me there."

Will stared at her for a long moment. "Rude."

"Bite me." She slid down a small ditch that had been too wide to step across, stubbing her toe on a rock at the bottom. Pain made her eyes water and she hopped on one foot so she could rub her toes.

"Aly—"

Aly raised one hand to him, the other rubbing her toes. Turning her head away so he didn't see her tears of frustration, she snapped, "Just leave me alone."

"You're being ridiculous." He huffed, thrusting his hands into his pockets and kicked at the ground. Another noisy huff as she decided to ignore him and rub her toes. He growled. "You can hate me later," he snapped and hopped down into the ditch. Two steps and he was beside her and Aly found herself thrown over his shoulder.

"Put me down!"

"I'm doing what I'm told," he said. "I'm getting you home. The faster we get there, the faster you get back to your life."

Struggling to get into a position where she could hit him, she kicked her legs. "I do *not* need to be carried!"

"On my back or over my shoulder. Your choice."

"I choose to walk."

"That wasn't an option."

"I hate you!"

His step slowed. "No, you don't."

Aly's teeth grated together. "Put me down!"

"Nope."

She itched to smack him to stop the smug tone of voice. "I have a gun and I'm not afraid to use it!" she threatened, not even sure she could reach the gun from her current position.

"That's fine," he replied, his attention elsewhere.

"That's *fine*?" she shrilled, incensed.

A tree trunk splintered near them, wood cracking as the tree fell. Aly caught sight of something big charging through the woodlands for them. Her stomach dropped to her toes and panic replaced the anger.

Will yanked her so she was in his arms rather than over his shoulder and propelled them into the woodlands. Aly wove her arms around his neck and held on. She tried to see but couldn't catch more than glimpses. "What is that?"

"Something I'd rather not engage," he told her. "Just hold on!"

Aware of every second Will ran, Aly was equally aware the thing chasing them gained ground. Where Will had to dip and dodge trees, the thing crashed through them. She didn't even want to consider how much strength the thing must have if it could break trees. Granted, most of the younger trees in the woodland were about as thick as her arm, but it was still a feat to break them.

No hiding place in sight, their only hope was to outrun and that hope was dwindling.

She worried. There was a limit to Will, she knew, as there would be a limit to anyone's stamina. Carrying her and running as he was, he'd exhaust himself before long and then what would they do?

The prospect of having to fight terrified her. "What are we gonna do?"

Will changed his grip on Aly so that the hand on her back was down toward her bottom and she was supported along one arm. With a free hand, Will leaped for a larger, sturdier tree, bounding up it like some sort of monkey. His climb was a lot less graceful than expected. He had to work for every foot of height. His knees knocked into her as he constantly changed his grip. Aly wasn't sure it was a good idea, seeing how fast the thing had mowed down trees, but she didn't have a better one.

Hidden among the foliage, Will planted her feet on a branch and pressed them both to the trunk. He heaved in several breaths before he held it and peered down to the ground.

The bark of the tree was rough against her back and Will's chest pushed against her to make them as small as possible. Aly was grateful Elaine's camouflage jacket helped hide her. Will's braced arms meant it was difficult to see down and Aly thought that was a good thing. She didn't want to see whatever panted and grunted below. A part of her said "gorilla" or "bear", but she knew it wasn't possible. Not when whatever it was below wore clothes.

Will's breath tickled her neck as he released it. He turned his head, peering down the other side of the branch and Aly got the impression the thing was under them. She dropped her head back so it rested against the bark and looked straight up into the sky. Concentrating on her breathing helped the pure terror bubbling inside her.

The thing below them roared. Aly heard a crunch and the sapling beside them fell. Aly had to cover her mouth with her hands to keep from screaming.

Will's hand landed over hers, his eyes boring into hers. With a tiny shake of his head, he mouthed "no".

Aly closed her eyes, feeling tears leaking from the corners. Even though he hid it well, Will's terror melted into her. She'd never seen him terrified before and she didn't want to now.

Will's hand lifted away as he returned to watching the thing, but she kept her hands on her mouth to muffle any sounds.

Another crack as another sapling tree was smashed. Aly flinched. Will tensed and he pressed against her so her face was on his shoulder. She felt rather than heard the rumble and *shh*. With a shudder, Aly shook her head as though her denial of what occurred could change it. Will's hand pressed against the back of her head.

Not knowing, not seeing how close the creature was, not knowing if it knew where they were and was toying with them, not seeing if the next tree it hit was theirs so she could brace took its toll on Aly. She had to know, had to see. She peeked out underneath Will's arm and caught sight of the thing.

It was wrong. Wrong. Everything was wrong. It didn't

flare up the tingles, but the wrongness swelled.

With mottled lips stretched thin over misshapen bone, the wrongness met her gaze. Two fists hit their tree and the reverberations trembled up the trunk to shake the branch they perched on. Aly screamed, her hands muffling the sound.

The fists arched and plummeted toward the tree. It shook again and Aly teetered from the force. Will spun her in a deft movement so her chest was against the tree and Aly grabbed at the trunk to anchor herself.

Will unclipped his shotgun. "Stay here," he said, and jumped off the branch before Aly was even aware he had moved.

"Wait! No!"

The shotgun fired and the wrongness roared. Aly wasn't in a position to see if Will had hit his mark. Peering down, she caught a glimpse of Will on the thrashing being's back. Branches snapped and small trunks crumbled against the flailing hands and Aly felt the tree being hit again.

It wasn't safe up here. It wasn't safe on the ground. But she couldn't see and at least on the ground she'd have a better chance of being able to dodge.

The gun was heavy in her pocket and she couldn't pretend it was a paintball gun. Shooting someone might become a necessity. It felt painfully real. Aly knew, once she'd had a chance to truly stop and think, the situation would knock her off her feet and she'd curl up with a large tub of ice-cream, a bunch of Snickers and marathon *Scrubs* with Grace. Until then, she had to endure. Her life depended on it. Their lives.

Fletcher was alive and she wanted to keep him that way. She couldn't do it stuck up a tree. Sliding down the trunk, she sat on a lower branch and looked around for the next branch to climb down to, spotting it below and to the right. With a bit of inching and precarious balance, she stretched out her foot to it.

With a loud thump, Will cried out in pain. Startled, Aly fell down to the next branch. She clawed at the trunk and managed to keep herself from falling completely out of the tree. Twisting, she tried to see why he'd cried out. "Fletcher?!"

"Stay put!" he called. She saw him extract himself from a large shrub some distance away, but her view was obscured by a broad, muscular back.

Some part of her knew it was egotistical to think she could help someone who'd been military, though even a second distraction could give Will an opening. "I can help!"

"How?" he called.

Aly heard two more shots. Her shifter sense flared, sparking down her back. With a sharp, in-draw of breath, she scrambled down to the lower branches of the tree. Crouching on the branch, she got a good look. Elaine had been right; this thing was like an out-of-proportioned hulk-beast covered in clothes and with a mop of sand-colored hair. It didn't have a face. Not a human one. Just a gap for a toothy mouth, a small mound with holes which might have once been a nose with gray scales flapped over it and two pale eyes. Faceless, straight out of nightmares; is that what Will looked like too?

She felt sick.

Brute strength; Aly could only imagine what would happen if one of those hits connected with Will. The Faceless swung his arms with no care for what lay in their path. Sometimes they broke through trees, sometimes the trees stopped the blow and there was a shower of something, perhaps blood, from the Faceless' arm.

She didn't want it anywhere near her. "I'm a sitting duck up here!"

"He's not exactly smart!" Will said, rolling to one side to avoid a swipe. Pausing on a knee, he lifted his shotgun and fired point blank.

The Faceless didn't stop coming. It didn't even seem to

register it'd been shot.

Will made a noise of utter disgust. Leaping out of the way, he holstered the shotgun. "Check your pockets, I need a knife!" He snatched a rock from the ground and threw it. It bounced off the Faceless without even making it flinch.

She patted herself all over, checking both Elaine's jacket and the pocket of her apron on her uniform, watching each of Will's frantic dodges with bated breath. Aly likened it to some sort of bullfight: the Faceless charged, Will dodged out of the way and the Faceless would turn and charge again. There wasn't much time between charges. The speed the Faceless possessed when chasing them had diminished to a shamble. It was playing with them, taunting them.

No knife, but she found a small flash drive hidden deep in one of Elaine's pockets. "Nothing!"

"Shit!" Will cast a sweeping glance around the woodlands. He shook out his hands, his fingers wriggling. "Okay. Okay." Grabbing one of the taller, straight saplings, he kicked it with the side of his foot and yanked at the same time, breaking the sapling off. He tore off the top twigs and broke off the top of the tree. Holding it like a spear, he held the spiky end toward the Faceless and braced. "You need to run."

"I'm not leaving y—"

Will jabbed at the Faceless with his makeshift spear the next time the Faceless charged. With a roar, Aly saw a gash on the Faceless' arm as it spun. "Six o'clock. Go!"

Aly turned to the side, preparing to swing down to the ground. The ground below the tree was torn up; saplings with snapped trunks and ferns decimated beneath feet. Will had led the Faceless far so away she wasn't in immediate danger of a charge taking out her tree.

"Aly, go!" Will held the Faceless at distance with his spear. The Faceless stopped and focused completely on Will, its body swaying from side to side. Their eyes connected and they both seemed to freeze in place.

Aly dropped from the tree and the Faceless twisted toward her. Not willing to take her eyes off it, she crept backward. The Faceless snorted and Aly thought it intended to charge. The Faceless was massive; one swat and she would surely be killed. All bravado faded as terror filled her.

Will drew out his gun in a fluid motion and fired on the Faceless several times. As the Faceless swung back to Will, he jammed the end of his spear into the ground, angling the point to the Faceless' chest.

Aly's eyes widened. Knowing she didn't want to see this, she bolted in the direction Will told her to run. Behind her she heard several thumps, then something screeched.

Aly panicked. Branches flicked against her, twigs scratched her thighs as she crashed through the wilderness. She made no effort to be stealthy or hide her path. Her mind was blank with fear. All she saw was trees and shrubs and bare patches of ground.

Had to run, had to get away. Panicked heart and mind, her hands stretched out ahead of her as she tried to ward off the oncoming foliage. It seemed to be getting denser, the trees thicker and sturdier and the fern clumps more frequent and Aly realized she could hear running water. A lot of running water, the gushing sound of it soon filled her ears.

Then the ground fell away and Aly skidded to a halt, dropping to the ground to stop her momentum, teetering on a tree-covered embankment down to a flowing river. Her chest heaved, the panic subsiding enough to allow her to wonder why Will had sent her in this direction. Was she supposed to cross that?

Picking herself up off the ground, she leaned on a tree trunk and peered down the embankment. Steep, rocks at the bottom, falling into flowing water. She didn't think she could cross it, not from here. Perhaps there was a better place downstream, beyond the waterfall.

Turning, she looked the way she had come, just in time to be scooped up by Will and forced to run. Without pause, he threw them down the embankment, skidding sideways on the leaf debris on the ground. Aly's descent was chaotic. Dragged by Will and unsteadied by the sliding leaves beneath her feet, she couldn't stop as they reached the rocks by the riverside. Will leaped into the water, dragging Aly in behind him.

Cold engulfed her. It was shallower than she expected, but she was off balance. Water clogged her eyes, flooded her mouth. She couldn't tell up from down. She kicked and clawed at the water, her body was dragged along by the current and she lost Will in the chaos of the waterfall. Tumbling and spinning, her feet scraped pebbles at the bottom and her shoulder hit a rock. Pain sliced and made her dizzy.

Her scream bubbled and left an emptiness in her chest. No time to think, no time to act, the surface remained a swirl of light and white and... so far away. Breaking the surface for an instant didn't allow her time to do anything.

Everything was rock and water. She tried to stay afloat but the water pulled her under. Half of her breath was water and Aly had to fight against her natural instinct to cough. Blood pounded in her ears and her chest ached.

She was going to drown. This had always been her greatest fear. Losing herself to water.

Something grabbed her, something stronger than the current and Aly realized she could feel Will's hand on her arm. He pulled her up and she found the surface. Spluttering, she tried to see around the foaming water.

"Keep your head up!"

She tried, but the current was strong and she was disoriented. Even getting her feet angled in the direction they traveled was a battle. Will's hand kept them tethered together. He was stronger than her and Aly knew she would have lost her grip on him long ago. She couldn't even keep her head above water long enough to cough for much-needed help.

With a yank, Aly crashed into Will. His arm roped across her chest and shoulder and kept her head up. "Stop panicking," he told her. "Breathe."

She gulped in a breath and coughed. The longer he held her above the water, the more she caught her breath.

"Easy. Now, angle your feet."

Now she wasn't fighting for every breath, it was easier to get her body to do as it was told. It still took a little bit of nudging with Will's feet before she could.

"There. That's it. Now, hang on. Thirty seconds, at most."

Longest "thirty seconds" of her life.

By the time the river calmed and allowed them to wade to shore, Aly was exhausted. Supported by Will, when they reached the shore, he dumped her on the muddy bank and collapsed beside her.

His chest heaved as he lay on his back. Aly shivered from cold and nerves and stared up at the sky.

"That was wrong. Just wrong," Will muttered. "The regeneration was too fast. They must burn out so quick."

Aly, not really knowing what to say, remained quiet.

"What would even be the point?" he continued. "There'd only be so much military programming Darcy could do with such a short span. They're untrained. Brute strength. Maybe that's it. Hard and fast and over before anyone's really aware…" He huffed out a breath. "They're slow and they're dumb. At least I know how to contain one now." Covering his face with both hands, he moaned, "Elaine, what have you gotten me into now?"

Aly blinked. Where was Elaine? Should they go find her?

With another sigh, Will rolled toward her and propped himself up. Stretching out his hand, he rested it on her stomach. "Are you okay?"

She bit her lip. "I'm… alive."

He chuckled without any real humor. "That's a start." He pressed his lips together, then pulled a face. "We need to move. Catch your breath for a moment."

"Already?"

"It's not safe here." Will sighed. "Sorry," he added as an afterthought.

She grimaced. "I don't like it when you apologize. Do it three times in one day and the world'll get hit by a meteorite or something."

Will snorted.

She adjusted her head, then lifted both her hands to place them over the top of his. He lifted his fingers and spread them and she wove her fingers between his.

"I'll have you home soon," he promised.

Aly frowned. "What about you?"

Will looked remorseful. "I can't go back."

"You really think I can just go back to that life knowing about all this? Knowing about you and what you can do?"

"You have to," he said. "I need you safe."

"I'll never see you again. You weren't even gone a month and people kidnapped me."

"They took you because of my presence; you'll be safer with me gone."

"Bullshit."

His lips pursed in frustration. "Aly—"

"You're a shapeshifter," she reasoned. "Even if Fletcher's gone, you're not. You could come back as someone else."

"It's not that easy. I can't just slip back into Bellhollow. I worked hard to earn a place there."

"A place you're so willing to let go."

Will sighed.

"Where are you going to go? What are you going to do?"

"I'll figure it out. I always do."

"I could come with you," she said without thinking.

His face filled with remorse. "You can't."

She nodded, too tired to really feel anything. "Yeah. Thought so."

"Aly—" His head snapped up and his breath escaped in a rush. Pushing up from the ground, he scooped Aly and lifted, then bounced up the closest tree. Larger trees close to abundant water meant the foliage was thicker and the ground below obscured. They were hidden, at least by Aly's reckoning.

Squatting, Will sat Aly on a branch and bounded up one higher, peering down. He held a finger to his lips.

Aly rolled her eyes at him. He reached down to squeeze her shoulder to show he understood.

"Keep looking! Search downstream!" came a voice.

Aly's jaw dropped open and she jerked forward, only to be stopped by Will's hand. He shook his head at her and tapped his lips.

Not understanding why he'd want her to remain silent, she gestured. It was Elaine's voice. He nodded to show he knew.

A grunt from below and something big passed beneath the tree and Aly gasped. That Faceless! It was after Elaine!

Will clapped his hand over her mouth and mouthed, "I know" to her.

"Stupid lug," Elaine snapped. "You were supposed to capture him; not try to kill him."

Aly's eyes widened. Will moved his hand away from Aly's mouth and back to her shoulder.

"Go look! That way!" Elaine scolded, then her voice changed to contrite and Aly got the impression she was talking on the phone. "Sorry ma'am. We seem to have lost him. Bastard jumped into the river." She paused. "Yes ma'am, I understand how important he is… We were waylaid, I had to improvise." Another pause. "The girl?"

Will tensed and Aly turned her head to stare at him.

"No. No one special," Elaine continued. "She's not Braddock's daughter, the genealogy didn't match… of course, I checked… The Purists are idiots. She was in the wrong place at the wrong time. I couldn't ditch her without Noah getting suspicious... no, setting a trap won't work. He'll do a dump and run... because that's what you trained us to do, ma'am. No attachments... Noah's nobler than the rest of us, ma'am, and he's been out the longest. I guess he felt he had to... I agree, it wouldn't hurt to keep eyes on her for a while. Jonah would be best... yes, ma'am."

Elaine paused and her voice started to move away. "We'll keep looking. There's a lot more river left. Full report by morning."

Will bent over and his hand dove into Aly's left hip pocket. Startled by the suddenness, Aly resisted the urge to squeak. The surprise turned to curiosity when Will pulled out the flash drive Aly had discovered before. Rolling it between his fingers, Will leaned his head against the trunk of the tree and exhaled. "We'll stay here for a while," he said in a low voice.

Aly didn't trust herself to speak, still too stunned by what had occurred. Reaching across, she took Will's hand. He didn't react with more than a reassuring squeeze, so she got as comfortable as she could to wait.

In truth, she was glad for the chance to pause. She felt like she'd done nothing but move non-stop since she woke up in that deserted mall. The short nap in the car had done little to recharge her batteries.

Now she was wet and stuck up a tree. She wondered what the water would do to her plaster. She wondered what time it was, the sun hung in the sky and seemed to be getting lower. Mid to late afternoon? Hopefully, they wouldn't spend the night in the forest, but she had no idea what they would do next. She wondered about a lot of things.

Elaine had lied. But to who? And what had been the lie? Were there other girls or had Elaine used that to get Aly to come along? Did Rex really have anything to do with her or was it another lie? Who did Elaine work for?

Rex? Darcy? Or both? Double agent, perhaps? What was on the flash drive and how did Will know she had it? Had they done their silent communication? Questions piled up in her mind with few answers. If she voiced them, would Will tell her, since he was so adamant he would leave? Would she forever wonder?

She couldn't decide if Will leaving was better than believing he was dead. She supposed if he left —when he left— she could always believe he was fine. She'd never know if something happened to him and therefore he would always, in her mind, be fine. Never dying. Living his life without her in it.

It was really hard to think and her head throbbed. It took all her concentration not to go to sleep.

Will eventually stirred. He lifted her hand to his mouth and pressed his lips against the back, then, as he pressed her hand to his face, he shuddered out a sigh. Sensing finality in the gesture, she curled her fingers, squeezing his hand. Will raised his eyes to meet Aly's and held her gaze.

He couldn't come back to Bellhollow. She had to return home alone because if she didn't, whoever was on the phone with Elaine would know she was important to Will. They'd use her against him. If she went with him, her family might be in danger. She had to stay, and he had to go.

So many things she'd wanted to say but words failed her. If she broke this moment, there might never be another. She couldn't even memorize his features to conjure up on a rainy day. Instead, she memorized the sensation of her hand against his lips. The longing in his gaze. The emotion his name etched in her heart.

Neither of them moved. A fly tangled in a web of feeling she couldn't make sense of, cradled in the intensity of his eyes. This was an end, not a beginning. She didn't want to say goodbye.

Withdrawing, he closed his eyes. One last linger of his lips against her hand, her skin tickling where he touched her, and he released it. Without speaking, he clambered up the tree as high as he could go. Aly guessed he was looking for a road or landmark or something, a guess which was confirmed when she tingled. Scuttling down, he said, "Time to get you home."

CHAPTER 20

Will left her on the side of the road a mile from a gas station. One moment he was beside her, then he simply stopped walking and, with one final squeeze, let her hand go. Aly dropped Elaine's jacket on the ground and kept walking. She didn't look back. He didn't call to her to stop.

She supposed it wasn't Will anymore. He would have shifted away from Will's form as soon as he could. She needed to get used to calling him Noah in her head. If she ever saw him again.

She hoped she would. Even though he might never set foot in Bellhollow again, she had to hope he'd make contact with her one day. Meet for lunch. See her at college. Email. He couldn't just throw away everything they'd been through to hide where he was.

Tired, hungry, in pain and clad only in her uniform and one shoe, she walked the mile in the dark. The attendant took one look at her disheveled appearance, bloody chin and bruised head and asked her if she was okay. That was all it took for Aly to break down in tears and ask for help.

A whirlwind of activity occurred, with her in the center. The local sheriffs arrived ten minutes later, sirens blaring and flashing lights, with an ambulance in tow. The attendant, a lovely woman by the name of Sue, prepared her a hot chocolate and a fresh sandwich—which didn't stay down.

Aly gave them her name, her address, and then said the last thing she remembered was finishing work and then nothing. She couldn't remember. She told them there may have been a car ride. There might have been a forest. She acted confused, repeatedly asking who they were; where she was; what time it was; why was she cold; and where her mother was.

Will told her to feign amnesia rather than concoct a story that would have holes. Add to that the bumps on her head, the bruising, it would seem plausible. She knew enough about concussion she could feign some of its more severe symptoms, with enough actual symptoms to make it plausible.

Then came the ride to the hospital. Copious tests, blood work, X-rays, and re-plastering of her wrist. Fletcher's waterlogged note had disintegrated when she tried to pull it out.

With DNA and other evidence collected, statements taken, all tests running, she was finally allowed to shower and sleep. They said "overnight observation" because of the amnesia and tomorrow they'd discuss releasing her. Her parents had been contacted and were coming.

No one said a word about any other missing girls and Aly knew she couldn't ask or it would blow a hole in her story. It made her wonder if it were true, or whether Elaine had lied to get them to go with her.

She shied away from any sort of sleeping pill or relaxant. Not usually a light sleeper, Aly found herself startling at every noise and following every set of footsteps that passed her door. So when Penelope creaked open the door, Aly was still awake.

"Mom," Aly breathed and sat up in bed.

Surprised to find her awake, Penelope wasted no time in crossing the room to gather Aly in her arms. There were no words and there didn't need to be. Buried in her mother's arms, Aly felt safe. It was all over. Done. She could go back to her life.

"We were so worried," Penelope said in a voice that was thick with tears. Hands petted at Aly's head, Penelope peppered kisses around her head and face.

"I'm okay," Aly murmured, smiling as Roger poked his head through the door and looked relieved. Roger crossed the room to them, placing one hand on both of their backs.

"I had to know," Penelope whispered. "They said you were asleep, but I had to check."

"That's okay."

"I love you so much."

Aly buried her face in Penelope's shoulder and held on tight. "I love you too, Mom."

Penelope pulled away, cupping Aly's face with both hands. "Are you okay? What happened?"

Aly shrugged and feigned a sheepish look. "I can't remember." She touched her ear. "Hit my head, everything's blurry." Not a complete lie either, some of the events were already bleeding together.

"Concussion?" Roger asked as he reached for her chin to tilt her head, being careful not to touch the cut.

"They said so, yeah."

He nodded. "It happens. Especially with traumatic events. I'm not surprised."

"Have you eaten?" Penelope fussed. "Did you sleep?"

"Did you?" Aly countered. "You look so tired. You didn't have to come; it's the middle of the night."

Penelope brushed Aly's hair behind her ear. "Wild horses wouldn't have kept me away."

"Where's Tim?" Aly asked, torn between wanting to see her brother and not wanting to traumatize him with her appearance.

"With Nan and Pop," Penelope replied, indicating Roger's parents.

"Did you talk to the police?" Roger asked.

"Uh-huh. Basic stuff so they could search," Aly said. "I have a detective's card to call if I remember anything and they said something about coming back in the morning."

"We'll be present for that," Roger assured her.

"Thanks."

"Oh," Penelope lifted away from Aly. "We have a bag of things you might need; where'd it go?"

"Outside the door," Roger said. He strode across the room and Aly heard him speak to someone outside briefly before he came back in with a bag.

As Roger placed it on the end of the bed Penelope said, "Clothes, toiletries, things like that."

"Thanks," Aly said, glad for the chance to have her own clothes. Her uniform had been taken as evidence and the hospital gown itched and made her self-conscious.

Roger gave her shoulder a squeeze. "She needs to rest," he reminded Penelope. "We'll come back in the morning."

"Oh, she shouldn't be left alone," Penelope fussed, and pointed to the armchair in the corner. "There's a chair, I can—"

"I'm fine, Mom, really. You should sleep in a proper bed."

"I don't—"

"I'm really boring to watch sleep. The snoring is atrocious." Aly said, plastering on a fake smile.

"She's got a point, Poppy," Roger said with a chuckle. "Give her your phone, Aly can call if she needs anything."

Looking both torn and exhausted, Penelope nodded. "All right. We'll be back first thing," she promised, kissing Aly's head.

"Soon as we can," Roger said, adding his own kiss.

"Call if you need anything at all," Penelope said, placing her phone on the bedside table.

Aly nodded, suddenly exhausted as well. "Can... can you stay until I fall asleep?"

Penelope nodded and stroked Aly's hair. "Of course."

While she was woken at various points during the night by nurses doing rounds or odd noises, Aly did manage to get some sleep. Being able to change into her normal clothes was liberating, as well as being able to move around her room. She waited until eight before calling Grace on Penelope's phone.

"Penelope?" Grace answered, sounding scared. "Is everything—"

"Hey, it's me."

"Aly!" Grace screeched. "Oh my God! Are you okay? Are you hurt? What happened? Where are you?"

"Slow down," Aly said, laughing at Grace's winded words. "I'm fine."

Grace's voice trembled. "I was so scared!"

"I know; me too. I think. I can't remember much."

"You can't?"

"Concussion," Aly said, not knowing how much Grace had been told.

Grace sucked in a gasp. "Oh, nasty."

"I'm okay, otherwise," Aly said. "Bumps and bruises and bug bites."

"You weren't… um… you know… were you?"

"No," Aly assured her, knowing exactly what she'd meant. The police had asked the same question, only blunter. "I wasn't."

"Oh, thank God." A soft noise and Grace's voice was muffled. "It's Aly, she's okay!" More noises then, "You're on speaker."

"Aly-cat?"

"Hey, Del," Aly said, smiling even wider.

"You literally scared the shit out of me," Del said, sounding relieved.

"Well, that's a gross image," Aly said, teasing him.

"Literally," Grace added.

"Hey, I got it right. No, not right?" Del said, sounding unsure, and Aly had this image in her head of him looking at Grace with a forlorn expression.

"No," Grace said, then giggled.

"You should literally just stop using the word," Aly said.

"Aww."

The humor in Grace's voice faded. "When are you coming home?"

"Today. I hope. Pretty sure. There's probably some legal stuff I need to do, but yeah. I'm outta here the minute the doctors clear me." She paused and tried not to sound needy. "Will you guys meet me?"

"Of course," Grace soothed. "We'll camp out on your porch."

"So what happened?" Del asked.

"I can't remember," Aly replied.

"Concussion," Grace said.

"I thought it was amnesia?" Del asked, confused.

"No," Grace corrected. "Well, yeah. Concussion is when you hit your head. Amnesia is forgetting. But concussion can cause amnesia."

"Right," Aly said. "I have a nasty bump on my head and everything's fuzzy—" Someone behind her cleared their throat and Aly twisted, thinking it was a nurse or doctor and went stiff.

Belinda waited. Not the Belinda who Aly remembered. Not one dressed in black and green combat clothes. This one wore pastels. Professional clothes. Skirt. Flats. Gray jacket. Pink shirt. Her appearance was so off-putting, so contradictory to what Aly remembered, she thought she was hallucinating.

In a polite and somewhat jovial voice, Belinda said, "I'm Special Agent Belinda Bell from the FBI. Do you have a moment?"

The FBI? Alarm bells went off. No shivers. Not someone impersonating. Not Fletcher, she'd know. She didn't think it was Elaine. So, it had to be the real Belinda, right? Did it matter since Aly feigned memory loss? "Ahh... Sure."

"Aly, you okay?" Grace asked, concerned.

"Grace, I gotta go. Talk to you soon." Aly hung up and said the first thing that came to mind, "Belinda *Bell?*"

She smiled, again contradicting everything Aly knew. "My husband finds it amusing too."

Aly offered up a trembling smile, uncertain and a little scared. "I'm sorry, that was rude of me. I have concussion, it makes it hard to think and my mouth wanders."

"I understand."

Aly didn't think Belinda could do anything to her here, and she knew she shouldn't take any chances. Belinda was scary, but she wasn't the scariest thing out there. Taking a step back, Aly flopped into a seat by the window.

Belinda nonchalantly blocked the doorway behind her. "How are you feeling? This must be upsetting for you. You seem remarkably well adjusted."

"That could be because I really don't remember what happened," Aly said.

"Nothing's come back overnight?"

Aly shook her head. "Sorry."

Belinda stepped farther into the room. Reaching into her pocket, she pulled out her phone and referenced it. "I read the police report. Sounds like a lucky escape. I have a few additional questions, if you don't mind."

Wary, Aly kept her fear to herself. "Shouldn't we wait for my parents?"

"Oh, this won't take long."

Aly chewed her bottom lip. "Okay."

"Your parents are Penelope and Roger Gale?"

"Yes."

"Are they here?"

"I think they're still at the hotel. It's still early and I don't think Mom got much sleep."

"Did you have help escaping?"

Aly was desperate not to react or show how scared she was. She hoped her acting skills were good enough to let her hide. "I have no idea."

"Do you think they let you go?"

"No clue. I wish I had more to offer, it would mean you guys could catch these bastards."

"Do you remember where you were taken?"

Aly gave a show of considering. "No. There's… flashes of someplace dark, but that's it."

"Were there any other people in this dark place?"

Aly wondered if this led toward the other girls who were taken. When she checked the news feeds on Penelope's phone earlier, the only kidnapping she'd been able to find was her own. "I don't think so."

Belinda nodded, regarding her phone again.

"Was it three or four people who took you?"

Aly got the feeling Belinda was trying to trap her to see if the amnesia was real. "Three. Well, three that I saw. There might've been a fourth or fifth in the van, but I didn't see them."

"Can you describe the van?"

"Black. I couldn't see any writing on it or anything."

"How did you escape?"

"I have no idea. They hit me with some sort of sleeping dart, next thing I know I'm in a forest."

"A forest?"

"Yeah."

"Was anyone with you?"

"No."

"Did you get the feeling anyone was around? Hairs on the back of your neck? Goose bumps? A general feeling someone was watching?"

Aly's mouth went dry and then overly wet and she had to remember not to swallow the sudden burst of saliva in case that was a tell. It sounded like, in a roundabout away, Belinda was asking about Aly's shifter sense. How would she know? "What, like the heebeegeebees? No."

"Hmm," Belinda hummed and made some notes on her phone. "You said three people took you."

"Yes."

"Can you describe them?"

"One of them was in the diner before I finished work. He left in a hurry. He had dark hair, dark clothes. Kind of a large nose. There is probably footage from my diner. Dirk's Diner in Bellhollow," she added for clarification. "The other two, I don't know. It was dark."

"I see. Do you think you could pick him out of a lineup?"

"Maybe."

Belinda glanced down at her phone. "Does the name Rex Braddock mean anything to you?"

Aly suppressed chills. She lifted her feet off the ground and hugged her knees. "No. Should it?"

Belinda's eyes narrowed a fraction as she regarded Aly. "What about Will Ward?"

"No. Are those the names of the guys who took me?" Aly asked. "Did you find out who? Did you catch them?"

"I'm simply following a lead."

"Oh. Can I ask why the FBI is involved?" Aly asked, suddenly aware she hadn't seen a badge.

Belinda smiled. "You can, but I'm not at liberty to tell."

"Oh."

"Can you remember anything else?"

Aly considered. "Well, I bit one of the men, I remember that. Hard enough that I could taste blood. Can you do something with that?"

"Perhaps. We'll add it to the list. Why do you think they took you?"

"I really don't know," Aly replied. "Honestly… I don't like thinking about it. It all seems very surreal."

Belinda closed the case of her phone and pulled out a business card. "I'll leave you my number in case you remember anything else. Or notice something strange or people following you."

"People following me?" Aly blurted, unable to disguise her fear anymore. "Do you think they'll try again?"

"With these sorts of events, it's a precaution.

Sometimes people become a little paranoid. If you do—and it's completely normal if you do—please feel free to call me. I'll brief your local police."

"My best friend's father is a deputy," Aly said.

"Then I'm sure he'll be keeping an eye on you," Belinda replied.

The feigned politeness grated on Aly. She didn't know what game Belinda played or whether she believed Aly's amnesia story. She started to feel like this would never end.

"If you remember anything," Belinda said as she put the business card on the bed. "Please do let us know. Any little bit of information helps."

"Of course," Aly said, forcing a smile.

Aly waited until Belinda left before she darted to the window to watch. She didn't relax until she spotted Belinda walking to the parking lot below and get in her car. With a sigh, she slumped in her chair and closed her eyes in relief.

Without any way to contact "Noah", Aly couldn't warn him Belinda was still out there. That she was FBI or someone impersonating FBI. She supposed it was her problem now, not his. He was out.

Gone.

Penelope's phone beeped, indicating a text message.

Thinking it was Penelope, Aly thumbed the phone to view the message.

It was from a blocked number with only a single line of text but it made Aly's blood run cold.

[Is she safe? –R]

CHAPTER 21

"Self-defense classes?" Roger asked, sitting at the dining table a few weeks later.

"Yes," Aly said, holding her toast to her mouth. "It's a new course. On Wednesday nights."

"Can I do it?" Tim took a large mouthful of his cereal. "I wanna beat people up too."

"That's not what it's for," Aly chided.

He pouted. "Aww."

Penelope glanced up from her cell. "Are you going to have time?"

"Of course," Aly replied. "Grace and Del said they'd do the class with me. Besides, I'm not leaving for Otis until August; it'll give me something to do over the break."

Penelope and Roger exchanged a glance. Penelope said, "Aly, we're really not comfortable about Otis. Don't you think you should try for something closer to home?"

"You signed the enrollment form," Aly pointed out. "Didn't you think I'd get in?"

Penelope said. "That's not the point."

"She's eighteen now. It's her decision," Roger replied and took a sip of his coffee. "We can't coddle her."

"And he wanted Yale, which is even farther away," Aly

added.

Penelope frowned. "Yes, but in light of recent events, don't you think—"

"I think," Roger said, changing the subject, "the self-defense class is a good idea."

Aly smiled. "Thanks." She took a large bite of her toast and glanced at the clock. "I gotta go or I'll be late." Pushing away from the table, she kissed her parents and ruffled Tim's hair. "We're at the lake until noon!" Aly called as she headed out the door. "I'll be back just after that!"

"Don't get sunburned!"

Aly rolled her eyes. "Promise. I have sunblock."

Her smile died as she reached the front door. Aly had felt in limbo during the past few weeks. At home, doing routine things, but she was changed. She was different, the world was different and it was hard to go back to her normal life knowing what was out there.

What was out there wasn't in Bellhollow. It seemed Bellhollow was a place completely devoid of shifters. Or perhaps they weren't as numerous as she'd thought they might be; maybe that had been why Noah had settled here. What was out there probably wasn't in Los Angeles either, but the memories in Bellhollow were too strong and Aly wanted to forge new ones.

Even her eighteenth birthday had felt hollow. She hadn't wanted a party and her parents respected her wish. Instead, she took a bunch of friends to the Happy Dragon for a feast, with an extra chair left vacant to represent the one missing.

Walking to her car, Aly scanned her surroundings. Belinda had been right about the paranoia. It wasn't bad, she didn't think, but anyone could be a shifter. Only Aly's awareness that they existed meant she could look out for them. People like Elaine and Noah didn't set off Aly's radar unless they shifted and Aly had no idea how many sets of clones there could be. She found herself checking her friends and family for signs of imposters and worrying about whether she could really tell.

Del had once sent her a video on rare mental illnesses and one of them was similar to the paranoia she experienced. Now Aly wondered if there wasn't something more to it.

She had to trust her tingles. Family, friends; none of them set her off. None of them acted weird. She had to trust they were who she thought they were.

Aly had Jonah to worry about. The surveillance Elaine spoke of. Her every action was supposed to be scrutinized and reported back. She hadn't seen any signs, but she didn't want to take any risks. She tried to keep things as normal as possible, but it was emotionally draining.

Since she couldn't be sure who was watching her: Jonah, Belinda… Rex… or what avenues they could use to spy, she couldn't do any research on her father. Leon Braddock could have been an alias. Or a coincidence. Or maybe Rex was an uncle? Curiosity overflowed, especially coupled with the messages Penelope received from the mysterious "R", but she was no closer to answers.

She wasn't even sure if she remembered everything which occurred in the forest correctly. There was a fog in her mind and she doubted her own accuracy. Like, her mother couldn't have possibly been there. And the Faceless, surely she'd imagined parts of that.

One thing she did know was Noah was still out there.

Her fingers touched the pendant around her neck. Dainty, elegant, it was a wire cage in the shape of a bee surrounding a yellow globe that glowed in the dark. It had arrived in the post for her birthday with a note in Fletcher's hand. Penelope had been wary, reasoning Fletcher must have ordered it before he'd died, but Aly knew better.

The pendant, added with the fact her new cell would occasionally receive a bee emoji from an unidentified number told her he was thinking about her. That made everything a little more bearable, even if he couldn't be with her.

She missed him. Noah-Fletcher-Will. Missed his presence, missed his voice and his laughter. Missed the way he smiled and his endless supply of Snickers. Even going to paintball felt so different now, so she stopped.

Missing him didn't stop her from living. She looked forward to Otis. While she did worry that it was too far away, she was excited about the study. Getting out on her own, living her life the way she wanted. Finding an apartment for her and Grace to live in, especially since Grace managed to secure a place at LA College of Music. Experiencing college life. She reasoned it would be the perfect time for him to come back.

She sighed and pulled into the parking lot at the lake. Grace was waiting at the edge, laughing with Del, Tamara and Lloyd. None of them were being terribly subtle about watching out for her. They'd all been overprotective, not that she blamed them.

At least they believed her. There were a few students at the school who said she'd staged her kidnapping for attention. Hidden away until her parents alerted the authorities and then basked in the media storm. Whispered rumors, people hiding behind their hands, turning away from her as she strode through the school. They sought out the media to tell tales while she hid, so who was it who wanted the attention?

She was glad when the attention died down.

She didn't know how to act around her friends anymore. The world was so big. Fletcher wasn't dead and her friends continued to tiptoe around him as a subject, or stare at her in shock when she mentioned him.

Fixing on a smile, she opened the car door, grabbed her gear and went to greet her friends.

"Hey, Aly!" Del said as she grew closer, a smile blooming on his face. "Tell Grace she has to come."

"Come where?" Aly asked, reaching them.

Lloyd rolled his eyes. "Madison-Lee's after party."

"Really?" Aly asked, unimpressed. "Prom isn't enough of a party for her?"

"You know," Tamara said, tossing her braided hair over her shoulder. "I don't think it even matters why anymore. She loves parties."

"She'll fit right in at college," Grace said, fixing the strap of her black bikini. "But I'm still not going."

Del gave her puppy dog eyes. "It won't be any fun without you. Literally."

"Finally," Lloyd said with a laugh. "Correct usage of 'literally'. All those years of tutelage paid off. We can move on to basic math. Now, Del, what's one plus one?"

Del scowled and Lloyd bolted, laughing over his shoulder as Del gave chase with "C'mere, you!"

"That's a first," Aly said, watching the boys chase each other.

"Statistically, he was bound to get it right sooner or later," Grace mentioned.

"Hasn't he gotten it right before?" Tamara asked.

"Probably," Grace said. "But we can still tease him."

Aly smiled as she watched them. Turning to Grace, she asked, "Why are you opposed to the party?"

"I'm not," Grace replied. "I'd just…" she shrugged, "rather do something else. It seems… tedious, I guess. We're nearly graduated and Madison-Lee's still in high school mode."

"She'll probably join a sorority as soon as she can to continue partying," Tamara said, then looked at Aly. "Thinking about going?"

Aly shrugged. "I agree with Grace."

"If this is what maturity is," Grace complained. "I don't want it."

"Lloyd and I are going to kick back in my rumpus room with a couple of good movies and popcorn," Tamara said. "We haven't done a good horror night in a while. We could hit Madison-Lee's party for a while and then all go back to my place."

Aly and Grace exchanged a glance. "You wouldn't mind?"

"Nah," Tamara said with a shrug, then winked. "I'll kick you out when you've overstayed your welcome."

Grace grinned. "A horror night is something I could get down with."

"Horror night?" Del called, pausing in his chase.

"How about it?" Tamara asked.

"Weren't you gonna ask me?" Lloyd complained.

"You don't mind, do you?" she asked, giving him a flirty smile. "I'll make it worth your while."

Lloyd laughed. "The more the merrier."

Del looked to Grace, who shrugged and nodded. "Definitely in!" he declared and bounded back and grabbed Grace and Aly's arms. "Aight girls, let's go swimmin'!"

Aly loved it at the lake, especially during spring. Even now, on the edge of summer, it was lovely, warm and green, and the water was gorgeous to swim in. The lake had a pontoon and a dock, both of which were good to jump from and were easy swimming distances from each other, making for exciting races. There were several walking tracks, as well as rocks to sit on and grassy picnic areas for families to eat. A popular haunt for the teens of Bellhollow.

They separated into friendship groups, but they were all together. Happy most of them knew for sure where they were headed the next year.

Placing their bags in a group, Aly shed her clothing and her sandals and followed Grace into the water. They splashed. They played. They dive-bombed off the pontoon. Grace and Del played chicken and lost dramatically. They played volleyball. They tossed a beach ball.

When she was tired of swimming, Aly spread her towel on the grass under the shade of a tree, pulled out her tablet and slipped on her wrist brace.

She'd started sketching Fletcher's Memory weeks ago, when she'd thought he was gone. She didn't see any reason to scrap it but the image had changed from when she'd first envisaged it. Instead of being dreary and gray, the tones were lighter, his posture held freedom, and he smiled. Wind-tousled hair, hands in the pockets of his jacket as he sat astride his motorcycle, a long road stretching out behind him toward sunset. She was proud of the lopsidedness of his smile.

With her cast now off, she'd had a chance to work on it and it was nearly complete. The colors of the sunset weren't quite right and she needed more detail on the motorcycle before she started animating the wind in his hair and the shifting light. She also needed to stop chewing on her pen or she'd have to buy another one soon.

Smiling at Grace's playful scream as she and Del had a water fight, her eyes wandered over to Tamara and Lloyd, then to Madison-Lee and Ethan, who were making out beneath the pontoon.

"Wow."

Aly frowned at the screen.

"I didn't know you could draw."

"You really don't know much about me," she muttered. "Carter, piss off."

"Yeah, yeah," he said, sarcastic. "Take the compliment."

"From you, it's not a compliment."

"Geez, all I wanted to say was that it was a good likeness."

She didn't reply.

"Can you draw me?"

"No."

"Aww, c'mon."

Aly pressed her lips together and refused to speak again. She zoomed in on some nondescript bush to ignore him.

"He... he was a good guy, Aly," Carter said with sudden seriousness. "I'm sorry he's gone."

Aly froze at the uncharacteristic remark. "Yeah... thanks..."

"Are you going to prom?"

She hesitated and wondered if this was a roundabout attempt to ask her out again. "Why?"

Carter was awkward. "Y'know Ethan, he had this idea..."

"I've already spoken to Ethan," Aly murmured, recalling the bumbling conversation she'd had with the quarterback regarding honoring Fletcher. "It's... a thoughtful gesture. I'll be there for it."

"Oh. Okay. Cool." And with that, he was back to his usual self. "You'll save a dance with me?"

"No, I really won't."

"Carter!" Mitchell, another member of the football team, bellowed from not far away and brandished a football. "Pick-up match! Loser does the pizza run!"

Carter moved away. "You're so going down."

Aly acknowledged Mitchell with a smile and received a nod in return. With a sigh of relief, she turned her attention back to her drawing. Another deep breath, steadying this time, she set to work. She would pause every few minutes and raise her eyes to allow them to relax while she stretched her cast-less hand. She smiled and waved at Grace and Del as they continued to have fun.

"That's really good."

Aly stiffened, not recognizing the voice.

The intruder slid down the trunk of the tree behind her to rest his back against the rough bark. "You romanced up the bike, though; it's missing a lot of the rust on the back. I liked that rust. Shame on you, Als."

As her heart took off racing, Aly jerked her head around.

It wasn't Fletcher's body, he could never come back in that, but this body had a strong resemblance. Slightly different face, more angular and older. Lighter, dusty brown hair instead of dark. Freckles dotting his nose and cheeks to match hers. But the eyes, his eyes were still that warm chocolate she loved so much.

Aly beamed.

ABOUT THE AUTHOR

Rikkaine Thompson lives in the Northern Territory of Australia with her wonderful husband, three boisterous children and a dog. *Shift* is her first novel. She is currently working on the next instalment *Twist*.

CONNECT WITH RIKKAINE

I really appreciate you reading my book. Here are some social media site you can find me at:

Follow my blog http://rikkaine.tumblr.com/
Follow me on twitter https://twitter.com/rikkaine

.